A SEA OF FEAR

Russell F. Moran

A Sea of Fear

Coddington Press

Copyright © 2019 by Russell F. Moran

www.morancom.com

Printed in the United States of America

ISBN 978-1-7338872-0-5

Covers and text design by LuAnn T. Palazzo
www.TheDesignDiva.net

DEDICATION

This book is dedicated to the men and women of the United States Navy.

ACKNOWLEDGEMENTS

As always, I thank my wife, Lynda, for her attentive reading, rereading, and editing of my many drafts, and for laughing at my jokes. Lynda is to me as Meg is to Harry. I also thank my friend and editor, John White, for his keen editorial eye. And I especially thank my readers, many of whom are a constant source of inspiration and encouragement for me.

AUTHOR'S NOTE

A Sea of Fear is Book Three of the Harry and Meg Series. Harry and Meg are two of my favorite characters, and I think of them as old friends. We've been on a lot of adventures together. I hope you will see them that way as well.

You will find a **Cast of Characters** after the last chapter of the book. It can be frustrating to come across a character on page 150, who you first met on page 20, especially if you've put the book down for a few days. I've seen this done in Russian literature, and I happily add a cast of characters to *A Sea of Fear* as well as my other novels.

PART ONE

Chapter 1

Commander Fenton, Commander Fenton, please report to the lobby."

Damn, this is a luxury resort not a friggin military base. Why do we need to be referred to by our old Navy ranks?

She walked into the lobby where I was waiting.

"I tried calling you on your cell phone, Meg, but you didn't answer."

"I accidentally turned it off. Hey, honey, why can't we knock off this nonsense of us being called by our old Navy ranks in public. It sounds silly in a place like this."

"The answer is marketing, hon. We've found that 70 percent of our guests are active or retired military. Hearing our Navy ranks makes them feel at home. It adds to the atmosphere of the place."

"Aye aye, Admiral–I suppose."

Meg and I own Leyte Hall, a luxury resort on Narragansett Bay in Portsmouth, Rhode Island. We both retired from the Navy two years ago. Meg was a commander and I was fleet admiral, the first five-star admiral since Chester Nimitz. After I served as Chief of Naval Operations, I was promoted to Chairman of the Joint Chiefs of Staff. Meg was *my* chief of staff. When we bought this place, we figured that my background and Meg's would help to attract military families, and we were right. We designed the resort to be a sort of Chautauqua, like that town in upstate New York that caters to "learning vacations," a popular trend. I designed a curriculum of naval history topics, courses I taught at the Naval Academy when I was a visiting instructor. We also run courses on appreciating opera, learning classical music, and various management topics. Sort of like *Adult Ed with a view.* Turns out we nailed it. Leyte Hall has turned a profit, a healthy profit, ever since it opened. Our accountants were shocked that we actually finished our first year in the black, something almost unheard of in the resort business. Building this place was Meg's idea, and like most of her ideas, it was a good one. Running a resort isn't as exciting as my years in the Navy, but it was starting to grow on me. Waking up in the morning and not guessing if you're going to attack—or be attacked, was a pleasant feeling, a different feeling, but pleasant.

A few short years ago, while we were still in the Navy, Meg and I sat on our back deck at our house in Virginia one Sunday morning. We had just finished a stressful year interdicting ships suspected of smuggling nuclear weapons. The operation concluded with a total naval and air blockade of Iran and North Korea. After almost nonstop action at sea, it was comforting just to relax and read the papers. Like a couple of displaced New Yorkers that we were, we enjoy reading the *New York Times* on Sunday. Meg came across a real estate listing in the business section. I'll never forget it, and I'll never forget Meg's reaction.

"Hey, listen to this, honey," she said. "Bed and breakfast overlooking Narragansett Bay in Portsmouth, Rhode Island for sale. The building is on one acre and is adjacent to a 15-acre parcel, which is also for sale."

A few years before that conversation, I had raised the idea

of us retiring from the Navy and buying a bed and breakfast. I can recall verbatim what I said. "Wouldn't it be nice if you and I could run a place and make people happy, rather than killing them."

Meg reminded me of what I said that day. So, we drove up to Portsmouth, inspected the building, which was a dump, and made an offer. The rest, as the old saying goes, is history. With Meg's huge trust fund from her wealthy dad, supplemented by our book royalties, we tore the place down, and built a world-class resort, not just a B&B. Meg likes to do things big.

"So, what did you want to see me about, honey—sorry, I mean Admiral?"

"I hate to bother you with something like this, Meg, but you're so on top of things I figured you should handle this problem. I just got a call that one of our supply companies has gone out of business, the outfit that provides all our linens including tablecloths. And the weekend fast approaches."

"Why didn't you call Tim Clancy, our highly-paid resort manager, Harry?"

"Remember, Tim's on vacation."

"Oh, shit. I'd better make some phone calls. Hey, aren't you supposed to give a talk at the Naval War College today? You'd better get going. I'll handle our linen problem."

———◆———

When I got back from my talk at the War College, Meg greeted me at the main entrance with a wide smile on her face.

"It's handled, honey. I interviewed three hotel supply companies. Naturally they're dying to do business with us. And get this. The prices from the company I chose are better than the prices we were paying. Hey, why the silly grin?"

"I just remembered something."

"What?"

"I love you."

"And I love you, baby."

"Gimme a kiss, Commander."

As a career military officer, I learned to put up with disappointment and to do without things. A long-planned vacation may need to be put off, a holiday postponed, a reunion delayed. I learned how to say goodbye to good friends. One time, I was looking forward to a big family gathering my folks had planned over the Christmas holidays. Fentons from around the country were due to get together. The day before the gathering, my ship was deployed to a hot spot in the Middle East, and my reunion consisted of emails. You never knew when you would have to man your battle station. So, over the years I disciplined myself to put up with that shit. But there is one thing I simply cannot do without—my wife, Meg. Sounds like a romance novel, but I find that I love Meg more each day that we're together. Over the years, I've accomplished some good things for the Navy, and the Bureau of Naval Personnel learned to trust me, and also to make concessions that I politely demanded. One of those concessions was to assign Meg to any duty station to which I was ordered, including ships. Meg went from being my aide to my chief of staff. Assigning naval personnel is always done with "the good of the service" as the top priority. The Navy learned over the years that "the good of the service" was amply served by having Meg at my side.

Now the Navy is behind us, but our relationship is still closer than ever.

Life is good. I'm with the beautiful woman I love, we have a successful business, and we get to enjoy making people happy. And we never have to man our battle stations. Call me combat scarred, but I couldn't help think, will life always be so good?

Chapter 2

Shepard Smith for Fox News, ladies and gentlemen. It seems that every few days I repeat the same report, and today is no different. Yes, it's another story about a cruise ship being attacked and sunk. Yes, another story of modern-day piracy. We have received a report that during the early morning hours, the Celebrity Line ship, *Majestic*, has been attacked by a gunboat while the ship steamed in the Caribbean. As in the other stories, the incident involved an attack on the ship with rockets and grenades, followed by the ship being boarded by heavily armed men. The cabins were looted, the passengers killed along with the crew, and the gunboat left the scene at a high rate of speed. These incidents are piling up at an alarming rate. Last night was the fifth piracy in one month alone. Our government appears to be at a loss as to what to do. All the incidents came with no warning that they were about to occur.

"We will be tracking this unfolding story closely, of course. Stay tuned to *Fox News* for the latest on these disturbing incidents. In other news…"

Chapter 3

Meg walked into our private dining room after she met with the new linen supplier she hired the day before. We were about to be served breakfast.

"Hey, Pickle Puss, why the frown?"

"I just got off the phone with Jake Arnold, the President's Chief of Staff. President Blake wants to see me at the White House, and asked that you come with me. Jake sounded really concerned about something"

"Oh shit, Harry, I saw this coming. I watched the report on the news this morning about the latest cruise ship piracy. I think I should give my nerves a break and stop reading newspapers or watching the news. Something tells me that's why the President wants to see you. When do we leave?"

"Right after breakfast. A CIA Gulfstream awaits us at Green Airport in Providence. Jake said the President wants to see us this afternoon."

"I know what he wants, honey, and so do you. He wants you back in the Navy. That little squirt of a country, Concordia, has got the government freaking out after all the ship attacks. Like it or not, it seems we're involved in a naval war. Harry, I almost lost you once, baby, and I don't want that to happen again."

We had decided to retire from the Navy after I was almost

7

assassinated at a party in my office, a small caliber bullet having connected with my skull. I would have been killed had Meg not drawn her service revolver and shot the would-be assassin before he could fire another round. We live an interesting life.

"Assuming you're right, and I think you are, we won't be involved in combat, Meg. We'll be at the Pentagon. I hope you'll take your old job as my chief of staff. I repeat, we won't be in combat."

"Harry, you were shot in the head at a fucking cocktail party, if you recall. You're the best thing that ever happened to the Navy, and our enemies took notice. Honey, we're having a nice life as innkeepers, and making a lot of money, too. Do you really want to go back to that shit?"

"The job hasn't been offered to me yet, of course, but how can I turn down the President if he requests it? I don't know, maybe it's in my blood."

"Honey, your sense of duty is one of the many things I love about you. Yes, it *is* in your blood. But why can't other people handle a crisis for a change?"

"I'm not the only one with a sense of duty, Meg, and you well know that."

"I know, I know. I loved being in the Navy with you, honey, and yes, I do share your sense of a call to duty. But I was just getting used to us being at peace."

"But we're *not* at peace, Meg. Our country is under attack. Hey, let's go. We should get to the airport."

Chapter 4

Meg and I were escorted into the Oval Office by two Marine guards. It was a rainy day, with nonstop thunderstorms, just a reminder of the stormy weather our country was facing. Usually, Chief of Staff Jake Arnold would show us in. Another indicator that we were at war, declared or not.

President Blake is one of my favorite people. He has a charming warmth about him, but when the country is in danger, Matt Blake knows how to kick ass. Had I not been in the Navy at the time, I would have volunteered to work on his presidential campaign. I couldn't help but notice that he looked oddly tired, not his usual robust self.

"Good afternoon, Harry, Meg. I guess you two are wondering why I invited you here."

One thing about Matt Blake, he gets right to the point without introductory small talk.

"Yes sir, Mr. President. Meg and I assume that you'd like us to take command of next year's Easter Egg hunt on the White House lawn."

He cracked up.

"Always the wiseass. One of the many things I miss about

you, Harry."

Jake handed the president a folder.

"Harry, I'm sure you've been keeping up with the news about the attacks on American shipping by that new country, Concordia. I recall that you had an encounter with a Concordian flotilla when you were the commanding officer of Carrier Strike Group 14."

"Yes, sir. Meg was with me, of course. We encountered a flotilla of 10 ships, including four frigates and six destroyers. I was amazed that they fired two missiles at us. A bright young lieutenant JG who served as my aide, had done research on Concordia and concluded that the country wanted to engage us. They did, although the Concordian admiral begged us not to open fire. We could have sunk the entire flotilla, but I took out only the frigate that fired on us, and let the other ships go on their way. It was quite an experience."

"Well, Admiral, Concordia isn't showing any signs of friendliness. We expect further engagements, although nothing as reckless as firing on a carrier strike group."

"Pardon me, Mr. President, but I believe you mean Harry. I'm no longer an admiral, just a humble innkeeper."

"And a pretty wealthy innkeeper from what I've heard. No, I didn't make a mistake by calling you admiral. I guess you're expecting what I'm about to say, but your country needs you—back in the Navy. Our country needs Harry Fenton on the battle line, not to mention his brilliant wife. Harry, I want you to put your five-star admiral pin back on. I'm not asking you to take your old job as Chairman of the Joint Chiefs of Staff, but a more active role. I'm appointing you head of U.S. Fleet Forces Command. When you go to sea, your flagship will be a ship you're quite familiar with, the *USS Gerald R. Ford*. I also want you to take command of Carrier Strike Group 14, your former job. I ask your talented wife to dust off her stripes and resume her position as your chief of staff. The country needs you two, Harry, it's that simple. You're the best damn fighting admiral in American history, and I'm asking you to lace up your gloves. We're faced with a little tinpot nation that has taken on the world's shipping industry as a target. Hell, until a few years ago nobody ever heard of Concordia. I still can't believe that it split off from Santa Mallarta, taking part of the seacoast with it."

"And Santa Mallarta still doesn't recognize Concordia," Jake Arnold chimed in. "They didn't try to stop the secession with military force because Santa Mallarta is still a financial wreck after the previous administration drove it into the dirt."

"The country's president, a chubby little creep named Orlando Bruno, is every bit as bad as the former head of Santa Mallarta, and in many ways even worse," President Blake said. "The country is pretty flush financially, with none of the debt like Santa Mallarta. When they mapped out the country's boundaries, they were careful to include most of the large oil fields that were once part of Santa Mallarta, along with a part of the sea coast. For reasons nobody can figure out, they seem to think of themselves as pirates. In the past month alone, Concordian gunboats have boarded five cruise ships. After they were done looting the ships and their passengers, they sank the ships. That's right, they just sank the goddam ships, sending their crews and passengers to the bottom. These people remind me of the MS-13 gang with their cruelty and violence. Also, they're pretty slick at hiding their identities. In one of the five incidents I just mentioned, the attacking gunboat carried a Liberian flag and was homeported in Costa Rica. There have been a few reports that Concordia has ships stationed in various countries in the Caribbean and the Atlantic, but so far, we don't have any hard evidence. When questioned, a captain admitted that his ship was from Concordia. I've been calling them gunboats, but they're pretty large, about the size of an American destroyer escort."

"Mr. President, Secretary Fleming is here. I'll send him in." Jake Arnold said.

Meg and I glanced at each other. I couldn't believe what was going on. We hadn't accepted the positions yet, but there we were being briefed as if I had already taken command. I think President Blake knows me well, maybe better than I know myself.

Meg leaned over to me and whispered. "I recall you saying that we wouldn't be involved in combat, Harry. Looks like the President has other ideas. I mean, holy shit, Commander of US Fleet Forces along with a carrier strike group? That's a combat job."

Treasury Secretary Otis Fleming is a tall guy, about 6'3" and carries himself like a college professor, which he was for many years. He wore a three-piece gray suit and had his glasses perched on the end of his nose. But why the hell was I being addressed by the Secretary of the Treasury? I wondered. I'd find out soon enough.

"Otis, I believe you've met Harry and Meg Fenton before."

"It's a pleasure to see you again, Admiral. You too, Commander Meg. Not many a man can take a bullet to the head and live to talk about it. You were lucky to have a chief of staff like Meg who knew how to handle a gun. President Blake has asked me to give you a rundown on some economic numbers that have come about because of the actions of one small country. I'm talking about Concordia, of course. Yes, it is a crisis, and yes, we could be heading toward an economic disaster especially if Concordia turns its sights on freighters and crude oil tankers. We've researched the results of the attacks on cruise ships. Bookings are off by 75 percent across all cruise lines, and the number will go higher with every ship that's attacked. It's simple to understand, and the operative word is fear. People avoid going to sea on a cruise ship for fear of their lives. Usually, the only thing you worry about on a cruise ship is rough seas. People are frightened they'll be killed on a pleasant sea cruise.

"Let's look at some numbers. There are just over 50 cruise line companies worldwide, accounting for 1,020,000 full time jobs and $41.1 billion in wages and salaries. Ancillary jobs and occupations that cater to the cruise industry include over 27,000 travel agents. Currently there are 449 cruise ships with another 27 planned to launch this year. The total economic output of the cruise industry is $126 billion. Add to these numbers the economic activity of ports of call. Some small Caribbean countries couldn't exist without regular visits from cruise ships. Over a recent five-year period, cruise vacation bookings were up 20.5 percent. That number began to change and is changing fast as we speak. I mentioned that bookings are off 75 percent since the attacks began. It isn't hard to see that the number will soon be 100 percent. No cruise line company is going to commit suicide by launching ships that aren't covered by bookings. To summarize, we have a problem—a big one."

"Soon there will no longer be a cruise line industry," President Blake said. "Our country needs a fighting admiral like Harry Fenton to kick some ass. Meg, what do you think?"

"I'd like to hear my husband's thoughts, Mr. President. Honey, I mean Harry, I mean Admiral, I mean holy shit, answer the President's question."

Blake cracked up.

I looked into Meg's eyes. Ever since we married, Meg and I have learned to communicate without speaking. All we need to do is look at each other and we know the answer to a question before it's asked. Sometimes I think that Meg and I disappear as two individuals and reappear as one person. Meg smiled and winked.

"The answer, Mr. President, is aye aye, sir."

"I expected nothing less from you, my friend. Harry, dust off the Fenton Doctrine—deprive the enemy of options. We're going to show that little rogue country what it's like to deal with the Fentons. I think of you as *America's Twofer*."

Chapter 5

On the Gulfstream on our way back to Rhode Island to tie up our affairs at Leyte Hall, I told Meg I wasn't worried about the details because she could organize a tornado. We made a good choice a few years back to hire a man named Tim Clancy as the manager of Leyte Hall, a guy with a reputation as a great resort manager. We hired him away from a hotel on Lake George. We even gave him 20 percent of the stock in the Leyte Hall Corporation to keep his mind focused. Tim is due back from vacation today, thank goodness.

Leyte Hall got its name from Leyte Gulf, at Meg's insistence. When I was the commanding officer of a carrier strike group, the ship slipped through a time portal, also known as a wormhole. Yes, as strange as it sounds, we traveled through time. My flagship was the *USS Gerald R. Ford*, the Navy's newest and biggest carrier, the same one that will once again be my flagship. We found ourselves in the year 1944, a couple of months before the Battle of Leyte Gulf. I knew the history of World War II well, having taught courses on the subject as a visiting instructor at the Naval Academy. I came up with an idea to save a few hundred thousand lives by sinking the entire Japanese fleet at Leyte Gulf. My thinking was that we could convince Japan to surrender without dropping atomic bombs on her. So, we hooked up with Admiral Halsey and his Third Fleet and laid out our plans. We sank every one of the remaining 40 Japanese ships, just as I intended. Japan capitulated a week later. So, we saved the lives of hundreds of thousands of men, women, and children because we never bombed Hiroshima or Nagasaki. We also avoided the remaining battles of the Pacific War. There never was a Battle of Luzon, Manila, Iwo Jima, or Okinawa. Yes, we changed history, I think for the better. Meg, a former investment company executive, was my chief of staff, and changed from financial maven to an outstanding naval tactician. She was a key to our success at Leyte Gulf, and even took command of an attack on the Japanese ship *Yamato*, the largest battleship ever built.

I married well.

That wasn't the only time we traveled to another era. Meg and I met when I was the captain of a corporate cruise ship after my first retirement from the Navy. She was a vice president of the company that owned the ship, the *Maltese*. We encountered a time portal and traveled back in time over 100 million years. The event became known as *The Maltese Incident*. I hadn't known Meg more than four days when I fell wildly in love with her. Besides her gorgeous looks, she's brilliant and had a way about her that made me want to be with her for the rest of my life. I still do. So, we got married in the ship's ballroom—100 million years ago. When we returned to the present, I was asked to reenter the Navy, with the rank of rear admiral. Meg followed me into the Navy, and we've never been apart since. You can't make this shit up.

Yes, Meg and I lead interesting lives. Strange but interesting.

I wanted Meg's honest input. Well, that's the only input she ever gives me. The last thing I ever want to do is make a decision that involves the two of us without Meg's complete agreement.

"Are you okay with this, honey? Please tell me you didn't agree just because your husband doesn't know how to say no to a superior."

"I'm totally okay with it, baby. I love the way President Blake referred to us as *America's Twofer*. That's the way I'm going to think of us from now on. I think this is going to be fun."

Only Meg could think of waging a naval war as fun. She gives new meaning to the term positive thinking.

"That's because we *are* a twofer, honey. We're a package deal."

"So, what are your thoughts, Harry? A blockade? You pulled off the blockade of Iran and North Korea brilliantly a few years ago when you were Chief of Naval Operations."

"A blockade won't work in this situation, Meg. That little country has spread its attack ships across the Caribbean, and now they're branching out into the Atlantic. For a small country, they have huge ambitions. Jake Arnold told me that they have ships stationed in dozens of countries, ready to charge into the ocean and raise hell. Did you notice that the President mentioned the Fenton Doctrine?"

"Yes, I did, Harry. *The Fenton Doctrine*, your wonderful idea to take away an enemy's options, just like you did at the Battle of Leyte Gulf. But it can be tricky when we don't know just where the enemy's located."

"Meg, I think 90 percent of this operation, whatever this operation is, will be based on intelligence. As soon as we get back to Washington, I want to meet with our old friend, Buster from the CIA."

A couple of hours after we arrived at Leyte Hall, Tim Clancy threw a big party for us just as he did the last time we came out of retirement and went back to the Navy. He must think we're nuts. He just may be right.

Chapter 6

Good afternoon, ladies and gentlemen, Wolf Blitzer reporting for *CNN*. There has been yet another piracy of a cruise ship. The *Sea Bounder*, a large ship owned by Norwegian Cruise Line has been attacked, looted, and sunk off the coast of Central America. This is the fourth such incident in the past two months. The first three involved attackers from the new nation of Concordia. We don't know yet if the nation's government was involved in any of the actions, including the one I'm talking about. At 4:15 p.m. Eastern Time, a group of pirates attacked the *Sea Bounder* with a storm of rapid machine-gun fire and small cannons. The attacking ship was a large gunboat, about the size of an American destroyer escort. Just as in the other incidents, this action was brutal and sadistic. A party of 20 men boarded the ship, mowing down anyone in sight. After they finished looting the passengers' staterooms, they climbed aboard their ship and escaped, but not before detonating four large bombs below the *Sea Bounder*'s waterline. The ship sank to the bottom with all passengers and crew. We received this report from a man in the communications office of the ship. I'm afraid the poor man is dead. The actual sinking of the ship was reported to us from a nearby vessel.

"With me in the studio is Randolph Perkins, Vice President for Public Affairs at Norwegian Cruise Line. Mr. Perkins, what can you tell us about these horrific incidents?"

"Horrific is the word, Wolf. From time immemorial piracy

has plagued the oceans, but these attacks are almost akin to terror, not just plunder and theft. Why would these people sink the ship, killing the remaining passengers, when all they had to do was escape with their contraband? These are stories of unimaginable cruelty. I simply don't understand their motivation."

"Mr. Perkins, please tell us the impact these incidents have had on the cruise ship industry in general."

"The impact is large and getting larger, Wolf. Cruise ship bookings are off by 75 percent, not only at Norwegian but the other cruise lines as well. People are beginning to fear the sea."

"Are you taking any steps to prevent these actions?

"Yes, we are. We've begun hiring people with experience in security, although we already have folks like that working for us. We've been recruiting retired soldiers, Marines, and Navy SEALs, all combat-trained veterans."

"I hope I'm not overstating the obvious, Mr. Perkins, when I say that passengers may not like the idea of armed combat on something as pleasant as a sea cruise."

"I won't kid you, Wolf. The bigger problem can only be solved by government intervention, our own as well as any governments that see cruise ships departing their shores."

"There you have it, ladies and gentlemen, yet another tale of horrible cruelty and violence. We will be tracking this problem closely and will bring you updates as we get more information."

Chapter 7

Captain, I think we may have a problem," First Officer Bill Toomey said to Captain Henry Magnussen. They stood on the bridge of the *Celestial Magic*, a Celebrity Line cruise ship.

"What do you see, Bill?" the captain said.

"That gunboat is approaching us about 300 feet off the starboard bow. It looks like one of those boats that have been pirating cruise ships."

"Sergeant Bennings, this is the bridge, please pick up." Sergeant Timothy Bennings, a former Marine, oversaw security on the *Celestial Magic*. He led a group of 30 combat veterans. Celebrity Line chose them for their experience and paid them well for their services.

"Yes, sir, Bennings here."

"Come to the bridge please. I think we're looking at one of those hostile gunboats that has been raising hell recently."

Bennings walked onto the bridge along with his second in command, Sergeant Loretta Prince. He looked at the gunboat with his binoculars.

"The boat seems to be going quite slowly," Bennings said.

"What is your plan, Sergeant?"

"My plan is what we've trained for. As soon as you called me, I alerted my people, who are positioning themselves along the starboard side of the ship now. We're heavily armed and can throw a punch."

Magnussen looked down at the deck. He saw a man with a grenade launcher tucked into his shoulder.

Captain Magnussen just nodded. A former military man himself, he didn't feel as confident as Sergeant Bennings. He kept staring at the gunboat.

"She seems to be maneuvering, sir."

"I agree," Loretta Prince said, "but if she means us harm, why would they maneuver so slowly rather than charge at top speed."

"It looks to me like she's taking aim at us," Captain Magnussen said.

"Oh, dear God," yelled First Officer Toomey, "tell me I'm not seeing that."

Two large torpedoes streaked toward the *Celestial Magic*.

"Prepare for impact," the captain shouted over the PA system.

The first torpedo struck the *Celestial* amidships, causing a huge explosion and sending belching smoke and fire into the air. The second torpedo struck the ship by its stern, disabling her steering. Two more torpedoes approached the ship, the first one hitting the starboard bow, destroying the bow thrusters. The fourth torpedo struck amidships again, causing another gigantic explosion. The *Celestial Magic* was adrift with fires burning furiously across her decks. The gunboat positioned itself directly abeam of the struggling ship. Two more torpedoes raced toward the big ship's hull.

Those last two torpedoes were intended to finish off the *Celestial Magic.* The ship rolled slowly to starboard and capsized. Within minutes the ship sank beneath the waves in 900 feet of water. All the passengers and the entire crew perished.

Chapter 8

The Cunard Line ship *Queen of the Winds* cast off its lines from a dock in Miami. At 16 decks high, weighing 220,000 gross tons, with a length of 1,100 feet, the ship was one of the largest afloat. She carried 6,200 passengers, close to capacity, which surprised the captain, given the recent stories of ship sinkings. He assumed that the bookings were the result of the huge discounts that Cunard offered. A crew of 300 served the guests. Her destination was Bermuda.

Captain Mike Flanagan, the skipper of the *Queen of the Winds,* retired from the United States Navy two years before. He had been the commanding officer of the *USS Port Royal,* a Ticonderoga Class missile cruiser. Captain Flanagan was passed over for selection as a rear admiral, and rather than wait for another round of selections, he decided to retire from the Navy after 24 years of service.

Captain Flanagan, who had divorced two years before, sat in his private dining room with a beautiful passenger who was on the cruise leading a college group.

"It's really great having you aboard, Nancy," he said, as he spilled water on his lap. Having been away from the flirting and dating scene for so long, he felt awkward as hell. Although never at a loss for words, he didn't know what to say to his pretty guest.

"Captain to the bridge, please, captain to the bridge," announced the squawk box. He was almost relieved that he could stop fumbling over his words with the lovely Nancy.

He stepped onto the bridge and was greeted by commotion.

"Captain, one of those gunboats that's been attacking ships is off our port beam. I tried to hail her, but she doesn't respond."

Captain Flanagan called below to the ship's security detail to order them to their emergency stations.

He and Florio Monez, his first officer, kept their binoculars trained on the gunboat. They saw a flare coming straight at them.

"Holy shit," the captain said, "that's a Harpoon missile coming at us."

The Harpoon anti-ship missile is 12.6 feet long, 13.5 inches in diameter, and weighs 1,523 pounds. The warhead alone weighs 488 pounds. It's designed to penetrate the hull of a vessel and detonate inside the ship. Depending on where it penetrated, one Harpoon missile could sink a ship.

The missile approached the *Queen of the Winds* streaking toward a spot just below the bridge. In the final moment of his life, Captain Flanagan wished he had remained in the Navy.

A gigantic explosion ripped through the ship's hull, destroying the bridge. Without navigation, she was adrift. Another Harpoon missile struck the aft part of the ship, destroying the engine room, and tearing a large hole in the ship's hull below the water line. The *Queen of the Winds* listed to port, capsized, and sank, taking the 6,200 passengers and 300 crew members with it. The gunboat turned and raced in the opposite direction at a speed of 25 knots. The crew of the gunboat broke out into laughter. They made no attempt to recover any contraband. That was not the purpose of their attack. Nor did they try to rescue survivors.

A large debris field covered the ocean where the ship went down. The debris included no human life.

Chapter 9

Juan Portillo, Minister of Trade for Mexico, sat in the office of Orlando Bruno, president of the newly formed nation of Concordia. What Bruno didn't know, and neither did his aides, was that Portillo was a spy for the CIA. The supposed purpose of the meeting, which Portillo found laughable, was to open trade agreements between Mexico and Concordia.

He noticed that Bruno spent a good amount of time staring into the distance and laughing.

"Mr. President," Portillo said, "my government is interested in a friendly trading relationship with your new country."

"That's good. You are nice peoples. I happy to be meetings with you."

Although they both spoke Spanish, Portillo was amazed at how Bruno mispronounced words and stumbled over phrases. He also noticed that Bruno never stopped smiling. Every few minutes he would break out into laughter.

"I'm sure, Mr. President, that your vice president, Hector Lopez, has told you about our thinking."

"Who he? I am not knowings a guy named Hector Lupo."

"That's Lopez, Mr. President. I believe his is the vice president of Concordia."

"He must be nice boy to have such a big job."

Portillo could see that the conversation was going nowhere, but his job was to spy, so he pressed on. He decided to steer the conversation, if that's what you could call it, toward a controversial subject.

"I'm sure you've heard the rumors, Mr. President, that the recent pirate attacks and ship sinkings may have something to do with your country."

"Pirates? You means like Captain Hook, the guy with a parrot on his shoulder?" Bruno said, laughing hysterically.

As a seasoned spy, Portillo was familiar with the behavior of someone on drugs. But he had never encountered a man who behaved like Bruno. He talked like an infant, or maybe a mentally-ill person, not like a man high on drugs.

The meeting wound down. It had lasted a bit over an hour, and Portillo noticed that Bruno's phone or intercom didn't sound even once.

"It was a pleasure to meet you, Mr. President. I'm sure I'll be seeing you again."

"Nice meetings you, Mr. Prombullo."

"That's Portillo, sir."

"Okay, fine. You nice boy."

Portillo went to the airport to take a flight to Washington for a planned meeting with CIA Director Carlini.

Chapter 10

When Meg and I returned from Rhode Island we went to our assigned apartment at the Washington Navy Yard. The apartment was huge, with four bedrooms and five baths. It was nicely appointed with naval history paintings adorning the walls. A patio out back was surrounded by a lovely garden. We immediately liked the place. Then I wondered how often we'd get to stay there. Soon we would report to the Norfolk Navy base and board my flagship, the *USS Gerald R. Ford.*

Meg wore my favorite perfume and looked especially beautiful that morning. I tried to snap my head back to the present, the urgent present, but then I realized that our meeting at the Pentagon was three hours off.

"Harry, have I mentioned lately how much I love you?"

"Well, babe, we have three hours till our meeting. Let's put that time to good use." I helped Meg out of her uniform, and she did the same for me. We climbed into bed for some pre-meeting excitement.

We arrived at the Pentagon at noon for a working lunch with Secretary of Defense, Michael (Mike) Jamison. Mike Jamison is a tall black man, about six feet five. He's well known for the force of his personality. He was President Blake's first appointment when he took office. Jamison served in the Senate for 16 years before taking this job. Before that he served 10 years in the Navy, leaving with the rank of lieutenant commander. The press loves the guy. He's known for his straight talk, honesty, and good sense of humor. He's also known as a tough task master and doesn't put up with any idleness from his subordinates.

Admiral Jack Pollard, my successor as Chief of Naval Operations, joined us, along with our old friend, Buster, the super spook. CIA Director Carlini couldn't be there because he was undergoing surgery for an impacted wisdom tooth. Buster, whose real name is Charles Atkins, also answers to the name Gamal Akhbar. He is and looks Middle Eastern. His parents are Coptic Christians from Egypt. He's the best damn spy I ever met, and I've known quite a few. We were served lunch in Jamison's private dining room, so security was not an issue. The large window in Jamison's dining room faced Southwest, avoiding the direct sun at noon. It cast the room in a pretty, peaceful glow, not exactly an appropriate setting for the subject of our meeting.

"I suggest that Buster bring us up to date on our little crisis," Jamison said.

"*Little* crisis?" I said.

"I know you've been involved in bigger ones, Admiral, that's why I said that. But let's not kid ourselves, we have a huge problem on our hands. Buster, tell us how bad it is."

"The situation is very bad, Mr. Secretary. Let's look at some numbers. Ever since Concordia broke off from Santa Mallarta, they sank nine ships. They began their activities with piracy. They would board a ship, rob the passengers, and then sink it. Two months ago, they stopped pirating the ships and began to simply send them to the bottom, using Harpoon anti-ship missiles, torpedoes, on-board bombs, and most recently, ramming their ship into the target vessel using remote control. These sick bastards went from being thieves to mass murderers."

"Buster," I said, "have you come up with a theory of what they're after? Piracy we can all understand. Pirates want to steal goods and money. But they're sinking ships as if it were some sort of vandalism on a large scale. Besides not stealing money, they *spend* a hell of a lot of money doing what they're doing. A Mark 48 torpedo costs $3.5 million, and a Harpoon missile costs $1.2 million. I'm sure those gunboats cost in the multi-millions. What the hell is going on? It doesn't make sense."

"Admiral Harry," Secretary Jamison said, "we've been brainstorming on that very question, and we've come up with a working hypothesis."

He let his words hang in the air. Jamison is an expert at getting people's attention.

"Well, Mr. Secretary, what is the hypothesis?" I said, breaking the awkward silence.

"Concordia wants to destroy the world's shipping industry, Admiral. As we sit here, the cruise line industry is steaming toward disaster. A couple of cruise lines have begun offering a week on a ship next to a dock. Just a fancy vacation spot with a view of a harbor. Of the 50 cruise lines that were in existence at the beginning of this insanity, 42 have declared bankruptcy. So, Concordia has almost succeeded in destroying one segment of the shipping industry, cruise lines. Buster, why don't you tell us what we've been hearing from our moles on the ground."

"You're correct, Mr. Secretary, the cruise line business is dying, taking with it 1,020,000 full time jobs and $41.1 billion in wages and salaries. The fall-off in bookings will soon hit the magic number of 100 percent. I think the only word that applies to this nightmare is catastrophic."

"Admiral Harry, as our country's top naval warrior, do you have some thoughts on the matter?"

"I do have some thoughts, Mr. Secretary, quite a few, actually."

"Of course, you do. That's why the president called our country's only five-star admiral out of retirement. Please enlighten us, my friend."

"I've been discussing this with Commander Meg here, my wife and chief of staff. After the first few attacks, we both thought about a naval blockade of Concordia. But as we all know, they've expanded their base of operations beyond that one country. Buster, please tell us how many other ports of call have been involved."

"So far only five other countries have been involved," Buster said. "When I say 'involved,' I mean that a seaport in each of those countries has launched an attacking ship. That doesn't mean the country from which an attack was launched is necessarily our enemy. Chances are that their governments had no idea what was about to happen. A rogue ship simply sets sail from one of those countries. If we see repeated attacks coming from a particular country, they've got some explaining to do. And President Blake isn't one to listen to bullshit explanations."

"I think Buster nailed it," Jamison said, "which doesn't surprise me. Matt Blake isn't just a great president, he's a brilliant diplomat. I've been involved in Matt Blake negotiations, and I've watched him carefully. The man has a magical way of getting his point across and bringing people to his point of view. I can imagine him sitting across the table from the infamous Orlando Bruno. I'm going to call the White House. I think President Blake needs to hear what we've discussed here today. Keep your calendars open folks. Our next meeting will be in the Oval Office."

Chapter 11

Alberto Cruz reported to the bursar's office of the HMS *Ocean Sovereign,* a Cunard Line cruise ship. The ship was large, over 1,000 feet in length, and could carry 5,500 people including passengers and crew, although only 2,800 were on board. The relentless attacks on cruise ships were taking a toll on bookings. Cruz had just been hired as an engineer. After filling out the check-in form, he took his bag and went to his room. Because he had an important executive job, he rated his own room, although a small one. He opened his bag and withdrew 16 small plastic bags each of which carried a white substance. He placed four of the bags into two large pockets in his jacket. He looked in the mirror on his door and satisfied himself that the bulges hardly showed. One of his responsibilities was to inspect the ship's hull to make sure no cracks appeared in the plates. When he got to the forward compartment, which was below the waterline, he carefully taped one of the bags against the hull. He did the same with the other three bags, making sure to place each of them 20 feet apart. He returned to his cabin to get the next four bags. He continued his way along the deck, taping each of the bags against the hull, returning to his room every few minutes to retrieve the next group of four bags. After he taped 12 bags along the starboard hull, he then went to the engine room, another one of his duty stations. He carried the remaining four bags with him. Looking over his shoulder to ensure that he wasn't being watched, he taped each of the bags inside a hatch on the housing surrounding the main engine.

Cruz looked at his watch. He needed to leave the ship in 30 minutes.

The stern of the *Ocean Sovereign* was equipped with a large moveable platform that would be lowered to water level when the ship stopped to let passengers enjoy the "marina," equipped with kayaks, small sail boats, canoes, and the ever-popular jet skis.

Cruz called to his two assistants, Juan Portera and Francesco Marquez.

"I want to test the marina platform to make sure it's working," Cruz said.

The two assistants manned the controls that lowered the huge platform to sea level. Cruz had asked the captain to stop the ship so he could test the platform. The calm sea would enable him to launch a jet ski.

"Yo, Alberto," Juan Portera yelled, "what are you doing on that jet ski?"

"I'm giving it a test. You guys can try it after me."

The two men looked at each other and shrugged.

Portera and Marquez lowered the platform to the ocean surface, with Cruz on his jet ski.

The jet ski was an expensive Seadoo RXP, one of the fastest on the market. As soon as it hit the water, Cruz gunned the engine, racing away from the ship at 60 MPH. He laughed hysterically as the Seadoo bounded over the waves.

Trevor Johnston, the ship's first officer, was making his rounds. He stood on the aft sightseeing deck. He noticed the jet ski racing away from the ship. He yelled down to the two men on the platform. "Hey, what the hell are you guys doing?"

"Alberto, our boss man, said he wanted to test one of the jet skis. That dude is nuts if you ask me."

Johnston called the captain on the bridge. "I just saw a jet ski racing away from the ship at top speed, Captain. This may sound crazy, but it looked like he was trying to escape something."

Jack and Martha Jenkins were celebrating their 25th wedding anniversary. They booked an interior stateroom below the ship's waterline as a way to save money and didn't mind that they had no view of the ocean. They still had two kids in college and their budget was tight.

They had better things to do than look at water, they both agreed. They skipped lunch, as they often did on the cruise, showered, and climbed into bed for some afternoon fun. In the final moment of their lives, they enjoyed a mutual orgasm.

First Officer Johnston heard and felt 16 muffled thumping sounds from below decks, each thump about a second apart. The *Ocean Sovereign* shuddered as the bags of highly explosive Semtex responded to their timers. The ship began to list sharply to starboard, hurling deck chairs and passengers down the suddenly sloped decks. Because of the 45-degree angle of the ship's list, it was impossible to launch life boats. All the panicked crew could do was hurl life preservers and hope some people would catch them.

In 15 minutes, the ship was floating on its starboard side, rapidly taking on water. Thirty minutes later, the *Ocean Sovereign* sank in 850 feet of water. Of the 3,100 passengers and crew aboard, 400 survived, clinging to life preservers.

Chapter 12

J ake Arnold, President Blake's Chief of Staff, took his place to the President's left. First Lady Dee, of course, sat at his right. Although she holds no official title besides First Lady, everybody recognizes Dee as a one-woman cabinet. She met Matt Blake when he represented her as a lawyer in a huge case involving the wrongful death of her husband, an investigative journalist. The case turned out to be more than a personal injury lawsuit. They uncovered a conspiracy that reached the highest levels of government. The case became simply known as *Sideswiped*, for the type of collision in which Dee's first husband was killed. The Blakes are a close, loving couple, something Meg and I easily recognized.

We sat opposite from them.

"Okay, folks," the President said, "this issue isn't getting out of hand. It *is* out of hand. Yesterday the tenth ship in two months was sunk. Only 400 out of 3,100 people survived. Now I'll call on CIA Director Bill Carlini, to update us on intelligence, and then I want to hear from Admiral Harry."

"Thank you, Mr. President," Carlini said. "As you know the CIA has quite a few people on the ground in Concordia, and the news isn't good. Although none of our moles has heard it from an official source, they tell us that the country is planning to ramp up its ship attacks. They believe the information they gathered can only point to that conclusion. The most disturbing thing we've seen with the last three incidents is that they can't be described as piracy. They are attacks with a single intent—to sink the ship. In the past two weeks we've seen a ship sunk by torpedoes, one by Harpoon anti-ship missiles, and one by on-board bomb placement using Semtex. You will recall that a small amount of Semtex—12 ounces—brought down a 747 over Lockerbie, Scotland a few years back. As short a time as four weeks ago, we thought we were dealing with a bunch of looting pirates. But recently they have made no attempt to steal anything. They just want to kill. In a word, this is terrorism. We believe that the goal is to cripple the shipping industry. That would plunge the world into economic chaos, even a depression. What's next? We don't know at this point."

"Do we know for certain where the ships come from, Bill?" the President said.

"A big problem, Mr. President," Carlini said, "is that the location of these attacking ships is not necessarily Concordia. As I've reported before, Concordia is flagging ships in a number of countries. The ships that don't come from Concordia are hard to identify. We couldn't even prove in a court of law that the recent attackers had anything to do with Concordia. But we know it's them because of our spies on the ground."

"Bill, can you tell us what is being done to protect ships against attacks?" the President said.

"Mr. President, we're in constant touch with all the cruise lines," Carlini said. "They're not taking this insanity sitting down, but there isn't a lot they can do. Cruise ships have always had security staff, and they're doubling and tripling the number of armed personnel. Some are hiring former soldiers, Marines, and Navy SEALs. Those people can help against a piracy, but don't do a damn bit of good against a torpedo or a Harpoon anti-ship missile. The security agents may as well not be there.

An extreme way of beefing up safety would be to install missile and gun batteries on all cruise ships, turning them into men-of-war. That's ridiculous, of course. I ask anyone in this room if you would want to go on a cruise with a missile battery next to your deck chair. Another crazy idea I've heard kicked around is that we should provide naval escort service for the cruise ships. But, as I'm sure Admiral Harry here would agree, that would give the Navy one mission only, taking it away from other vital operations. Besides that, the cost would be enormous."

"Admiral Harry, your thoughts?" the President said.

"We've been in tough spots before, Mr. President. What we don't know now is the command and control. In other words, we don't know who the management team is. Once we find out who they are, Bill Carlini's folks can start to pay a few visits. For my part I intend to use submarines. It won't be easy, and it won't be foolproof, but it does present a tactical possibility. If we're correct that Concordia uses satellites to check for nearby warships, submarines will overcome that problem. But even though our modern nukes can cover a lot of ocean, it's a big ocean. I've deployed three strike groups to the Caribbean and three to the Atlantic. I'm going to request two additional strike groups from the Pacific. I hope those idiots in Congress are proud that we saved money by stripping our Navy to its bones."

"This little shit country is wreaking havoc with our foreign policy," President Blake said. "If you need additional appropriations, Harry, come directly to me."

As he said that, President Blake drilled his eyes into mine, as if to emphasize what he said about appropriations.

"Admiral Harry, it's time to take your gloves off."

Chapter 13

Luis Brunilla and Hector Lopez, two high ranking officials of the new country of Concordia, sat in an outdoor café on the island of Grenada, off the coast of Concordia. When certain matters need discussing, they would never meet in their new homeland. Brunilla was obsessive about security.

"Have you heard from...?"

"Shut up, Hector. You must never say his name in public. Absolute secrecy is essential."

"But there isn't anyone within 50 feet of us, Luis. What's the problem?"

"The problem is one of discipline. We must never say his name, not even to each other, and I don't care if we're in a boat 100 yards offshore. It is a matter of training ourselves to maintain secrecy."

"Well, I'm expecting a call from him in two days, Luis. You and I should go over my report. You know how furious he gets if he doesn't hear the smallest detail from me."

"Okay, let's review what you will be reporting. Keep your voice low, Hector."

"I think my report will make him happy as it does us, Luis. So, let's see. Ten ships sunk in two months. The last three are what he wants to hear. We sank three ships without boarding. One we hit with torpedoes, one with Harpoon anti-ship missiles, and one was sunk by a bomber who worked on the ship."

"It amazes me that we can afford such weapons. My God, we even have five diesel submarines. It's comforting to have that man's money behind us. It's not only comforting, it's essential because we need to use sophisticated weapons. Our brief policy of piracy may have gotten us some valuable contraband, but our days of boarding a ship and then sinking it are over. All the cruise ship companies have inserted armed security personnel onto their ships. Any piracy action from now on will involve huge gun battles. But they can't do much against a torpedo or a missile. With every ship we hit, we get closer to our objective, I mean *his* objective."

"Let's go over the objective once again, Hector. When I first heard of it I thought the idea was crazy. But I now see what it means."

"It really isn't complicated, Luis. We are a very small new country. We have revenue from oil, but it isn't enough to get us where our friend wants us to go. His objective is to bankrupt the world shipping industry and then take it over. Soon we'll begin attacking freighters and tankers. In a few months, the world will beg us to come to a negotiating table. Then we will take over what is left of Santa Mallarta and move on from there. In a year or two Concordia will no longer be a small powerless country. We will be a major actor on the world stage."

"You put it dramatically, my friend, but you are right. Even the Americans will sidle up next to us after we bring the world to its knees."

"I like the way you put it, Hector: Bring the world to its knees."

"Let's now review our next attack."

Chapter 14

On a warm July day, the Royal Caribbean cruise ship *Oceanic Magic* departed its homeport, Cape Liberty, in Bayonne, New Jersey. Although the ship could accommodate over 5,000 passengers, only 1,100 were aboard, just over the break-even point for the Royal Caribbean treasury. The recent piracies and ship sinkings were taking a severe toll on the cruise ship industry. The destination for this cruise was Freeport in the Bahamas.

On the second day of the cruise the slight drizzle stopped and beautiful sunshine bathed the ship.

Frank Howard and his wife Diana were taking their first vacation in a year. Frank had retired from the United States Navy a year before with the rank of captain. Diana was a freelance journalist.

Although he spent 26 years in the Navy, with most of his tours at sea, he still loved the ocean. He enjoyed the stress-free environment of a cruise ship, where he didn't have a mission to control. Diana was nervous about cruising because of all the highly publicized stories about ships being pirated and sunk. Frank convinced her, as a lot of people had convinced themselves, that the ship attacks seemed to be focused on the Caribbean, and they were in the Atlantic.

They had lunch in one of the ship's restaurants. Frank even

allowed himself a Martini, something he'd never do on a Navy ship. The ship's loudspeakers pumped out a medley of Beatles songs, his favorite group.

"Hey, handsome," Diana said. "I haven't seen you so relaxed in a long time. Maybe after lunch we should go to our stateroom."

"What for?"

"You have to ask what for? Gimme a kiss and finish your drink. I'll show you what for."

They walked holding hands along the outer deck, catching some fresh air as they headed toward their stateroom.

"What the hell am I seeing?" Frank said, loudly.

"What is it, honey?"

"That's a periscope I'm looking at."

"Maybe it's one of our subs catching a peek at this pretty ship."

"That's damn reckless behavior by the captain of that boat. I almost want to announce general quarters to send everyone to their battle stations. What a yahoo."

"Oh, dear God, honey. What's that in the water?"

Four torpedoes streaked toward the middle of the *Oceanic Magic.* The first one hit just below the spot where Frank and Diana stood. They were killed instantly by the ensuing explosion. Each of the remaining three torpedoes found its mark. The four explosions tore huge holes in the ship's hull, and she began to list to port. In fifteen minutes, the mighty ship slipped beneath the waves in 1,200 feet of water. A Coast

Guard cutter steamed toward the debris field, having heard the ship's distress calls a few minutes before.

Ten people survived, clinging to life jackets.

Chapter 15

So, how's my favorite Mexican trade minister, Juan?" Bill Carlini said as Juan Portillo sat at the conference table. "You've got the deepest cover of any agent in the CIA."

"Working with you guys is a lot more fun, Bill. I see that Buster is here. That's good, because now I can blow two minds, not just one."

"So, tell us about your meeting with the infamous and mysterious Orlando Bruno."

"I'll get right to the point and fill in from there. Orlando Bruno is not in charge of Concordia. He's a prop, a wall ornament. From my background research, I know that Spanish is his native tongue. That said, he can barely speak the language. To say that he's a flake is an understatement. I think he's mentally ill. His language and appearances told me that he is not in command of *himself*, much less the nation of Concordia. Orlando Bruno is just a puppet, a marionette, and we don't know who's pulling the strings. Before I met with Bruno, I had a brief meeting with Hector Lopez, the vice president of Concordia. Bruno told me he never heard the guy's name before. When I gently brought up the subject of piracy, he got hysterical laughing and asked if I meant Captain Hook, 'the guy with a parrot on his shoulder.' Gentlemen, I'm afraid we're back to square one with that country. Right now we don't know who's minding the store, but it sure as hell isn't

Orlando Bruno."

"Do you think he was on drugs, or maybe drunk?" Buster asked.

"No. As you well know, Buster, we've been trained to the hilt on how to spot someone under the influence. The poor guy, and yes, I mean the poor guy, is mentally unfit. Somebody sat him in his office and puts out memos in his name. In the hour I spent with him, neither his intercom nor phone sounded even once. The guy is place keeper. I hate to come here empty-handed, but there was nothing to get my hands on. I recommend that we station a few top operatives in Concordia."

"Well, gentlemen, this meeting has gone as far as it can go. Great work, Juan. I now have to report to the President. I can't believe that Concordia has been around for a few years, and only now do we find that we don't know who's in charge. We've got to find out, fast."

"Mr. Director," his assistant said over the intercom. "I suggest you turn on the TV. There's been another ship sinking."

"Did I mention—fast?"

Chapter 16

Wolf Blitzer for *CNN*, ladies and gentlemen. We're just getting reports that yet another cruise ship has been attacked and sunk. The *Ocean Explorer*, a ship from a cruise line of the same name, has gone down 100 miles off Cape Hatteras, North Carolina. She carried only 1,100 passengers although she has a capacity for over 5,000. Also aboard was a skeleton crew of 200. Cruise bookings, as we've been reporting for weeks, are way down, and it's getting worse by the day. The latest statistic we've heard from the Cruise Lines International Association, the industry advocate and watchdog, is that cruise bookings are down 90 percent. We have on the line by satellite hookup, Coast Guard Commander Dwight Brooks, commanding officer of the Coast Guard Cutter, *USCG Waesche*, which is on the scene of the disaster. Please tell us what you see, Commander."

"Wolf, what I see is sickening. Because the ship went down so fast, there isn't much of a debris field. We managed to rescue 15 people, that's 15 out of a total of 1,300 aboard, including the crew. One man, a third mate on the ship, said that he saw four torpedoes racing toward the portside of the ship. He ran across the deck to the starboard side, managing to save his life. He said that the ship went down in less than 20 minutes. No other vessels were in sight, so we can assume the torpedoes were launched from a submarine."

"Thank you, commander, and Godspeed for your safe return. Ladies and gentlemen, someone or some group has declared war on the world's cruise ship industry. What began a few months ago as piracy, has now become mass murder. This is a new form of terror that has blindsided the governments of the world, including our own. Tomorrow we're going to give you an update on the bookings crisis from the Cruise Lines International Association. I don't expect it to be a happy update.

"In other news…"

Chapter 17

Francois Petain sat at his table in the market area of Labadee, Haiti. His table was covered with souvenir items that he fashioned himself. Petain earned a good income from selling his wares, far above the average wage in Haiti. He loved the sight of a cruise ship coming into port with its cash-laden passengers.

Labadee is located on the northern coast of Haiti. Royal Caribbean Cruise Line has a lease which gives it the exclusive right to dock its ships at the port. Since 1986, Royal Caribbean has contributed the largest share of Haiti's tourist revenue. The company employs 300 locals and allows 200 other people, such as Francois Petain, to sell their goods in the market area for a fee. In the months of January and February alone, 34 ships of Royal Caribbean visit the port, along with thousands of passengers eager to shop. Without the ships' passengers and their dollars, Labadee would be an area of subsistence farming.

Francois Petain sat and waited. He looked at his watch. The Royal Caribbean cruise ship, *Harmony of the Seas* had been scheduled to dock three hours earlier.

Jacques Alois, the manager of the marketplace, stood by the tables with a megaphone.

"My friends, I have bad news, I'm afraid. I have just received word from Royal Caribbean headquarters that *Harmony of the*

Seas will not be visiting us today. They also told me that all scheduled visits have been cancelled until further notice. You may wish to pack up your wares and go home, because we will not see any customers today. I will let you all know if there is any change in future plans.

Francois Petain packed his goods. Like all the other vendors at Labadee, he had followed the news reports of the ship sinkings, and the horrible toll on the cruise ship industry. As he pulled his wares in a cart behind him to his modest house, he recalled that he grew up in a life of crushing poverty. A tear ran down his face as he realized that he and his family will soon return to that life.

Chapter 18

The shrill sound of the boatswain's pipe sounded throughout all four ships of Carrier Strike Group 14.

"Attention all hands, attention all hands. Stand by for Commander Meghan Fenton, the wife and chief of staff to Admiral Harry Fenton."

"Good morning everyone," Meg said. "As you all know, Admiral Fenton has just taken command of this strike group in addition to his duties as Commander of U.S. Fleet Forces. President Blake likes to keep the admiral busy. My husband and I briefly retired from the Navy, as you have heard, but I'm happy to say that we're both proud to be back, serving the country we love. I just wanted to say hello and to introduce Admiral Harry."

I never tire of watching Meg grow and mature as a leader. There was a time when she was shy in front of a microphone. No more. She could address a crowd of thousands and keep everyone in the palm of her hand. But Meg has one problem. Although my beautiful wife is quite an athlete, she's clumsy as an ox. She tripped over a floor mat as she handed the microphone to me. She steadied herself by grabbing the edge of a desk.

"Good morning, everyone, and thank you for the introduction, Commander Meg. Yes, President Blake wants to keep me busy as well as every man and woman in the Navy.

The reason we'll all be busy is because of one small country, a new country, an evil country. I'm speaking, of course, about Concordia, a nation that seems hell-bent on attacking the world's shipping. In the few short years since she seceded from Santa Mallarta, Concordia has become a word of fear, a word of hatred. She attacks ships with abandon. What started out as piracy, has now become nothing less than mass murder. She is no longer content with looting and gathering wealth but has turned to wanton violence. With the help of you fine men and women of the United States Navy, I intend to put a stop to this nation's criminal acts. In the days ahead of us you will see naval combat, the likes of which many of you have never experienced before. We are at war, a war that I intend to win. That is all. Carry on."

"That was perfect, honey. Another one of your 'Give 'em hell Harry' speeches. Combat frightens me, but with you in command, I have nothing to worry about, and neither do the others. By the way, I love it the way you say 'carry on' after you give a talk. For some crazy reason it makes me feel horny when I think that you and I will 'carry on' later."

"Thanks for your kind words, babe. You give a pretty good speech yourself. I just wanted to level with everybody that the days in front of us are not going to be easy. And yes, I love the idea of you and me carrying on."

So, I had my old command back. Carrier Strike Group (CSG) 14 consists of the aircraft carrier *USS Gerald R. Ford*, my flagship, the guided missile cruiser *USS Vicksburg* (CG-69), two Arleigh Burke class destroyers, the *USS Oscar Austin* (DDG 79), and the *USS Arleigh Burke* (DDG-51). But there's a difference this time. I'm also the Commander of U.S. Fleet Forces, formerly known as the Atlantic Fleet. Instead of just one group, CSG-14, I have seven others under my command. Thank God Meg is my chief of staff.

We were tied up to the pier at Naval Station Norfolk, the homeport of the *Ford* and CSG 14. After my talk, Meg and I sat in my office with Captain Peter Barrington, commanding officer of the *Ford*. The Secretary of the Navy had met with Barrington and me and made it clear that, although Peter is the CO of the *Ford*, his duties are normal shipboard operations. In practice, I will have command of the *Ford*.

"Well, we've got our orders," I said. "Steam and interdict. We'll have plenty of satellite intelligence, but as we know, Concordian attack ships like to hit fast—hard and fast. We have five of our nuclear subs on the lookout for Concordian subs. This will be a complex operation. You know who we need?"

"I agree," Meg said.

"I can't believe you two," Captain Barrington said, laughing. "You answer each other's questions before they're even asked."

"You will find, Peter, that Meg and I sometimes blend into one person."

"So, can you fill me in on the question—and the answer?"

"Admiral Harry asked the question, 'Who do we need?' We both know the answer—Leonardo Murphy."

"Oh, yeah, that genius guy. Didn't I read that he served as your aide when he was in the Navy?"

"The one and only," I said, "the smartest human being I ever met. He likes nothing more than to solve impossible problems, and that's what this Concordia mess is beginning to look like— an impossible problem."

"But he's no longer in the Navy," Barrington said. "Do you

think he'd agree to be a consultant?"

"Meg and I correspond with him all the time. After active duty he remained in the Naval Reserve. He now holds the rank of lieutenant commander. He's a good friend and a patriot. He also craves some excitement when he's not inventing the better can opener. I'd be surprised if he doesn't jump at the chance for some active duty time with us."

"I'll call him," Meg said. "Better yet, you call him, Harry. He's your biggest fan. No way would he turn *you* down."

Chapter 19

Leonardo Murphy is the most amazing person I've ever met—and by far the smartest, with the second highest IQ ever recorded. When he was 12 years old, he launched a satellite into space without a rocket. He's now just shy of 30, and makes headlines constantly with his latest inventions. I read somewhere that he owns 75 patents on all sorts of objects and computer programs. The CIA and FBI hired him as a consultant when he was a teenager, and although a lot of it is classified, he pulled off some amazing stunts as a computer spy. I couldn't have been happier a few years ago when he joined the Navy and was assigned to the *Ford*. Although he had just gotten a PhD in physics from Harvard at age 20 and could have had his pick of jobs, he wanted to follow in his parents' footsteps as a naval officer. Besides having an oversized brain, he's a patriot as well. In his four years on the *Ford*, he reworked our onboard database and made it the envy of the Navy. He also got his wings as a fighter pilot. On one occasion I will never forget, I was on the bridge when a rocket was fired at us. His quick thinking and reflexes saved my life when he wrestled me to the deck before I could be hit. For that brave action, he was awarded the Silver Star for gallantry. Needless to say, I'm quite fond of this young genius.

"So, did you talk to Leonardo, Harry?"

"He said yes before I finished the question."

"Oh my God, that's fantastic! Do you think it will be okay with that pretty wife of his?"

"Apparently, Leonardo and his wife, Janice look at you and me as role models. She joined the Navy and holds the rank of lieutenant JG in the reserves. He wants her to join us on the *Ford*. From everything I've heard about Leonardo since he left the Navy, Janice Murphy is his right hand and his intellectual partner. They're a twofer—like us. So, I readily agreed to have Janice serve as well. You've got some work ahead of you with the Bureau of Naval Personnel, honey, but I've never seen anybody better than you in getting around bureaucracies."

"I'll have the paperwork done before dinner."

Chapter 20

On a warm August evening, The Carnival Cruise Line ship, *Splendor of the Seas*, cast off from the dock in Galveston, Texas. The itinerary was the coast of the Bahamas, with Prince George Wharf in Nassau as its first stop.

Although the ship can accommodate 3,000 passengers, she was light, the lingering doubts caused by the recent ship attacks having beaten down bookings. Only 950 passengers were aboard, almost exactly the break-even point financially. Carnival management had considered cancelling the cruise but decided at the last minute to let it happen. A crew of only 200 was aboard. The dining rooms where table service was offered were closed. The only way to dine was to stand in line at the cafeteria buffet. Second helpings were discouraged. Management tried to tell the passengers that they were only trying to provide a healthful environment and fewer calories were a good idea. But the obvious reason was that the ship didn't stock the normal amount of food.

The ship left the Gulf of Mexico, passing Florida to port.

Franz Hoffman was the captain of the *Splendor of the Seas*. He had served for over 25 years with Carnival, and this would be his final cruise. Although he was 60 years old, his hair was jet black with no hint of gray. His family moved to the United States when he was 10 years old from Stuttgart, Germany. Even after 50 years, he still had a slight German accent.

"Are you as nervous as I am, Captain?" First Officer Walter Lansbury asked.

"I don't know how nervous you are, Walter, but I will admit that, yes, I'm nervous. The ship attacks have moved from the Caribbean and now the terrorists attack ships anywhere."

"I notice that you refer to the attackers as terrorists, Captain."

"What else can you possibly call them, Walter? They attack and sink ships for no apparent reason. When they were pirates, at least we could understand the reasoning behind their actions—they wanted to steal money and goods. But now it's simply violence and murder. If this wasn't my retirement cruise, I think I would have declined the assignment, as more and more captains are doing. But I'm a positive-thinking person. I intend to show our passengers, the few who are aboard, a wonderful cruise. I just wish to hell the government would realize that there's a goddam war going on and get the Navy involved. Every pundit you listen to thinks these bastards are trying to destroy a huge industry—the cruise line industry. Hell, if that isn't a matter of national security what is?"

———◆———

The *Splendor of the Seas* was 100 miles from its destination, Nassau in the Bahamas. The ship steamed at a leisurely 12 knots on a calm summer day. Orders from the home office insisted on slow speed to save fuel. The profit and loss numbers, because of the massive cancellations of bookings, had the top executives more worried than ever.

"Captain, that ship appears to be headed straight toward us. Look off the port beam, sir."

"I agree, Walter. From the angle of the ship it does look like he's aiming for us. Track his course on radar."

Five minutes later, Lansbury was gripped by fear. Radar showed that the other ship was aiming for the *Splendor* on a collision course.

"Give me an ETA on the possible collision, Walter."

"Ten minutes, Captain."

"Give me an announcement and then hand me the microphone, Walter."

"Attention everyone, attention everyone. Please stand by for an important announcement by Captain Hoffman."

"Ladies and gentlemen, I'm going to be blunt. We're tracking a ship that appears to be on a collision course with the *Splendor of the Seas*. Please go to your muster stations immediately to board a lifeboat. Bring your life jacket with you. You're going to hear the emergency alarm in a moment. Remain calm and follow the directions of the crew. Please go immediately to your muster station."

The captain's announcement was followed by a loud emergency alarm.

"I think we're going to see a panic, Captain."

"Can you blame them? I'm feeling a bit panicky myself. Let's see if we can outrun that bastard."

"I doubt it, sir. It looks like a large and fast gunboat, the same type that's been involved in most of the other incidents."

Captain Hoffman called the engine room and ordered all ahead flank speed—but the gunboat kept closing on the *Splendor of the Seas*.

As the gunboat came within 100 feet of the *Splendor* on her starboard side, it abruptly turned, aiming for a direct hit rather than a glancing collision.

"Prepare for impact," Captain Hoffman yelled into the microphone. Those would be the last words he ever spoke. The gunboat collided with the hull of the *Splendor* directly below the bridge, causing a massive explosion. The explosion was large because the bow of the gunboat was packed with explosives.

Nobody was aboard the gunboat. It was controlled remotely by a drone that flew above it.

The blast created a gigantic hole in the starboard hull of the *Splendor*. She sank in 25 minutes.

Of the 950 passengers only 200 survived, those who were fortunate to get into a lifeboat. Another 200 managed to remain afloat in their lifejackets. A massive shark attack ensued. Even though a Coast Guard cutter raced to the scene, it was too late to save the floating victims.

The *Splendor of the Seas* was the last cruise ship to be sunk. Booking cancellations had reached 100 percent. Concordia had achieved its primary goal, to cripple the cruise lines. Now, the country would focus on the rest of the shipping industry.

Chapter 21

I walked into Meg's office, next to mine. God, how can this woman be so neat when she has at least five balls juggling int the air at any one time? I couldn't imagine a better chief of staff.

"I guess you've heard the news by now," I said.

"Yes, a news flash just popped up on my screen," Meg said. "I assume you're talking about the attack on the *Splendor of the Seas*. I just got this photo from the Office of Naval Intelligence. Some brave guy snapped a shot of the attacking ship just before it hit. Come and have a look, honey. As you can see it's a close-up of the bridge of the attacking ship. It's empty. ONI thinks this was a remote-controlled collision, probably directed by radio signals from a drone. Harry, I think this may be the official end of the cruise line business."

"That sounds dramatic, but it's also accurate. Each ship attack resulted in more and more booking cancellations. From the briefing memo I read this morning, I believe the sinking of the *Splendor* will bring the number of cancelled cruises to 100 percent. That little shit country has pulled off something nobody could have imagined. Come on, hon, a car awaits us for a trip to the base airport."

"Where are we going?"

"Wanna guess?"

"The White House?"

"Yes, I just got a call from Jake Arnold. The President wants to meet with us as well as CIA Director Carlini and our favorite spook, Buster. Jake sounded upset. I think we're going to talk war."

———◆———

Our driver pulled the car under the porte cochere which provided cover at the main entrance to the West Wing. It's hard to believe that the porte cochere wasn't added until 1969. Before then, people would get soaked entering the West Wing in the rain. It was pouring as we drove up at 11:15 a.m.

Jake greeted us at the entrance, and we walked to the Oval Office. It's always a gripping experience to be at the seat of the world's superpower, a superpower that was feeling its limits as a result of the little country of Concordia.

"Good morning, Harry. Good morning, Meg," President Blake said. He likes to be informal and not use titles. Of course, we address him as Mr. President, even though we're old friends.

"Harry, please fill us in on your plans as a result of our last meeting."

"Mr. President, the Navy currently deploys 12 carrier strike groups, two in the Sea of Japan, and 10 in the United States. As I recommended before, four strike groups will be stationed in the Caribbean and four in the Atlantic, including my CSG-14. That leaves us with two groups that can be deployed in the Pacific if Concordia expands its area of operations. With satellite surveillance we can identify a threatening ship or gunboat, assisted of course by information from the commercial ships themselves. All ship captains in the designated areas of operation have been given an emergency radio channel to call for help if necessary. At any given time, there are 52,000 ships at sea all over the world. That number is lower, of course, because of all the cruise lines that have gone bankrupt."

"Harry, how fast can a strike group get to a threatened ship?"

"I intend to answer a call for help by launching attack aircraft. The F/A-18 Super Hornet, for example, can fly at Mach 1.6, or 1,190 kph. The Hornet has a range of 1,275 nautical miles which can be extended with external fuel tanks. One Hornet can take out any of the large gunboats we've seen Concordia deploying, even a destroyer."

"The Hornet is my favorite plane," Meg said.

"And from what I've heard, you're one hell of a fighter pilot, Meg," the President said.

"Harry, do you think this plan can put an end to Concordia's operations?"

"Nothing is 100 percent, sir, but this plan will severely hamper their anti-ship operations. But we need to keep in mind that Concordia monitors satellites just as we do, and they monitor ship locations. Another thing I expect from them is the increased use of submarines with torpedoes. Safe to say, sir, Concordia's job will just get harder, a lot harder, but they will be tough to deal with."

"As I've said before, give 'em hell, Harry."

Chapter 22

Hey, it's a beautiful day, honey. Let's get a little exercise and take a walk on deck."

"Speaking of beautiful, hon, close up the second button on your uniform. Your lovely boobs are giving me a hard-on."

"We'll need to address ourselves to that hard-on problem later."

"I look forward to it. Button up, baby."

"Harry, I just saw a car pull up with Leonardo and Janice Murphy. I alerted the OOD to send them up here to your office."

Leonardo and Janice walked into my office and saluted. Leonardo had kept himself fit, and his uniform was flawless. His wife Janice stays in shape too, obviously, because her uniform also fit perfectly. Janice is a lovely woman with natural blond hair. She's the sister of Ellen Bellamy, the TV host of *The Ellen Bellamy Show*. She looks a lot like her older sister. Meg and I got a laugh when Leonardo told us that he was madly in love with Ellen Bellamy when he was a little boy and appeared on her show. Ellen Bellamy takes credit for introducing Leonardo and

Janice. She jokingly called herself Ellen the Yenta.

"Leonardo and Janice, you two have done some great work for our national security. My friend CIA Director Carlini told me about some of the wonders you pulled off, editing his story for security reasons, of course. Our old friend Buster, who I know is also a good friend of yours, filled me in as well. It's great to see you again, Leonardo, and I'm delighted that we get to meet your wife. I don't know if Leonardo shares his outgoing emails with you, Janice, but this guy can't shut up about you. I'm glad our old friend married such a wonderful woman. I just wish that Meg and I could have been at your wedding, but as you know NavOps had other plans for us."

"I should mention, Admiral, that both of us have our top-secret clearances up to date," Leonardo said. "As you know, my dad is the head of the Joint Terrorism Task Force and he keeps the paperwork current in case he needs us for something. Admiral Harry, when I asked what you needed my help with you said one word—Concordia."

"Yes, they were raising havoc the last time you were in the Navy, Leonardo, and their hell-raising gets worse by the day. As I'm sure you've heard, Concordia has turned the cruise ship industry into burnt toast. Have you had a chance to research the latest on our little friend?"

"Yes, sir, I've done a lot of current research and I've also done some thinking."

"You've done some *thinking*?" Meg said, laughing. "Like an eagle did some flying."

"What is the major thing you've discovered, besides the fact that the Concordian navy keeps getting bigger?"

"I believe I've found out who's in charge, sir."

Meg and I both slapped the table at the same time.

"My God," Meg said. "That's been the biggest secret since the pyramids. Who is it?"

"You may want to take a sip of water before I tell you. None other than Bartholomew Martin is running Concordia."

"Holy shit," Meg said.

"I concur with Commander Fenton," I said. "Holy shit. Bartholomew Martin, the 46th President of the United States is up to his old crap. How did you find out?"

"The way I find out about most things I research, sir. I devised a computer algorithm. I hacked into their computers and found countless references to a man whose name was never disclosed. He is usually referred to as 'The Man,' and often as simply as 'He' or 'Him,' always capitalized. I read numerous references to his insistence on calling people by their first names, a characteristic that we learned a long time ago about Bartholomew Martin. What clinched it for me were the phone calls I tapped into."

"How do you tap into a phone call?" I asked.

"Long story, sir. If I set my mind to it, I'd be a pretty good gangster. I found out how to do it when I worked for the CIA. So, when speaking on the phone, Concordia leadership isn't as careful as when they email. I speak fluent Spanish, as you know. I counted no fewer than 10 mentions of the word Bartholomew, all in contexts that convinced me it's him."

"I can't believe he was never prosecuted for that huge climate blackmail scheme he concocted," Meg said, "the one that was nicknamed *A Climate of Doubt*. But, unfortunately, the son of a bitch is still on the loose?"

"Martin's billions keep him well insulated from the law," Leonardo said. "Bartholomew Martin now resides in Concordia."

"Leonardo, I called you only four days ago. How did you find out all this stuff in so short a time?"

"You know me, Admiral. I like to work fast."

"I need to take this to the White House."

"Careful, honey," Meg said. "Don't forget the chain of command. Navy Department first, then Defense, then the White House."

"No, I want to keep this carefully under wraps. I'm going directly to the White House. Sorry, Leonardo and Janice, you haven't even unpacked yet, but suddenly we need to take an immediate trip to Washington."

"I'll arrange for our flight," Meg said as she picked up the phone.

I called Jake Arnold, the president's chief of staff. I didn't say anything on the phone, but I insisted that I needed to see President Blake. They all know I don't bullshit, so they were okay with not hearing the details. I did ask Jake if he knew of a Leonardo Murphy.

"Of course, I do," Jake said. "The White House knows Leonardo quite well."

Chapter 23

We arrived at the White House at 1500. I was surprised that Jake invited Janice into the Oval Office for our meeting along with Meg, Leonardo, and me. Obviously, the name Murphy rings bells at the White house.

"So, Admiral Harry, please summarize this urgent meeting for me," President Blake said.

I took a deep breath. I felt like I was holding a hand grenade and was about to pull the pin.

"Two words, sir," I said. "Bartholomew Martin."

President Blake didn't say a word, nor did Jake Arnold. They sat there as if posing for a picture.

President Blake spoke. "Are you certain it's Bartholomew Martin?"

"Yes, sir."

"Admiral Harry, how did you come across this knowledge?"

"Sir, nothing is secret from our friend Leonardo Murphy over here. I suggest we let Leonardo tell us what he knows."

"Tell me you figured it out with a software algorithm, Leonardo," President Blake said.

"Yes, sir, like most of my projects, this one involved an algorithm. I spent a few days working the 'Concordia Leadership' algorithm, and then I hacked into phone messages, using tricks I learned at the CIA. I became convinced that Bartholomew Martin is the man we're interested in."

"And how long have you been working on this project, Leonardo?"

"Four days, sir, ever since Admiral Fenton asked me to take active duty with his strike group."

"Leonardo, some day, and that day will probably never come, I will have a talk with you without being totally amazed. Great work, as usual. How many times have I said that to you in the past?"

"You embarrass me, Mr. President."

"Don't be embarrassed. Your work in recent years has kept our country safe. I want you to continue. I leave you in the able hands of one the greatest military leaders our country has ever produced, Admiral Harry Fenton. I'm sure that Admiral Harry will help you focus, not to mention Commander Meg and your charming wife, Janice."

———◆———

Sometimes I allow myself a pat on the back. Asking Leonardo Murphy to come back to active duty deserves a big pat. One for Meg too. Having Leonardo on my staff is like carrying the entire Internet in my head.

We had just buckled up for our short flight back to Norfolk.

"Admiral Harry, I'm embarrassed to ask this question, but I'll ask it anyway. I've just spent an intense few days researching

69

the leadership of Concordia and I came up with Bartholomew Martin. But I must admit that there's a lot about the man that I don't know. I was a kid when he was president. I've got a lot more research to do. For openers, can you fill me in a bit about the man?"

"That goes for me, too, Admiral," Janice said. "I really don't know a lot about this guy."

"Allow me then, to give you two a crash course on the amazing and mysterious Bartholomew Martin."

"He's the most evil scumbag on earth," Meg chimed in.

"My Chief of Staff likes to get right to the point, and she just made a good one. The man is evil, pure evil. When President Blake first ran against him for president, it looked like Blake would win easily. That's when Bartholomew's minions embarked on a gigantic campaign of lies and slander. In a few short weeks, the Martin gang convinced the American people that Matt Blake was not only soft on terrorism; he encouraged it. Just before the election, a group of sickening attacks on amusement parks occurred. Hundreds of children were killed. It was later discovered that Bartholomew's people planned and executed the attacks. Of course, his battalions of lawyers kept the suspicion away from him. Then the Martin campaign unleashed a brigade of women who accused Blake on TV of sexually molesting and raping them. What looked like a coming landslide for Blake turned out to be a win for Bartholomew Martin. He also brought with him a veto-proof majority of both houses of Congress."

"That's when the fun began," Meg said.

"Yeah, fun indeed. In one election, Bartholomew Martin became America's first dictator. Legislation consisted of executive orders, sealed off from attack by his lackeys in

Congress. Individual rights were snuffed out daily. Legal gun owners had their weapons confiscated. The dreaded 'knock on the door,' became an everyday reality."

"I do remember my parents complaining constantly about 'that bastard,' their nickname for Martin," Leonardo said. "Because they were both senior law enforcement officials, they got to see the results of his actions."

"Yes, law enforcement people soon found that they had a simple set of rules to follow—enforce Bartholomew's dictates. I wanted to do whatever I could to oppose him, but as a senior naval officer there wasn't much I *could* do. My moneybags wife over here did take action."

"I donated a million of my trust fund to the next campaign of Matt Blake."

"What brought about the opposition to him?" Janice asked.

"Bartholomew overplayed his hand. You can't stomp on the rights of the world's most freedom-loving people without opposition. A groundswell of support began to emerge for the second presidential campaign of Matt Blake. Bartholomew Martin's people reacted as expected—with a campaign of lies, slander, and violence. By that time, however, law enforcement got fed up, and conspired to work against Martin, as did a majority of the American people. The news media people, who had been tucked safely into Martin's pocket with his billions of bribe money, finally started to act like responsible journalists. A landslide in Blake's favor resulted. I'll never forget watching the election results with Meg. As they tallied the popular and electoral votes, it became certain that Matt Blake would win easily. Everyone expected the traditional concession phone call from Martin. It never came. That bastard, as your parents aptly referred to him, didn't show the simple decency of conceding in the face of overwhelming numbers."

"But even though he was voted out of office," Leonardo said, "it seems that he still constantly seeks power. I couldn't believe what I read about that *Climate of Doubt* conspiracy that he pulled off, although it was never legally pinned on him."

"Yes, the *Climate of Doubt,* one of the most ambitious operations in the history of terrorism. Martin used his billions to plant his key people into a company that controlled a space station and 20 satellites. They manipulated the satellites to turn away the sun's rays back into space. The result was what almost became a new ice age."

"How much money does this guy have, Admiral?" Janice said.

"According to Forbes, Bartholomew Martin is one of the richest men in the world with a net worth of over $200 billion."

"Wow, that's even more money than *we* have, Lee," Janice said.

I cracked up. I knew the Murphys were loaded and Janice just confirmed it. The numbers we kicked around were beyond my thinking as a humble sailor, even with Meg's huge trust fund.

"So that's Bartholomew Martin, folks. Thanks to you, Leonardo, we now know that he's the one we have to contend with in the suddenly powerful nation of Concordia—a despot who will stop at nothing in grabbing power."

"And something tells me he's got a target painted on President Blake's back," Meg said.

"I don't doubt it, hon. One of Bartholomew's key traits is his desire for revenge. He saw the White House as his private fiefdom, and I'm sure nothing would make him happier than to occupy the Oval Office again."

"Admiral, what do you want me, I mean us, to focus on?"

"Leonardo, having worked with you in my previous command, I've learned not to box in your brilliant mind. I want you and Janice to tell us everything about Concordia— everything, especially her naval armaments. I intend to beat that bastard, and to do so, I'll need mountains of intelligence. President Blake told us that the CIA and FBI are at our disposal. With your dad as head of the Joint Terrorism Task Force, we'll have some inside help. And let's not forget our mutual friend, super-spook Buster."

"We'll get this done, Admiral," Leonardo said.

"Okay, were coming in for a landing," I said. "CSG-14 is scheduled to deploy in two days for the Caribbean. A Caribbean cruise would normally sound like a nice idea, but we know who's lurking in the ocean."

"Harry?"

"Oh, yeah. I want you on the bridge, Leonardo, as officer of the deck when we cast off in two days. I want the crew to get to know you, and what better way to show them your leadership than taking the con as we set to sea."

Leonardo looked amazed at this typical Harry and Meg communication. All Meg said to me was, "Harry," and I knew she wanted to recommend that Leonardo stand watch as officer of the deck.

"I'm sure you haven't forgotten anything, but I'm going to ask Meg to serve watch with you to bring you up to date. Janice can serve as assistant junior officer of the deck. I want her to be completely familiar with our operations so she can help focus that brain of yours. It's a pleasure to have you back aboard, Commander Murphy."

Chapter 24

The *Ocean Advance*, operated by NYK Line, the Japanese shipping giant, is typical of modern car carriers. The ship is huge, two football fields in length with a cargo capacity of 21,443 tons. It can carry 8,500 new cars. Also known as a ro-ro, for roll-on roll-off, the ship is one of the work horses of the modern shipping industry. At an average retail price of $34,000 per car, her precious cargo tallied up to $289 million.

The ship's American captain, Hugo Winter, had been with NYK Line for 20 years. He would tell anyone who listened that he considered the thousands of cars in his ship's hold as his "children." His job was to deliver the vehicles to their destination in perfect shape, with no scratches or dents. The ship's 22 crew members saw to that, encasing the vehicles with fenders or bumpers, just as on a boat or ship to protect it from the dock. One of the captain's critical tasks was to avoid storms, lest his "children" get bumped and bruised.

The *Ocean Advance* cast off its lines from the port city of Tahara, 41 miles south of Nagoya, Japan. The sea conditions were moderate as the ship steamed toward the Philippine Sea, enabling Winter to maintain an average speed of 18 knots. Getting to the show on time was another important part of Winter's job. The ship's destination was Port Newark, New Jersey, which meant they would steam through the Panama Canal, a distance of 7,865 nautical miles, with a sailing time of

18 days.

"Good morning, Captain," First Officer Jorgen (Joe) Schweitzer said. "Weather reports indicate good sailing. Did you see the news report about another cruise ship that sank?"

"Yes, I did hear about that, Joe. I remember when I first got my license, I considered applying for work on a cruise ship. Seemed like a pleasant way to make a living. I'm damn glad I didn't, otherwise I'd be unemployed now. After that last attack, the cruise line industry is now officially dead. You take over, Joe. I need a nap."

After 11 days, they were a week away from the Panama Canal. First Officer Schweitzer walked onto the bridge and handed the captain a cup of coffee.

"It's a beautiful day, Joe. Why don't we have our coffee on the open bridge. We have a trailing wind of 18 knots, so it will be calm."

They stood looking at the ocean, something seasoned mariners never seem to get enough of. "Captain, was zur Hölle ist das?" Schweitzer shouted in his native German.

"Speak English, Joe. What do you see?"

Schweitzer handed him his binoculars and pointed toward the port bow.

"Dear God almighty. Those are torpedoes, four of them."

Winter ran inside the bridge and grabbed the microphone. "Incoming torpedoes" he shouted, something he never expected to announce.

None of the 22 crew members knew what to do. Torpedo attack drills are something they never engaged in. One of the men jumped into a huge Toyota Land Cruiser SUV, not sure why, but it looked like it could afford some kind of protection.

The torpedoes, each armed with a highly explosive 292 kg warhead, sped toward their target.

One torpedo crashed into the hull just below the bridge. In the final moment of his life, Captain Winter realized that his "children" would never see their new homes.

In 20 minutes, the *Ocean Advance* sank in 2,050 feet of water. 12 men, lucky to be on the ship's starboard side, escaped in life rafts. But in their panic, none of them remembered to carry anything other than a short-wave radio. They had no water. Their sun-scorched bodies would be discovered five days later by an American Coast Guard cutter.

Chapter 25

Luis Brunilla and Concordia vice president Hector Lopez huddled for their weekly meeting on the island of Grenada.

"We've achieved the breakthrough he was looking for," Vice President Lopez said.

"By he, you mean…"

"Dammit, Luis, do not say his name out loud. I hope I don't have to warn you again."

"Okay, okay. But nobody is anywhere near us."

"It doesn't matter, Luis. Secrecy requires discipline and keeping his name to ourselves is the discipline required."

Lopez waved to a waiter.

"We must celebrate, my friend. Join me in a glass of rum?"

"I could down a whole bottle after what happened two days ago. We have made the big graduation step. The cruise ship industry is dead, and we've now moved on to bigger game. In one action alone, we sank a gigantic ship carrying 8,500 new cars. Counting the ship, we've done over a billion American dollars in damage."

"To change the subject, Hector, how is our president,

Orlando Bruno, faring."

"Please don't bring up such a crazy matter. The poor bastard doesn't know up from down. That cocktail I gave him a few months ago has done its work. I'm surprised that Orlando even knows his own name. He certainly doesn't remember mine. Every time I see him, it's as if we just met. At first, I thought that keeping him on as a figurehead was a bad idea, but it wasn't my decision to make. I just follow orders like everyone else. But in a way, having him in place will keep the Americans quiet, because if any of their officials meet him, they will not fear Concordia. Soon they will find they have much to fear from us, so having Orlando Bruno occupy a chair will give us time to do what we must."

"And we shall do it."

Chapter 26

Good morning, James, I trust you have good news for me."

"Good morning, Bartholomew. Yes, I have a ton of good news."

"James, let the good news speak for itself. I dismiss your characterization of it as a *ton*."

Bartholomew Martin was meeting with his assistant, James Brent, at his luxury seaside mansion in the city of La Punta, Concordia. As always, he referred to another person by his first name, never a nickname. James Brent was James, never Jim. He also detested adjectives and adverbs. He hated it when a subordinate said that a program was great or stupendous, or that he had a "ton" of good news. He avoided subordinates' exaggerations that way, leaving the facts for him to analyze.

Bartholomew Martin, the 46th President of the United States, was the prime-mover in the secession of Concordia from Santa Mallarta, and was the country's chief of state, although that fact wasn't known to the world. He arranged for Bruno Orlando, a former army colonel, to be fed a concoction of chemicals that resulted in a permanent state of severe dementia. Orlando was 56 years old at the time his mind disappeared. Orlando's tenure helped to keep up the myth that Concordia is a harmless country.

Martin still hadn't gotten over losing his re-election bid to Matt Blake. The presidency of the United States was Bartholomew's highest achievement. He intended to retake the seat. But first he needed to work through a complex plan to gain power over the world's shipping.

"So, James, please give me your report."

"The cruise ship industry is virtually nonexistent, Bartholomew."

"Virtually?"

"Well, to be more accurate, the cruise ship industry no longer exists."

"And when will Concordia launch her first cruise ship?"

"In exactly six months, Bartholomew. In a recent raid, we managed to salvage a ship without serious damage. All her passengers and crew were killed, of course. She is undergoing renovations as we speak. Our engineers are redesigning the ship, so it won't be recognizable when we relaunch her. Also, we have our secret subsidiary making bids on the remaining cruise ships. They will soon become part of our fleet."

"Soon?"

"Our chief engineer says that we should have at least 25 seaworthy ships within 12 months."

"Tell me about the rest of the shipping industry, James."

"As you know, Bartholomew, we sank 10 industrial freighters. But our military planners have devised a new operation, and it will begin next month. We have developed a highly effective poison nerve gas that breaks down rapidly after it kills the targets. This will enable us to take a ship intact to our facilities and it will require few renovations except for cosmetic changes. The gas will be delivered by helicopter drones. Anyone who hasn't been killed will be severely disabled. Our attack crew will then safely board the ship and sail it to Concordia or one of our facilities in another country. I believe it's accurate to say that within two years, the world's shipping industry will be controlled by Concordia."

"Tell me about the American Navy's activities, James."

"Our spies have confirmed that Admiral Harry Fenton has come out of retirement and is in charge of all naval operations in the Atlantic and the Caribbean. His title is Commander U.S. Fleet Forces. He also has taken on his previous role as the commanding officer of a carrier strike group. President Blake once observed that Harry Fenton is America's greatest fighting admiral. He's a dangerous man, Bartholomew."

"Yes, he is. Too bad that our hired assassin only managed to shoot one round at the admiral's head a while back. I understand that Fenton's wife, a Navy commander, shot and killed our man."

"Yes, Bartholomew, that is true."

"Well, the Fentons have some interesting days before them. The next time we won't miss our chance to kill them both."

"So, that is my report, Bartholomew."

"Good day, James. I expect another report in exactly one week. If anything out of the ordinary comes up before then, don't hesitate to call me."

"Yes, sir, I mean Bartholomew."

Martin walked out onto his large deck overlooking the sea. He lit a cigar. So, he thought, America's greatest fighting admiral will soon be in for the fight of his life.

Chapter 27

Meg and I sat drinking coffee after a meeting of the Joint Chiefs of Staff in Washington. Although I was no longer chairman of the joint chiefs I was invited because of my role in the upcoming operations. Meg and I were staying at our apartment in the Washington Navy Yard, our regular location for visits to Washington.

"Do you think these friggin meetings ever get anything done, honey?"

"No, Meg, I don't. Sure, they're necessary because the country always has a lot on its plate, but the joint chiefs are almost irrelevant to our Concordia problem. It's a Navy show all the way."

"And how do you think the show is going, hon?"

"Not well, as we saw the other day when that Japanese car carrier was sunk. Submarines, just as in the days of World War I, are a bitch of a problem. We're getting close to bringing the situation under control with sensor devices all over the oceans, but the project is far from complete. Meanwhile, we need to monitor the actions of our busy carrier strike groups. Every day I thank God that you're my chief of staff, honey."

My secure phone rang.

"Admiral Harry, I think I have some good news for you, sir."

It was Rear Admiral Mike Finnegan, Commander of Carrier Strike Group 16. He was calling from his flagship, the *USS Abraham Lincoln.*

"I can use some good news, Mike. I'm here with Meg. I'll put you on speaker."

"Hi Meg."

"Hi Admiral Mike. So, what's the good news?"

"We got a satellite alert that a destroyer was threatening a large ore carrier. I launched four F/A 18s and sank the bastard."

"Did you encounter much resistance?" I asked.

"He launched anti-aircraft missiles but missed us. I think your plan is working, sir, but we still have a lot more to do. In a way it's simplicity itself. We get satellite feed showing a threatening vessel and launch aircraft."

"Did the captain of the ore carrier call for help?"

"Yes, he did, and that's a crucial part of this operation. Without a call from a threatened ship we're left to look at any ship that approaches another one and guess if it's a hostile act."

"Thanks for the heads up, Mike. I'm going to relay this good news to President Blake. Well done, my friend. Carry on."

"I think it's so cute the way you say, 'carry on' at the end of a speech or a conversation with a subordinate."

"That's because I like to carry on. You?"

"Yes, I do. Hey, honey, it's 1830. Why don't we go to our room and, well, carry on?"

"You never run out of great ideas, do you?"

Chapter 28

CSG-14 was preparing to deploy to the Caribbean in three weeks, right after Christmas. Our original orders were to leave before Christmas, but I put a stop to that. Bad for morale. Meg and I were in my office going over plans for our next deployment. The phone rang and Meg picked up.

"Hi Father Rick, it's great to hear from you. I'm here with Harry. Let me put you on speaker."

Father Rick Sampson, an Episcopal priest, was the chaplain of the *Ford* and CSG-14 the last time I commanded it. He's a good friend. When Meg and I celebrated our fifth wedding anniversary, Father Rick officiated in a ceremony where we renewed our vows. He's the pastor of St. Mark's Church in Manhattan.

"Father Rick, it's great to hear from you," I said. "If you ever find your way down here to Norfolk, we'd love to see you."

"That may happen soon, Admiral Harry, which brings me to the reason for my call. My future son-in-law is the musical director of the Norfolk Chorale Society. Every Christmas season they put on three performances of Handel's *Messiah*. He called me and said they'd love to perform on a Navy ship to honor our people in uniform. I suggested the *Ford* and told him I'd pass it by you first."

"That's a fabulous idea, Father Rick. We're in port until right after Christmas. Meg and I love the *Messiah*. We try to catch a performance every year, depending on where we're deployed, of course. When we ran Leyte Hall, we'd arrange for a performance by a local chorale group in the grand ballroom. Are you planning to join us?"

"Janet and I would love to be there."

"Great. A lot of our officers are on leave, so we have room for you to stay."

"The music director is Jeremy Patton. I'll tell him to call you."

———◆———

On December 15, the Norfolk Chorale Society was piped aboard for their performance. I couldn't have been happier. For me, the *Messiah* is one of the major highlights of the Christmas season. Pure musical beauty. The thought that Handel composed the *Messiah* in 24 days always amazed me. They performed in the hangar deck. It felt kind of weird to listen to a group of people singing the praises of God and peace, surrounded by weapons of war. But, as Meg always reminds me, our job *is* all about peace—keeping the peace.

The performance took an hour and a half. Many of the crew had never seen the *Messiah* performed before. Nevertheless, everybody stood without prompting for the Hallelujah chorus, a timeless tradition.

It was a wonderful event, and I felt at peace. Now, I reminded myself, it's time to prepare for war.

Chapter 29

The shrill sound of the boatswain's pipe carried across the ship, followed by the announcement, "Shift Status," meaning we were shifting status from being in port to cruising underway.

"This is Lt. Commander Murphy, I have the con," Leonardo announced to the crew in the pilot house, advising them that he had control, or *the con*. I stood outside on the open bridge. I was impressed that Leonardo remembered the details of standing watch as OOD underway. I fully expected him to remember everything about the job. But even with a photographic memory like Leonardo's, anything can happen when you're underway in wartime.

"Attention on deck," Leonardo yelled as I stepped onto the bridge with Captain Mike Dormand, CO of the *Ford*.

"As you were," I said.

"Nice to see you, Lieutenant Janice," I said. She looked nervous as hell. It was her first time on the bridge of a ship underway. The only onboard experience she got at OCS was on a "Yippy" or Yard Patrol Boat, a small craft used for training.

"Meg, why don't you show Janice a few ropes," I said.

I heard Janice say, "This is so friggin exciting."

———◆———

"Commander Murphy, we have three targets four miles off our starboard beam. They're steaming in formation," came the announcement the radar room.

"Admiral Fenton? Captain Dormand? General Quarters?" Leonardo asked.

"You know what to do, Leonardo," I said. Mike Dormand nodded his agreement.

"General quarters, general quarters," Leonardo barked into the microphone. "All hands man your battle stations. This is not a drill. I repeat, this is not a drill."

"Hail them on the radio," Leonardo said to the junior officer of the deck (JOOD). "If they're steaming in formation, they're most likely military. Air Ops, this is the bridge, launch a drone to fly over those three ships on our starboard side."

We looked at the video feed from the drone. No insignia at all on the ships, but plenty of armament. We got no reply from the radio contact. Leonardo, with his perfect Spanish, grabbed the microphone.

"Identify yourself," he said in Spanish. "If you do not respond we will open fire on you." He then repeated himself in English.

"We are from the Concordian Navy," a man radioed back excitedly in English. "We are proceeding to Concordia. Please hold your fire." So much for the normal Concordian secrecy.

"I think we should launch a Hornet to give them a little extra convincing," I said. "What do you think, Mike?"

"I concur Admiral. Commander Murphy, I'm ordering a Hornet to be launched."

"Aye aye, sir."

"Leonardo, I'd like to go over those armaments we're looking at on the drone video feed."

"I'll take the con, Commander, so you and the admiral can look at the video."

"This is Captain Dormand," Mike yelled into the pilot house, "I have the con."

A Hornet took off and circled the Concordian patrol.

"Do you see anything that jumps at you, Leonardo?" I said. "I see a few things, but I want your opinion."

"They're loaded for bear, Admiral. Those two missiles forward of the wheelhouse are ship-to-ship weapons. They look like they're Harpoons. The other weapons that we see on this ship alone are surface-to-air missiles."

He turned to Janice.

"Those are definitely Harpoons, honey, I mean Commander."

I guessed I looked surprised at Janice's weapons knowledge.

"As I said, Admiral, Janice and I work together closely. It's something I learned from you and Commander Meg."

Meg smiled from ear to ear.

"Your call, your shot, Mike," I said to the captain. He leaned into the pilot house. "Maintain course and speed. Air Ops, this is the bridge. Prepare to launch another Hornet."

Neither Mike Dormand nor I wanted the Concordian captains to get any stupid ideas.

Chapter 30

After the exciting afternoon, Meg and I invited our new shipmates to have dinner with us in our private dining room.

"So, Janice," I said. "How do you like the Navy? You saw more action today than many a sailor sees in a whole career."

"It was exciting as hell, and also scary. I'm a school teacher and a novelist, and I usually don't see this kind of action. Today was a different experience. And I got to watch my brave hubby do his thing."

"Something tells me you've got a novel cooking in your head after what you saw this afternoon," Leonardo said.

"Novel? How about a whole series? When we worked for the CIA and FBI, Lee and I did have some excitement, but nothing like today."

"I'm actually glad this happened," I said. "The Murphys got a first-hand view of what our country is up against."

"I have a hard time understanding how such a small country can cause so much havoc in the world," Janice said.

"Leonardo's research gave us the answer—Bartholomew Martin. When he's at the controls, normal planning, including naval tactics, are out the window. And as we found out when he tried to use climate change as his personal weapon of terror, he's never out of surprises. Leonardo, you've put us ahead years, pal. Problem is, we don't know how much time is left before that bastard takes over the world's shipping. After that, God knows what he'll be up to, but we can be sure of one thing—it will involve our country. That son of a bitch will stop at nothing to get his way. I hope I'm not putting too much pressure on you."

"Admiral Harry, Janice was being overly humble when she referred to herself as a simple school teacher and novelist. Yes, she is those things, but there's something you should know about the two of us. We love being spies. Some of our greatest times together were when we worked as consultants for the CIA and the FBI. I may have an oversized brain, but Janice here is amazing at picking the fly shit out of the pepper. Don't worry about putting pressure on us. We do our best work when the heat's on."

"I'm glad to hear that Leonardo, because the heat is definitely on."

Chapter 31

The *Sabrina I* is a Portuguese bulk carrier, classified with the odd name, Handymax. The ship is equipped with five holds and is designed for transporting bulk goods such as grain, ore, coal, or cement. She can store up to 400,000 tons of bulk in her huge holds. The ship is 190 meters long, or 624 feet. A crew of 30 are embarked. On this voyage she carried iron ore.

As the *Sabrina I* approached the coast of Brazil, the captain noticed something in the sky heading toward the ship. As they got closer, he saw that it was a flight of helicopter drones. Three of the six drones flew over the deck, dropping bottles of gas near anyone in the open. The gas, newly developed by Bartholomew Martin's scientific research team, is every bit as lethal as sarin, and 500 times more deadly than cyanide, but it has the benefit of dissipating rapidly, enabling an occupying force to board a vessel shortly after an attack. The 10 men on deck immediately succumbed to the gas and all died in less than a minute. The other four drones carefully approached the air intake funnels and fired the lethal gas canisters into them. The gas quickly penetrated all areas of the ship. All 30 crew members were dead within 10 minutes. After 15 minutes the gas was spent, an inert substance.

A helicopter, launched from a nearby destroyer, landed on the deck of the *Sabrina I*. The helicopter carried the replacement crew. The ship, the newest asset of the Concordian merchant fleet, changed course and steamed for the coast of Concordia.

When he was informed of the acquisition of the *Sabrina I*, Bartholomew Martin sat on his deck and lit a cigar. He laughed hysterically.

Chapter 32

Meg and I were on the flag bridge, reviewing plans. My squawk box sounded.

"Admiral, it's Leonardo. Janice and I have something important to show you."

Leonardo and Janice walked onto the bridge. He snapped a sharp salute. Janice snapped a passable one.

"Good morning, Admiral, good morning, Meg. If it's okay with you, sir, I think it's a good idea to come to you when we've found something important rather than waiting to deliver a full report."

"I'm perfectly content to accommodate the speed of your thinking, Leonardo. Fire away whenever you have something. So, what have we got?"

"I'm amazed that the Concordians are being so loose with their communications. They make it easy to spy on them. What we've just found is a shocker. It seems that the ship attacks have taken on a new phase. Their goal is to preserve a ship rather than destroy it. They accomplish that by attacking a ship with debilitating nerve gas rather than rockets, bombs, or torpedoes. They've figured out a way to deactivate the gas quickly, enabling a replacement crew to safely board a recently-attacked ship. The gas they use, and I haven't found a name for it yet, is every bit as deadly as sarin, but becomes inert shortly after killing the targets. They just captured a huge Portuguese bulk carrier named *Sabrina I.* It is now safely tied up with its cargo at a port in Concordia. A bit more research will tell me the name of the port. It seems clear, sir, that they want to build their own shipping industry a lot quicker than they planned before."

"That tells us that they want to convert ships of other nations into Concordia's own fleet. You're right, that will shorten the time to launching their fleet and amassing huge wealth. There's another problem with this new method of attack. What do you think, Leonardo?"

"Detection, Admiral. Our satellites were able to pick up explosions. We weren't able to prevent the attacks, but we were able to destroy Concordian ships soon afterward, as we've done on a few occasions. But now they poison the target with long-range drones, launched from a ship over the horizon. Then they send the replacement crew in a helicopter. Not much for a satellite to see."

"Anything else, Leonardo? I can't believe how far you've gotten in just 24 hours."

"Yes, sir, there is something else. I see clear indications that Bartholomew Martin has formed a secret dummy corporation, the purpose of which is to bid on ships from bankrupt cruise lines. The name of the company is the Darnell Corporation."

"I thought you said it was a secret corporation."

"As you've seen before, Admiral, it isn't easy to keep a secret from me. I recommend that you contact the CIA, sir. This Darnell Corporation will require some intense scrutiny."

"I'll contact the CIA right after our meeting. Great work as usual, Leonardo. You too, Janice."

Chapter 33

The Darnell Corporation had just incorporated in Delaware, a popular location for newly-formed corporations because its corporate laws are lenient and its fees reasonable, with no corporate income tax. The board of Darnell consisted of only three people. Although it was not disclosed, the funding for the corporation consisted of $25 billion from an unknown source. Its corporate charter said, "Commercial Shipping."

Michael Peterson, CEO and board chairman of Darnell, sat with the two other members of the board, Dwight Lang and Jonathan Smith. Neither Lang nor Smith knew where Darnell received its funding nor how. Only CEO Peterson was privy to such secrets. Although the normal due diligence expected of a board member would require they know this information, they were satisfied not to pry because their annual salaries as board members were $500,000 each.

"Dwight, what's the latest on our talks with Cunard and Holland America?" Peterson asked.

"We've offered Cunard half a billion each for the *Queen Mary II*, The *Queen Victoria*, and the newest ship, the *Queen Elizabeth*. Judging from the looks on the faces of the board members, I expect our offer to be accepted by tomorrow. The company is out of cash and they don't have much of a choice. For the 15 ships owned by Holland America, I've offered three million for each of the ships in the fleet. I expect an answer by the end of the week. As we discussed, we're prepared to sweeten the deal by half a million if necessary. I've offered Royal Caribbean $250,000 each for its 25 ships, a package of 6.25 million. I don't believe there are any other bidders out there, other than scrap metal companies, which pay pennies on the dollar to break a ship. By next week I think we'll be in the cruise line business with 43 ships."

"By *we*, Dwight, do you mean the Darnell Corporation?" Jonathan Smith asked.

"We shouldn't bog ourselves down with questions," Chairman Peterson said. "Good work, Dwight. I'll pass your words up the ladder."

Of course, Dwight Lang didn't know what ladder Peterson was referring to, nor did Smith.

Chapter 34

Carrier Strike Group 14 steamed in the Caribbean, 300 miles east of Concordia.

"I'm going to launch a flight of six drones, Mike," I said to Captain Dormand. "I want six drones aloft at all times, so we can have lots of eyes in the sky. As soon as they return, I'll launch another six."

"Aye aye, Admiral. Let me know what you need me to do," Dormand said.

I was being overly polite and intentionally so. Although our orders give me tactical command of the *Ford* as well as the other ships in CSG-14, I wanted Captain Mike to know I respect his position as CO of the *Ford,* and I always let him know my thinking and what I planned to do. He's a good guy and a good captain. No sense pissing him off over small stuff.

"I just wanted to remind you that I'm going for a training flight at 1400, honey," Meg said.

"Be careful, babe. You're a terrific pilot, but I always worry about my sweetheart racing around the clouds."

"Aren't you going to order me to 'carry on'?"

"I'm saving our plans to carry on for tonight."

"In that case, I'll make sure to be back on time."

I stood on the open deck of the flag bridge and watched as Meg taxied to her launch position. I wasn't kidding her when I said she's a terrific pilot. That said, my stomach is always in a knot when I watch her take off. When she got the launch signal, she and her Hornet shot off the flight deck like a rocket. I remember the time we were cruising off Guam when a terrorist bomb exploded on the aft flight deck as Meg was coming in for a landing. My view of her plane was replaced by a wall of fire. Within seconds I saw her bank left and avoid the explosion. I felt as if my life had drained out of me. Like all carrier pilots, Meg is required to take training flights to maintain her proficiency. That knowledge does nothing for the knot in my stomach.

"Follow my lead, Jack," Meg said to Lt. Jack Morton, the other pilot on their training flight. She had command of the flight.

"Roger that, Meg. We're going to through the normal drill, yes?"

"Yes, a few high climbs, a few rolls, and a few acrobatics. I hope you didn't eat too much for lunch."

Chapter 35

I think we can call it a wrap for today, Jack," Meg said over the radio as she leveled off after a deep dive drill.

"It's always a pleasure taking training flights with you Meg," Jack said. "In my humble opinion you're the best pilot on the ship."

"Hey, what the hell is that, Jack? Look below at three o'clock."

"It looks like that gunboat is attacking the freighter, Meg. I see the freighter listing heavily to starboard. She's going under."

"That's a typical Concordian destroyer," Meg said. "No insignia at all, but it's the same type of ship that's attacked all those other ships over the past two months. I thought they were going to rely on poison attacks. Let's drop down for a look."

"Holy shit," Jack said. "The freighter just capsized. She done for."

"Lima Juliet, Lima Juliet, this is flight Alpha Bravo, over."

"Read you Alpha Bravo, what's up, Meg?" the OOD said.

"Put me through to Harry...I mean Admiral Fenton."

"Hi, Meg," I said. "Are you two coming back to the ship?"

"Harry, we just saw a Concordian destroyer sink a small freighter. I request permission to attack."

She requests permission to attack? The love of my life had just asked me to send her into harm's way, a way that includes rockets, bullets, and cannon fire. Okay, time to act like an admiral, not a worried husband.

"Permission granted. Hey, be careful, honey, I mean Commander."

"Jack, I'm going to attack with Hellfire missiles. Follow me and drop a 500-pounder amidships."

"Aye aye, Meg."

"Holy shit, that son of a bitch is armed to the teeth. Look at all the rockets on deck."

"Meg, go left—go left—go left," Lt. Morton screamed into his mouthpiece.

Meg banked left and managed to duck a surface-to-air missile by six feet. She circled around and fired a volley of Hellfire missiles at the ship's bridge. Lt. Morton followed up by dropping a 500-pound bomb in the middle of the ship.

"I'm circling for some BDA (Battle Damage Assessment), Jack. Follow me."

She fired three more Hellfires just forward of the aft gun turret, where she knew the ship's magazine was located. A huge explosion ensued. The destroyer listed heavily to port, capsized and sank.

"Our work is done here, Jack. Let's go home."

"Lima Juliet, Lima Juliet, this is flight Alpha Bravo. We're beginning our landing approach."

"Roger, Alpha Bravo, we have you on visual."

Meg then began the part of flying that she hated—landing on a carrier deck.

One of a pilot's most critical jobs when coming in for a carrier landing is to "call the ball," indicating to the landing crew on the flight deck that she has a visually accurate view of the "meatball." The ball, or meatball, is an orange orb of light emitted from the optical landing system on the carrier's flight deck. A green horizontal row of lights (known as the datum) indicates proper glide slope. If the ball is below the datum, the aircraft is low, and if it's above the datum, the plane is high. When the ball is in proper view, the pilot repeatedly says, "Roger Ball."

Meg Roger-Balled her way to a perfect landing, grabbing the arresting wire with her tail hook, slowing the jet from 150 mph to zero in two seconds.

I was struggling to be the stiff-upper-lipped admiral. Every inclination in my body wanted to run to the flight deck, pick Meg up and hug her. Instead I said to the air officer, as calmly as I could, "Please ask Commander Fenton and Lt. Morton to report to the flag bridge."

As they walked onto the bridge, I threw away any sense of decorum. I picked Meg off her feet and hugged her.

"I thought you two were going on a training flight," I said. Stupid comment, but I needed to break the ice.

"Admiral, if I may, sir," Jack Morton said, "your wife here is one hell of a pilot."

Yeah, I thought, and I'm scared shitless every time I see her take off.

"I've invited Captain Dormand to join us for your debriefing of the incident," I said. "I've also asked the Murphys to be here. I want Leonardo's brain to absorb everything you have to say."

When Dormand and the Murphys entered the bridge, we let Meg and Jack tell their story. We recorded the session to be transcribed for the records later.

When Lieutenant Jack told about a rocket missing Meg by a few feet, I thought I'd throw up. Meg, *my* Meg, came within inches of dying a horrible death. I pride myself on keeping my emotions private. It's something I need to do in my position. But when I heard about that missile streaking six feet away from her, and how I almost lost the love of my life, I put my face in my hands and let go of a sob. I don't think anybody minded. Everybody seems to know how close Meg and I are. With tears streaming down my face, I reached over and grabbed Meg's hand. No fucking way am I sending her into battle again, although I didn't say that, of course.

After listening to the account, Leonardo chimed in. "Obviously they haven't abandoned their old tactic of attacking and sinking a ship. Their poisoning activities are just another arrow in their quiver. Hey, I just realized that the first time I flew in an F/A-18 I was with Meg. She convinced me to get my pilot's wings. It doesn't surprise me that Meg saved the day."

Yeah, and almost got fucking killed.

After the debriefing, Meg and I were alone on the flag bridge. She walked up to me and put her hands on my chest, our faces touching.

"Say, Admiral, I believe you issued an order earlier that you and I should 'carry on' this evening."

"Yes, and I want to do just that. But for right now, I just want to hold you. I want to enjoy the feeling that you're alive and in my arms. I was worried about you, baby. Please don't scare the shit out of me like that again."

"I'll try not to, honey. Hey, let's go to our room and carry on."

Chapter 36

Michael Peterson, CEO of the Darnell Corporation, sat on a chair on the huge deck of Bartholomew Martin's mansion in La Punta, Concordia. His chair was much shorter than the one Bartholomew sat on, resulting in Martin towering over his guest. Martin designed his furniture arrangement for that purpose. On Bartholomew's orders, Peterson wore a heavy disguise. He had a pillow under his shirt making him look much heavier. His head was covered by a blond wig, and his eyes were made up.

"So, tell me about the Darnell Corporation, Michael."

Well, sir, it's a done deal."

"Sir?"

"Sorry, I meant Bartholomew. Besides myself, there are only two other members of the board, as you ordered. We have acquired title to 43 cruise ships. The only renovations necessary are cosmetic changes to make them look different from the ships they once were. I am in the process of registering the ships in 12 different countries, and I'm arranging for their new homeports. I expect the bookings to begin slowly as we discussed, because the public is still concerned about cruise ships being attacked. People still look at the ocean with fear. But that will change over time, given the normal heavy demand for cruising vacations."

"Tell me about the security measures you have taken with the Darnell Corporation."

"Other than a few clerks in the Delaware Division of Corporations, nobody knows about the existence of Darnell. Our attorneys have put many layers of paper between you and Darnell."

"So, Michael, you're convinced that nobody knows about the Darnell Corporation—nobody?"

"Of that I'm certain, Bartholomew. Nobody knows that Darnell exists, and certainly nobody knows that it has any connection with you."

"And when do you expect the first cruise?"

"The *Sealestial,* formerly known as the *Regal Princess,* is under the ownership of yet another corporate entity, Seascape Cruise Line, Inc., based in Miami, Florida. Our travel agency, which has only one client, will soon begin to advertise for passengers."

"Thank you, Michael, for your attention to detail. We shall meet again shortly."

After Peterson left, Bartholomew lit a cigar.

"So, it's working," he said out loud, laughing. "It's working. Nobody knows the Darnell Corporation exists."

Chapter 37

What I find interesting about this Darnell Corporation, Janice, is the layers and layers of cover to obviously keep it a secret. The lawyers who set this up knew what they were doing."

"You mean they *thought* they knew what they were doing, honey. They didn't know they were up against the brain of Leonardo Murphy."

"Well, now that we have the key, we can unlock the door and look inside whenever we want. And I notice that they've set up a bunch of subsidiary corporations, obviously serving as Bartholomew Martin's shipping empire."

"Hey, I'm scheduled to meet with Meg to bring her up to date, Lee. Want to join me?"

"No, hon, I want to keep going. You know me. When one of my algorithms gets on a roll I like to keep it rolling."

◆

"Good morning, Janice," Meg said. "Have you and Leonardo found any new stuff to keep blowing our minds?"

"Just a lot of further evidence that Bartholomew Martin wants to put the world in his pocket. Lee keeps discovering more and more shadow corporations that are rolling up the world's shipping industry."

"I notice that you call him Lee. Are you the only person he doesn't insist on calling him Leonardo?"

"Yes, I'm the one and only. He doesn't have many hang-ups, but his first name is one of them."

"You know, Janice, you and Leonardo joining us has made a gigantic impact. Needless to say, we're happy you two are aboard."

"Lee never would have dreamed of turning down Admiral Harry's request that he return to active duty. I think it's safe to say that Lee is the admiral's biggest fan. When we got engaged, he never shut up about you two and his days in the Navy. I don't know if you've noticed, but Lee and I have patterned our marriage around yours—two people totally in love, dedicated to each other and to the mission. Lee and I are that way too."

"That's sweet of you to say that, Janice. We're amazed at how you feed off each other's ample brains. Keep up the good work. We need you and our country needs you."

"Lee has taken it as his personal quest to nail that evil scumbag, as you aptly call him, and I've signed up for the quest."

"Admiral Harry and I join you in the quest, Janice. Bartholomew Martin wants to rule the world. Not going to happen on our watch."

Chapter 38

After Meg's encounter with that Concordian destroyer, my brain on full alert. I need to cover more ocean, but only have four ships in my area of operation. I contacted the Secretary of the Navy and the Chief of Naval Operations and got the okay to deploy another strike group, CGS-17. That group would steam 100 miles from us. My objective is to sink Concordian ships, but no way in hell will my Meg be involved. As you were, Admiral. *Loving husband has the con.*"

"Hey, handsome, that was fun carrying on last night."

"Yes, it was. I'm still out of breath."

"That means we need to work out more often."

"Roger that, baby."

"To change the subject to something less exciting, Harry, I think your idea of deploying another strike group was excellent. We need to cover a lot more ocean than we can with only CSG-14."

"Yeah, between CSG-17 and us we're going to blanket the skies with spy drones. Once we see something suspicious, I'll launch aircraft—and that doesn't mean *you.* I want my Chief of Staff next to me—and occasionally in bed with me."

"Occasionally?"

"Okay, a lot. Hey, don't get me started, we haven't had breakfast yet."

"So, let's have breakfast and then screw."

"Hey, you certainly are a horny little lady, aren't you?"

"With a handsome hunk like you, it's easy to be horny."

"Hey, we have a lot of work to do."

"After we're done, can we *carry on* tonight?"

"Yes, that's a direct order. Now please stop stroking my leg under the table and let's order breakfast."

———◆———

"Admiral Harry, it's Leonardo. Can we come up to see you, sir?"

"Sure, come on up. I'll buzz Meg. She's doing an inspection of the hangar deck but I want her to be in our meeting."

After Leonardo and Janice sat down, Meg walked in, tripping over the edge of a chair, steadying herself by grabbing my shoulder.

"How's my favorite ballerina doing?" I said.

"Hey, wise guy, stop picking on me. I may be clumsy, but I get the job done," Meg said, laughing.

The Murphys cracked up.

"Janice and I think Concordia is planning something, something big. And for once, it has nothing to do with shipping. I see a ton of Internet chatter about political matters. I think some big plans are underway."

"Bartholomew Martin always likes to keep people off balance," I said. "Have you uncovered anything specific?"

"Only that it has something to do with Santa Mallarta, the country that Concordia was once part of."

"From what I've read, Santa Mallarta is on its ass economically," Meg said. "I'd say the country is ripe for an overthrow. You don't think Concordia would dare try something like that, do you, Leonardo?"

"I don't like to make predictions unless my algorithm leads me that way. Let Janice and me continue to monitor things and we'll report back shortly."

"Okay, we'll see you guys soon," I said.

"Hey, Admiral," Meg said, "aren't you supposed to say, 'that is all, carry on.'"

"Behave yourself, wiseass," I said, laughing, as Leonardo and Janice walked out.

"Actually, honey, I think the words 'carry on' are our little secret. I get all tingly every time I hear you say it."

"I believe you are the foxiest chief of staff in the history of the United States Navy."

"I try my best. And just think, when lying in bed next to you I never trip over anything."

Chapter 39

Hi, Leonardo, it's Meg. Our old CIA pal, Buster, just arrived on the COD (Carrier Onboard Deliver plane). Admiral Harry wants to meet with you two and Buster in his office."

Buster wore his Navy uniform. Besides being a spy, Buster is a commander in the Naval Reserve.

"Good to see you again, my friend," I said. "I know Leonardo is dying to talk to you. Bring us up to date on what's happening at Langley."

"In all my years at the CIA, I've never seen it on such a war footing. Well, we *are* at war, although undeclared. Admiral Harry, I can't tell you how relieved we are that you've unfurled our secret weapon. That would be Leonardo here."

"Hey, will you guys quit flattering me. I inherited my brain, and I'm happy to put it to use for my country. No way would I have turned down Admiral Harry's invitation to come on active duty."

"It's hard not to flatter you, Leonardo," Buster said. "Because of you we handled some of the biggest intelligence challenges we ever faced. Hell, you even started with us as a consultant when you were a little boy. You almost prevented the horrors of 10/7, and you would have if only some of my asshole colleagues at the CIA listened to you."

By 10/7, Buster was referring to a massive terrorist attack on the United States on that day a few years ago, an attack far worse than 9/11. Planes were blown out of the sky, massive skyscrapers toppled to the ground, trains derailed, and over 59,000 people died. Leonardo warned about the timing, but nobody listened to him. He was only 13 at the time.

"So now we're busy deciphering the cryptic messages you send me, Leonardo."

"Obviously my messages need to be cryptic, Buster," Leonardo said.

"Amen to that. So, let me tell you what we're up to at Langley. I can't tell you everything, of course."

"Buster," I said, raising my voice a bit, "yes, you can tell us— *everything*. I can't imagine us not having a need to know what's going on."

"I'm sorry, Admiral, you're absolutely right. Sometimes my spook instincts interfere with my ability to communicate. I'll tell you everything that's happening."

Meg reached over and gave him a pat on the shoulder.

"Thanks to Leonardo's amazing breakthrough recently," Buster continued, "we're no longer in the dark about who is running Concordia. We know it's Bartholomew Martin."

"The most evil scumbag on the planet," Meg said.

"You'll have to pardon Meg, Buster," I said. "She automatically says those words whenever she hears the name Bartholomew Martin."

"No problem, Admiral. I think Meg has come up with the perfect description of the man. As we all know, Martin is a man of constant surprises, and his surprises always get our attention. We at Langley don't like surprises. Hell, one of the primary roles of the CIA is to *prevent* surprises or at least anticipate them. That's why Leonardo's role is so critical. With his brilliant mind and his algorithms, he can predict the future. When this Concordia shit started, we all thought we were dealing with a little pipsqueak nation bent on causing trouble. Well, it certainly is that, but it's a lot more. We've been seeing activities in the States that tell us Bartholomew Martin is behind them. The man wants power, that we knew, but we're seeing some shocking stuff that tells us he wants to assume power in the United States as he has before. We know he hates President Blake. His actions over the years have made that quite clear. Security at the White House has never been tighter, and for good reason. Assassination is one of his favorite tools, as Admiral Harry here can attest to."

"How long do you expect to be on the *Ford*, Buster?" I said.

"Director Carlini wants me to stay aboard indefinitely so I can coordinate our intelligence gathering with Leonardo."

"You're welcome to stay as long as you wish," I said. "We'll put out word that you're a visiting officer from the Office of Naval Intelligence. Your uniform will help to keep your cover on tight. Okay folks, our meeting is over. We'll be getting together again soon."

"Harry?"

"Oh yeah. That is all. *Carry on.*"

Meg winked and blew me a kiss. Who would have thought that two little words could make a woman feel frisky?

Chapter 40

The nonstop stress of our activities was starting to wear on me. After a light dinner, I took a shower and lay down on the bed in my bathrobe. I fell asleep within seconds. Suddenly I awoke. I felt a strange sensation, a pleasant sensation. I pried my eyes open and raised my head. I saw a blond head bobbing up and down.

"Hey, what are you doing?"

"Do I really need to explain what I'm doing?" Meg said, looking up.

"No, no, no. That was just a rhetorical question. Don't let me interrupt you. Carry on."

She looked up. "I love it when you say that, honey."

After a few minutes, I didn't want it to end too soon.

"Hey, come up here, baby. I want you in my arms."

She slowly moved up the bed and straddled me with her beautiful legs, inserting me into her.

After a few more minutes, we mutually climaxed.

She nestled her face against my neck.

"Wow, do I love to carry on," she said. "How about you, Admiral?"

"I thought you'd never ask. In a few minutes I'm going to show you again how much I love it."

Earlier that day, Meg, with her incredible attention to detail, told me about her plan to handle the constant stress we were under. Sex. Constant, vigorous, amazing sex.

Meg has a talent for great planning ideas.

Chapter 41

H ey, handsome," Meg said, "why the hell did you assign me the mid-watch? I thought we had plans for tonight."

Meg was referring to her watch duty as officer of the deck. The mid-watch goes from midnight to 0400 in the morning.

"Oh shit," I said. "I mustn't have been paying attention when I gave my recommended watch list to Captain Mike. Don't worry, I'll ask him to assign it to Leonardo. Janice can stand watch with him as JOOD."

"Good. I think it's important that we stick to our destressing schedule," Meg said as she reached under the table and stroked my leg.

"I totally agree, Commander. Hey, you look especially glowing this morning."

"I'm still glowing from last night, baby."

"I think you should handle the watch list, hon. I'll talk to the captain about it. You wouldn't make the dumb mistake that I made."

"And I won't be assigning myself to any watches after hours."

"Have I mentioned recently how much I love you, Meg?"

"You can never say it enough, honey. I love you too. Gimme a kiss."

This carrying on business was getting to be fun.

———————————◆———————————

"This is Lieutenant Commander Murphy, I have the con," I announced to the watch standers in the pilot house.

Janice stood next to me. It was her first watch as junior officer of the deck.

"I think it's so cool, Lee, the way you make that announcement to the pilot house."

"Well, I didn't intend to be cool. It's standard Navy procedure. It's important that the other people on the bridge know exactly who is in charge."

"And my handsome hubby is definitely in charge. Hey, Lee, you really like this Navy stuff, don't you?"

"Well, I'd rather be back at our house in New York working on our projects, but our country needs us here."

"You're such a patriot. I love you. Is it okay for me to say that as we're standing watch?"

"It certainly is okay, just keep your voice down."

"Bridge radar room, bridge radar room, Lt. Tomlinson speaking."

"Go ahead, Lieutenant," I said.

"Commander, there are three destroyer-sized ships steaming four miles off our port quarter."

"What's their heading?"

"Same as ours, sir, 230."

"Keep them under careful surveillance, Lieutenant."

"Aye aye, sir."

"Janice, please convey that message to the other ships in our group."

"Foxtrot Tango, Foxtrot Tango, this is Lima Juliet, come in." Foxtrot Tango was the group code name. Each of other the ships also had their own radio codes.

When they all checked in, Janice said. "This is to inform you that three destroyer-sized ships are steaming four miles from our position on our port quarter on the same heading as us."

"Roger that, ma'am. We have them on radar. Awaiting your orders." The OOD of the *Arleigh Burke* said.

"This is Lima Juliet. Take no action now, just keep tracking them on radar."

"That was fabulous, honey," I said softly. "You're turning into a salty pro."

"Yeah, and I get to be called *ma'am.*"

"Air ops, bridge, air ops, bridge," I called to the Air Operations Department.

"Air ops aye, Commander."

"Launch three drones and send them over the coordinates of those ships four miles off our port quarter. I want to see if we can figure out what they're up to."

"I'd better alert Captain Dormand and Admiral Harry,"

Janice said.

"Good thinking, hon. Do it."

"Admiral Fenton and Captain Dormand said to keep close watch on them and call again if the situation changes," Janice said.

"I don't blame them. No sense racing to the bridge just because of a sighting."

I looked at the video feed from the drones.

"Hey, something's new," I said to Janice. "Those ships all have Concordian insignia on their decks. Looks like they're decided to come into the open. Jot that down for our notes, Janice."

I wasn't worried. I knew what the Concordian captains knew. If they opened fire on the *Ford*, it would be the last command they'd ever give. I wasn't worried, but I was nervous as hell.

Chapter 42

I'm scheduled to do an inspection of the magazine today, Harry."

"It'll have to wait, hon. I just got a message from the White House. President Blake wants to see us. He said to bring Buster along too."

"Washington is 1,200 miles from our current position," Meg said, "within range of our COD. I'll order it gassed up and made ready."

———

We arrived at the White House at 1500 (3 p.m.). Chief of Staff Jake Arnold greeted us at the entrance, along with four Marines carrying M16s. Oh yeah, we're at war.

The President was sitting at a small table with First Lady Dee.

They both stood to greet us. Classy people.

"Harry, Meg, Buster, we've got a problem, a big one. After the last election it seems that the ratio of assholes to intelligent people in Congress has gotten wider. Both the House and Senate appropriations committees are sitting on the money. Their attitude can be summed up as follows: 'We shouldn't worry about a puny little dictatorship and we certainly shouldn't spend much money on the matter.' Harry, when you requested the deployment of four additional carrier strike groups, you got it. But the cost is huge, and Congress is balking."

"The problem has grown bigger, Mr. President," I said.

"Yes, it has, and what Leonardo has found should have every member of Congress hitting the panic button. My God, none other than Bartholomew Martin is running the show in Concordia. He's just about wrapped up the cruise ship industry as his private club, and now he wants to control the world. And he's not just your garden variety megalomaniac. What he's done with the shipping industry has put him well on his way. You folks know what the problem is, and many other thoughtful people in our government do as well. We know that bastard from his past actions. Hell, he almost plunged the world into an ice age with that wild *Climate of Doubt* conspiracy.

"And get this. Leonardo sent a message to Jake this morning. You haven't seen it yet because you were on your way here. The message is simple. A new political party has just been formed. The name of the party? The Reformers, the same name that Martin ran on when he won the election against me. I'm convinced that Martin wants to win this office again. This is my second term, as you know, so the son of a bitch will take his hateful rhetoric to some other candidate. I wish to hell I had a crystal ball so I could show the congressional idiots what the future will look like with Bartholomew Martin pulling the strings."

Meg and I looked at each other when he spoke about looking into the future. She nodded her head. We were having one of our wordless conversations. I looked at her with an expression that said, "Should I?" She nodded vigorously.

"Mr. President, I think I may have a crystal ball."

"Don't kid around, Harry. What do you mean?"

"Do you recall that time travel journey that Meg and I took a few years ago? We slipped through a wormhole in Nantucket Sound and went three years into the future, a future that had witnessed an EMP detonation over the United States."

"Then we went back in time and my Harry saved the world." Meg embarrasses me sometimes.

"And almost got assassinated for his efforts," Jake Arnold said.

"So, I have a radical proposal, Mr. President. We'll find that wormhole off Nantucket and travel three years into the future, a future that Bartholomew Martin is working on right now."

"Meg, what do you think of your husband's idea?"

"She loves it, Mr. President."

"Oh, right. I noticed that you two were having one of your wordless conversations a few minutes ago. You two amaze me. So, Jake, Buster, Dee? What do you think of the Fenton plan?"

"I think it's brilliant," Dee Blake said, "what we've come to expect of Harry and Meg. I don't think we have a choice."

"But what if you find that nothing's changed much, that Bartholomew Martin hasn't had enough time to roll up his plans?" President Blake said.

"I hate clichés, sir, but 'nothing ventured, nothing gained.' If we don't find a fearsome future, it's on to Plan B. And I have no idea what Plan B is."

Chapter 43

I can't believe we're doing this, honey," Meg said. "I mean looking for a wormhole—on purpose?"

Meg, Buster, and I were meeting in my office to plan our trip to the future. I invited Leonardo and Janice too. I'm going to invite them to travel with us. The choice would be theirs, of course, but I didn't doubt for an instant that they'd jump at the chance.

First, I explained our crazy plan to Leonardo and Janice.

"Travel through time?" Leonardo said. "The answer is *aye aye, sir.*"

"Count me in too," Janice said. "My God, Lee, you'll get to update your mathematical book on time travel with actual observations."

"Okay, the first thing we need to understand is that this mission is absolutely top secret. We're not going to take the *Ford* or any other ship from CSG-14. The President told me to arrange for CSG-14 to return to Norfolk for some R&R. When we get to Rhode Island, we'll stay over at Leyte Hall, the place Meg and I own in Portsmouth. Then we'll rent a boat to take us to the wormhole."

"I'll call Tim Clancy to make the arrangements for our stay," Meg said, referring to our resort manager.

"Needless to say, we don't know what we'll find there," I said. "Our plan is to head for Martha's Vineyard after we go through the wormhole. We may see a typical American town, or we may find something that's been Bartholomew Martinized. Our objective is to observe and report back to the White House. We'll wear civilian clothes so as not to raise any questions. Leonardo and Janice, you two are key to this mission. God knows how good you are at observing things. Our friend Buster, here, will put his spy talents into high gear."

"I know who we hope we'll find, Harry," Meg said.

"Yes, I agree."

"Agree to what?" Buster asked.

"Roger Cramer and his wife, Janey," I said. "Maybe we'll get lucky."

"I met them when you came back from your time trip," Buster said. "They're bright and articulate people, the perfect ones to deliver information. Let's just hope they're home."

"This is the month of May," I said. "I know they go to their vacation house as often as they can in the warmer months. If they're not on Martha's Vineyard, maybe we can look them up at their home in Providence, which isn't too far."

———◆———

We landed at T.F. Green Airport in Providence at 11:30. Tim Clancy had arranged for a limo to take us on the 20-minute drive to Leyte Hall in Portsmouth. Our cover story was simple. Meg and I just wanted to take some accumulated leave time for a well-needed vacation, and also to check up on our property and show Leyte Hall to some friends.

Meg had called ahead to a yacht charter company in Newport and rented us a 60-foot Grand Banks, a beautiful boat with three staterooms. We didn't know how long we'd be gone so we wanted some amenities for comfort. Unlike the older trawlers that Grand Banks is famous for, this one can get out of its own way with a top speed of 35 mph. The boat's name was *Forward Lookout,* which I thought was appropriate for our mission.

Buster, always full of surprises, told us he had extensive boating experience as a gunboat captain when he was on active duty in the Navy. I appointed him captain of the *Forward Lookout.*

Before shoving off I called a meeting in the boat's huge lounge.

"Okay, everybody, here's the drill. Our sailing plan is to head south into Rhode Island Sound and then head east toward Nantucket Sound, passing Martha's Vineyard to port. We'll aim for the coordinates of the wormhole about five miles east of Martha's Vineyard."

"You actually kept a copy of the wormhole coordinates?" Leonardo said.

"Yes, when I was Chief of Naval Operations, I instituted a firm policy of publishing the coordinates of any wormhole that's been discovered."

"My Harry thinks of everything," Meg said.

"Thanks for the compliment, hon, but it was *your* idea. After we go through the wormhole we'll head back to Martha's Vineyard and tie up in Edgartown, the same place that Meg and I visited our last time. With any luck, we'll then go to Roger and Janey Cramer's house and find them home. As we all know, we have no idea what to anticipate. In the strange workings of wormholes, we expect that we'll find ourselves three years into the future because that's what happened last time. This could turn out to be a boring mission, or, on the other hand, we may see some amazing changes to our country. Let's all plan on taking lots of photos and make comments into the recorders on our phones. Okay, let's cast off. Captain Buster, you have the con."

As we approached the wormhole coordinates east of Martha's Vineyard, I figured I'd give a wormhole lecture to the uninitiated.

"Buster, you've been through this before. Leonardo and Janice, you're about to experience one of the weirdest events of your lives. In a few minutes, the boat will start to rumble, like we're cruising over logs. Then it will get dark, pitch dark. After two minutes, the rumbling will stop, and the daylight will return."

As if on cue, we hit the wormhole. Janice screamed with delight as she wrapped her arms around Leonardo.

We rounded the Cape Poge lighthouse, then turned left to head south to Edgartown.

As we approached Edgartown, the boat fell silent. Nobody spoke a word; not me, not even Meg.

"Holy shit," Meg finally said, breaking the silence. "Holy fucking shit."

At the top of the marina near the road was a 40 by 60-foot billboard.

"Embrace Reform Now," read the gigantic letters, "Before It's Too Late."

Under the words was an enormous photograph of Bartholomew Martin. Under the photo were the words: "Join President Martin in Embracing Reform."

"*President Martin,*" I said. "I guess one of our questions has been answered. How far did the bastard get?"

We walked along Planting Field Way toward Roger and Janey Cramer's house.

"Hey, look at the date on the newspaper in the window of that store," Janice said. "Looks like you were right on target, Admiral Harry. We're exactly three years into the future. Two and a half years after the last election."

"Let's go straight to the Cramers, Harry. Neither Roger nor Janey are answering their cell phones. The message on each says that the number is no longer active. That's weird."

"You two will like the Cramers," I said to Leonardo and Janice. "They're both professors at Brown University, Roger in physics and Janey in math."

We walked three blocks to the Cramers' house, a pretty two-story structure done in classic New England architecture. Unlike the first time Meg and I time-traveled to Martha's Vineyard, the place was alive with people. We noticed a lot of cops on every street corner. What's *that* about, I wondered.

We were 10 feet from the entrance when Roger and Janey Cramer came bursting through the door. "Admiral Harry and Meg," they both screamed as they wrapped their arms around us. It's a nice feeling when old friends greet you with joy.

"Thank God you two are okay," Roger said.

"Why do you think we wouldn't be okay?" I said.

"Don't you know what's happened in the past few years? Oh, wait a minute. Tell me you've time traveled again, and you don't know what's happened to our country."

"Yes, Roger, we've time traveled again. Back in 2021, Bartholomew Martin had been raising hell. President Blake agreed with us that we should visit our friendly old wormhole a few miles from here. Our mission is simple, and our question is simpler: What is going on?"

"Hey, it's time for lunch," Roger said. "You guys are our honored guests. And, wow, do we have a lot to tell you!"

"Let me guess," Meg said. "Raccoon?"

Roger cracked up. Meg was referring to the first time we met Roger, who was alone and hunting small game to stay alive. At that time, he offered us a meal of fresh-caught raccoon.

Roger already knew Buster. I introduced Leonardo and Janice Murphy.

"Wow, Leonardo Murphy?" Roger said. "I've read four of your books. My God, you're a genius. In a few short years you've turned the world of physics on its head."

We all sat down around a huge country kitchen table for a lunch consisting of fried chicken, shrimp, and various salads.

"So," I said, "from that gigantic poster by the marina we see that Bartholomew Martin is President of the United States."

"He certainly is. Welcome folks, to a totalitarian dictatorship. This is not the same country you left three years ago."

"Who did he run against?" Meg asked.

"Governor Philip Boland of Maine was his Republican opponent."

"I never heard much about him," Leonardo said.

"That's because he was a quiet guy, not one to bathe in publicity. The Republicans had a hell of a time finding somebody to run against Martin, and the Democrats couldn't find anybody. As you know from his previous campaigns, Martin likes nothing more than to turn an opponent into an object of fear and loathing. Shit, some of Martin's lying campaign ads would lead you to believe that Boland was a child-molesting axe murderer.

"Was the race close?" I asked.

"It started out that way. Each week the polls would see-saw between the two. Then one week before the election, Governor Boland and his wife were killed in a car accident. The police report indicated that the accident was 'suspicious.' As you know, Bartholomew Martin doesn't like to leave things to chance. So once again, Martin had his way, including veto-proof majorities in both houses of Congress. His billions in bribe money did the trick."

"What's it like?" Buster asked.

"Just like his first administration, our country is now a land of executive orders. But this time it's worse—a lot worse. When Matt Blake defeated Martin in a landslide, Bartholomew disappeared for a while. It's as if he studied what he should have done the first time to hold onto power."

"What are some of his main actions?" Meg asked.

"First, he started with the military, which he perceived as a threat to his dictatorship. He ordered all senior officers from every branch of service arrested. That's why Janey and I were so happy to see you two. None of the arrested generals and admirals have been heard from in over two years. An old friend of mine from the Office of Naval Intelligence, said that he's seen solid evidence that Bartholomew had them killed. Thank God you decided to go wormholing, Admiral. Janey and I assumed you were dead, and if you decided to let history play itself out on the other side of the wormhole, you would be exactly that—dead. Bartholomew then put in his own hand-picked people to run the military. Whoever the hell they are nobody seems to know."

"Next came gun control, actually gun confiscation. Bartholomew likes a docile population, and nothing promotes docility more than taking away people's weapons. I'll never forget the 'knock on the door.' Actually, it was a pounding on the door. Two guys were there from the Office of Public Peace. Don't laugh, they really call it the Office of Public Peace. Janey and I own, or I should say, owned—past tense, two handguns, a rifle, and a couple of shotguns. We were given receipts and warned never to try to purchase another gun, under penalty of death. You heard me—*death*. Meg, you mentioned that our cell phones don't work. That's because the Federal Office of Personal Communications confiscated every single cell phone of every citizen in the United States, and the government then assigned new numbers to the phones. Yes, the government assigned the phone numbers and has access to the cell phone of every person in the country. Here's the latest propaganda message I was texted just this morning: 'Join President Martin's campaign of Public Safety.' Of course, public safety, as everyone knows, means keeping your mouth shut."

"What about private property rights?" Buster said.

"There are none, it all belongs to the government, except for minor personal effects like tooth brushes. Our cars? They belong to the government. Our houses? Another 'knock on the door' came from the Office of Deeds. Along with guns, every deed on every piece of real property now resides in Washington. And it's not just the paper deeds. In one single executive order, the title to every bit of real property was transferred to the government. Janey and I owned this place free and clear, but we now pay rent to the government. Investment accounts? All owned by Washington. So, I guess you're wondering about the idea of just compensation. Such constitutional niceties fall deaf on Martin's ears."

Is there any opposition, at all?" Buster asked.

"With his vast billions, Bartholomew Martin takes good care of his lackeys. Picture the photos you've seen of adoring military men cheering on 'Dear Leader' in North Korea. Totalitarian dictatorships are like that, and that's exactly what we have in what was once the United States of America—a totalitarian dictatorship."

"Roger, Janey," I said, "I think it's obvious what you two need to do."

"Something tells me you're going to ask us to go back to the past with you, Admiral," Roger said.

"Oh my God, yes," Janey shouted. "When do we leave? Because of Admiral Harry and the rest of these folks, we have a chance of undoing what's been done, or at least preventing it from happening."

"Admiral, do you have any idea how we can prevent this?" Roger said. "We know that Governor Boland didn't have much of a chance against Martin, especially because he got killed in a mysterious car accident."

"Those decisions have nothing to do with me," I said. "Knowing Matt Blake like I do, I'm sure he and his advisors can find a solid candidate to run against Bartholomew Martin."

"Harry?" Meg said.

"Maybe."

"Maybe?"

"Later."

Everybody cracked up. Witnessing a Fenton one-word conversation takes some getting used to.

———◆———

Roger and Janey threw a few things together and we all headed down the road to the dock. We boarded *Forward Lookout* for our short journey to Leyte Hall in Portsmouth after we cross the wormhole. This was Janey's first trip through a wormhole and she appeared to get a big kick out of it. I briefly considered putting everybody up at Leyte Hall, but then I realized we didn't have a moment to waste. We took a limo to Green Airport and boarded a CIA Gulfstream that Buster had ordered. So, our mission to Martha's Vineyard was a success, I figured. But then a thought intruded. Now what?

Chapter 44

I called ahead to the White House and let Jake Arnold know we would have the Cramers with us once again.

"I don't expect you to tell me the whole story, Admiral Harry," Jake said, "but was your journey to the future enlightening?"

"Beyond enlightening, Jake. We saw a cluster fuck that's difficult to imagine. You may want to serve some stiff drinks at our meeting."

"As you know, Admiral, the President and First Lady are teetotalers, but you're welcome to bring a flask if you wish."

Jake had just reminded me of one of the reasons I was so fond of the Blakes. Before they met, both Matt and Dee Blake were alcoholic drug addicts. Of course, the Bartholomew Martin campaign tried to make the most of the Blakes' past. But the country soon learned of the Blakes' heroism and dedication to helping other people slay their dragons. The Blakes are great people.

———◆———

President Blake sat behind his desk in the Oval Office and we sat in a semi-circle in front of him. He had met the Cramers before, so we didn't waste a lot of time with introductions.

Roger and Janey Cramer told *THE STORY*. It took about an hour. Blake kept shaking his head from side to side in wonder at what he was hearing.

"No private property ownership, no gun ownership, no civil rights?" President Blake said. "When Commander Meg refers to Bartholomew Martin as the most evil scumbag on earth, she says it well—and accurately. So, you've seen the future, and we know that we can't let it happen. Folks, we're going to take a short break and then Jake and I are going to go into executive session with Admiral Harry and Commander Meg. Thank you for your time and attention. We will be meeting again soon."

———◆———

We had an early dinner with Buster, the Cramers, and the Murphys. We sat in a private room at the back of The Lafayette restaurant near the Blair House. Although Meg and I have an apartment nearby and so does Buster, we were all staying overnight at the Blair House, the White House guest hotel, courtesy of President Blake.

"I think our revelations caused a shock wave at the White House," Roger Cramer said.

"Shock wave?" Buster said. "More like a goddam earth quake."

"I suppose you can't tell us about your executive session with the President," Leonardo said.

"Actually," Meg said, "the subject of our meeting will soon be known across the country."

"In that case, can't you share it with us?" Buster said.

Meg stood and walked behind me. She put her hands on my

shoulders. "I'll not only share it with you guys, I look forward to sharing it with the world."

"Well, don't keep us in suspense," Roger said.

"Yeah," Janice said. "I can tell you're about to make a big announcement, Meg. So, what is it?"

"Harry is running for President of the United States."

Chapter 45

It was good our room was private and closed off, because it suddenly broke out into bedlam, shouts, and cheering. They all took turns hugging me and pumping my hand. It was great to be among good friends.

Janice, tears running down her face, hugged me. "Oh, my God, yes Admiral Harry, *yes, yes, yes!*"

"Admiral Harry," Buster said, "I have a good imagination, but I can't imagine a better candidate than you. You will keep our country safe, my friend."

"The last time I was this happy was when I married Janice," Leonardo said, as he gave me a bear hug.

"Speech, speech, speech," they all began to chant.

"Talk to us, President Harry," Janey Cramer said.

Everybody in the room, men and women, were dabbing tears from their eyes. It was such an emotional scene, I started to fill up myself.

"Leave it to Meg," I said, "to make this announcement in front of the perfect group of people, our dear friends. Meg and I have led an amazing life together. It's about to get more amazing. We're happy with our careers in the Navy, and the reason we're in the Navy is because our country needs us. What we saw and heard on the other side of the wormhole made us both realize that our country needs us once again. When I'm called to duty, I always answer the call, and so does Meg. And I *am* being called to duty as President Blake made clear. No way will I allow Bartholomew Martin to destroy our country as he almost did once before. I'm a fighting admiral, and I'll fight that son of a bitch to the end. At this point, all I can say is, I won't let you down—and neither will my beautiful First Lady here."

After another round of cheering, the room quieted down to animated conversations.

"So now we begin the grueling task of traveling and raising money," Meg said.

"I wouldn't worry about fund raising, Meg," Leonardo said. "According to *Forbes Magazine,* Janice and I are worth over $75 billion. I know where some of that money is going."

I almost choked when Leonardo said that. Seventy-five *billion?* His patent royalties and stock trading have obviously paid off over the years. Looks like my campaign already has one thing it needs—money.

"Admiral Harry, can you tell us any details about your executive session at the White House?" Buster asked.

"Sure," I said. "When Meg and I walked back into the room there were two others present. I recognized Hiram Gibbons, Chairman of the Republican National Committee, and Karl Rove, former political right hand to President George W. Bush, and one of the sharpest political minds in the country.

"The president said he invited Hiram and Karl to be there in the event our trip to the future proved startling. Well, it was beyond startling as we all know, and as the president discovered from Roger and Janey Cramer.

"Harry," President Blake said, "you and your friends have shown us a future that we simply cannot tolerate. I refuse to see our great nation become the private plaything of that malevolent bastard."

"I'll never forget what President Blake said," Meg chimed in. 'Harry, you're a warrior, one of the gutsiest leaders in our country's history. You're the man to take on that slimy fuck, and you know it.' He actually said that. President Blake *really* wants Harry in the Oval Office. Karl Rove then ran some numbers. We all know how Karl Rove likes to run numbers. Rove held up a white board on which he had scribbled some numbers with a magic marker. Rove is famous for the simple touch of a white board rather than an iPad. He handed the board to President Blake.

'Well, Harry,' the President said, 'it seems that you're one of the most popular people in the country, and that includes me, I'm embarrassed to say. America loves you, Harry. You sank an enemy fleet at the Battle of Leyte Gulf on one of your time travel ventures. You're the stuff of history, Admiral Harry, and I want you to lead us to a history we can be proud of.' President Blake is quite fond of my Harry."

"And that was that," I said. "President Blake asked me to run for president."

———◆———

I've known a lot of excitement in my life, and so has Meg, but nothing tops this. I briefly thought about Bartholomew Martin, but then forced the thought from my head. Sometimes it's just good to savor the moment. I wondered how long the moment would last.

Chapter 46

Good afternoon, ladies and gentlemen, Shepard Smith here for *Fox News*. I have a huge announcement about a breaking story. We've been reporting for weeks that both the Republican and Democratic parties seem to be struggling to find a candidate to run for President of the United States after President Blake completes his second term next year. Rumors have been swirling for months that Bartholomew Martin may throw his hat in the ring and seek another term of office. Martin, as you will recall, was defeated by Matt Blake in his reelection campaign seven years ago.

"We've been told by many political insiders that people are just plain unwilling to run against Martin because of the well-known dirty tricks his party used against his opponent. Many a would-be candidate just didn't think it was worth it to have his reputation destroyed in the Bartholomew Martin smear machine.

"Well, for the Republicans the wait is over. None other than five-star Admiral Harry Fenton has announced his candidacy for president. Admiral Fenton has a resume that's staggering. He's the former Chief of Naval Operations and Chairman of the Joint Chiefs of Staff. He's the first five-star admiral since Chester Nimitz, the World War II hero. Not long ago, President Blake convinced Admiral Fenton and his wife, Commander Meghan Fenton to come out of retirement and rejoin the

Navy to help with the problems caused by the small nation of Concordia. And now Harry Fenton is once again retiring from the Navy to run for the highest office in the land.

"Admiral Fenton and Commander Meg Fenton amazed the world a few years ago by traveling through time, convincing us that time travel is a very real phenomenon. The Fentons wrote a book about their journey to a prehistoric time entitled *The Maltese Incident,* a tale that gripped the world. That wasn't their only time-travel experience. When he was the commanding officer of a carrier strike group, Admiral Fenton and his wife time traveled again, along with his flagship, the *USS Gerald R. Ford.* The ship went back to 1944, right in the middle of the war in the Pacific. Admiral Fenton joined up with Admiral Halsey and defeated the Japanese Navy at the Battle of Leyte Gulf, where he destroyed all 40 ships in the Japanese fleet, bringing a hasty end to the conflict. He rewrote the history of World War II as we knew it. The Fentons own a luxury resort in Portsmouth, Rhode Island, known as Leyte Hall, a name picked by Meg Fenton to honor her husband's achievement in that long-ago battle.

"Admiral Fenton was almost assassinated a few years ago when a would-be killer fired a gun at Fenton's head at a party celebrating another of the admiral's achievements. Fortunately, his brave wife, Meg, drew her service revolver and shot the man before he could fire again.

"So, there you have it, folks, a genuine war hero is running for President of the United States."

Chapter 47

Bartholomew Martin met with his aide, James Brent, at his home in La Punta, Concordia. As an almost immutable rule, Bartholomew would only meet with one person at a time. He jealously guarded his privacy at his mansion.

"So, James, the newspapers tell us none other than Admiral Harry Fenton is running for the presidency. Too bad we didn't kill the man when we had our chance. What can you tell me about our organization's campaign efforts?"

"You chose some excellent political operatives, Bartholomew. We have campaign staffs in all 50 states, and they're busy gearing up for your run."

"Yes, they are excellent operatives. The enormous amount of money I pay keeps them focused. We didn't expect to see a lot of people lining up for a run, but this Admiral Fenton business puts a new light on the subject."

"It does, indeed, Bartholomew. A recent poll by the *Washington Post* shows that Fenton's approval ratings are higher than even President Blake's. You'll be facing the first real war hero since Eisenhower. It will be quite a challenge running against him."

"And what are our operatives doing about this new situation, James?"

"We have lined up no fewer than six women who will come forward with stories that will make voters think twice about their sainted war hero's stellar reputation. The women have been paid handsomely already, through secret bank accounts of course."

"Shortly I will be moving to my Manhattan brownstone so I can be close to the campaign efforts. No one knows about my house here in La Punta, I assume."

"Rest assured, Bartholomew, that your presence in Concordia isn't known by anyone."

"Good. Admiral Fenton will soon discover the unpleasant consequences of opposing Bartholomew Martin."

Chapter 48

I t's a good thing Meg and I are accustomed to excitement, because we were about to discover just how wild a political campaign can be. Ever since I made my announcement, I went through periods of self-doubt. I'm a military leader, I thought constantly. I take orders and I give them. What the hell do I know about politics? I started to think maybe my decision to run was a mistake. Whenever that happens, I just ask Meg for a hug. She always centers me, and I did need some serious centering.

We were scheduled to meet with Karl Rove, Hiram Gibbons, head of the Republican National Committee, and Max Hastings, the famous political consultant, the guy who managed President Blake's two campaigns. Hastings is known by most political experts to be the best campaign manager on the street. Hiram Gibbons wanted Max to be my campaign chairman, but first sought my permission. I readily gave that permission, of course. When I'm running an operation, I expect people to listen to my advice. I can do no less with Hiram Gibbons, a guy who knows a lot more about this stuff than me. We would meet in Gibbons' office at Republican Headquarters.

"Good morning, Admiral, Good morning, Commander Meg," Gibbons said. "You're about to start the wildest ride of your lives."

"Let's make it Harry and Meg, Hiram," I said. "We're going

to be working closely so no need for titles."

"Well, soon I hope to address you as Mr. President. Let me start this meeting with some great news, great and amazing news," Gibbons said. "I just got off the phone with Frank Bertone, Chairman of the Democratic National Committee. They're not putting up anybody to run. Instead they're cross-endorsing you, Harry. They're as scared shitless of another Bartholomew Martin presidency as we are, and they think you're the guy to beat him. I'm now going to turn this meeting over to the two best political consultants in the business, Karl Rove and Max Hastings. You met Karl the other day. You'll get to know Max quite well in the next few months."

"Harry and Meg," Max said, "I first want to say that it's an honor and pleasure to meet you both. It isn't often I get to sit in a meeting with two genuine American heroes. I've spent a lot of time reading up on you two, and let me just say, I'm impressed beyond imagination. But our purpose today is not to praise you, although you're well-deserving of praise. Our purpose today is to let you know what to expect in the next few months."

"A storm of supersonic bullshit," Gibbons said.

"Hiram's right," Max said. "You two come from a world of discipline, honor, and gallantry. You're about to enter a process that will make the Battle of Leyte Gulf look like a softball game. Your opponent is not only a dishonorable son of a bitch—he will stop at nothing to get elected, and that means a mountain of lies aimed at you both. In a few short weeks, I predict that we'll see a parade of women on television interviews, talking about sexual affairs with Admiral Harry. One or more of them will accuse you of molesting them when they were underage, portraying you as a statutory rapist. I must flat-out ask you an embarrassing question, Harry. Meg may want to leave the room."

145

"No, Meg stays. There's nothing I can say that she can't hear."

"Okay, Harry, so here's my question. Have you ever had an out-of-wedlock dalliance with any woman?"

"Yes, two to be exact, both after my first wife died, and both before I met Meg. They were brief relationships, no longer than a few months each. I was at sea a good deal of the time."

"If I may interject," Meg said. "Harry told me about them, and the most amazing thing is this. Both wrote him letters, which Harry shared with me, praising him for his naval heroism, and both expressing regret that they ever broke up with him. One of them even said, 'Please give my regards to your wife. She's a lucky woman.' I totally agree with her. I *am* a lucky woman. I don't expect to see anything from those two ladies, except maybe a campaign contribution."

"I just heard what I expected, Harry. I've heard you and Meg referred to as 'America's Favorite Couple,' 'America's Twofer,' and I can see why. You're both known for your dedication to each other, and also for your courage. You're going to need it, as Matt and Dee Blake found out. Meg, I've heard you refer to Bartholomew Martin as the most evil scumbag on earth. That is the most accurate description I've ever heard of him. He is pure unadulterated evil, and he's not afraid to exercise that evil in getting his way."

"Max, you mentioned a parade of women telling lies about Harry," Meg said. "Can you be more specific?"

"Yes, Meg, I'm going to do that. I make these predictions based on what we've seen from Martin in his campaigns against President Blake. Martin has a ton of money to throw around bribes, and these women will be highly compensated for their lies. Expect to see their stories corroborated by 'witnesses,' who also will be well-paid. Meg, your loving husband here will be accused of the vilest acts imaginable. It will test your marriage."

"Nothing in the world can test my marriage to Harry. Nothing."

"So, what can we do to counter the lies?" I said. "Simply deny them?"

I looked at Max Hastings.

"Sue the bitches," Max said. "In retrospect, that's what Matt Blake should have done. Sue them, sue their corroborators, sue anybody having anything to do with them. We'll show the world that we're not afraid of legal discovery, where all the evidence comes out. We *want* the evidence to come out. Of course, you'll immediately deny any allegation, but we want to follow it up with an immediate lawsuit for slander, and I mean *immediate*. News commentators will be impressed with your willingness to put yourself right on the line in a court of law. Harry, you're known as a fighting admiral, and that's exactly what you'll need to do. Come out fighting and sink a few ships—I mean a few lying bitches. Remember the Fenton Doctrine—take away the enemy's options."

"We'll give 'em hell, Harry," Meg said as she squeezed my hand.

Hiram Gibbon's assistant walked in and handed him a piece of paper.

"Sorry to interrupt, Mr. Gibbons, but I thought you'd like to see this immediately."

"Holy shit," Hiram said, smiling. "I repeat—holy shit."

"Don't keep us guessing, Hiram," Rove said. "What is it?"

"The Fenton for President campaign has just received its first contribution. Five billion, that's billion with a friggin 'b,' from a gentleman named Leonardo Murphy. Did I mention, *holy shit?*"

"Harry," Max said, "you've got some big fans in your corner."

"Our next order of business, is your choice of a running mate. In our system of politics, the running mate has one job—to help the main candidate get elected. Harry, here's a list of six people who we've discussed. The decision is yours, of course, but we'd like you to know that these people have all been chosen for their name recognition and ability to help you get votes."

He handed me the list. I was slightly familiar with each of them, helped by the brief autobiographical sketch they provided after each name. One name jumped out at me.

"Jack Riordan, Governor of Florida. He and his wife were our guests aboard the *Ford* when we anchored off Pensacola Naval Air Station for maneuvers. I was impressed by the man's knowledge of history, as well as his infectious enthusiasm. I then read up on the guy. Seems he's doing a great job as governor and is popular as hell."

"Harry, we didn't want to point you in a particular direction, but he's the number one pick of Hiram, Karl, and myself. Florida's a big electoral state, and as you said, he's popular with the voters. We don't need your decision right now because I'm sure you want to discuss him with Meg, but we think he's the perfect guy for the ticket. I've gotten countless inquiries from people who want to be on the ticket with Admiral Harry Fenton. Riordan didn't approach me, but I approached him with a feeler question. I think he'd love to be your running mate, Harry."

"He's got my vote, guys," Meg said. "I was with Harry when we met him on the *Ford*. I think he'll be a terrific running mate."

———◆———

Meg and I decided to have dinner by ourselves, something we wouldn't be doing too often in the months ahead.

"Honey, we've done a lot of exciting things in our lives. Your running for president tops them all. I'm looking at it positively, as I always do. I think it's going to be fun."

"On another subject, I'm not looking forward to the parade of lying women," I said.

"Harry, I think Max Hastings's idea of suing them immediately is perfect," Meg said. "We'll call their bluff as soon as the lies leave their lips. No overpaid lying bitch is going to get away with telling stories about my Harry."

"Hey, hon, we should turn in. We have another big day ahead of us."

"Aren't you forgetting something?"

"Oh yeah, *carry on.*"

"I'd love to, handsome. Let's go to our room."

Chapter 49

Wolf Blitzer for *CNN*, ladies and gentlemen. I've just received news of a rapidly breaking story. The government of Santa Mallarta has been toppled in a violent coup. At least 200 people have been killed in an eruption of gunfire on the steps of the capital. Santa Mallarta has now been taken over by the new nation of Concordia, which had split off from Santa Mallarta just a few years ago. The new combined country will be known as Concordia. Its headquarters will be located in the old Santa Mallartan capital of Delfuegas.

"A special meeting of the United Nations General Assembly has been called for tomorrow.

"Concordia is a mystery nation. When it first split from Santa Mallarta it seemed to take on as its national purpose attacking and sinking ships. The cruise line industry, as you know, is a thing of the past because of Concordia. And the strangest thing of all is that nobody seems to know who, or what group, is running the country. We tried to get a Concordian official on the line to make a statement, but our phone calls were not returned.

"Stay tuned for more news on this developing story. In other news…"

Chapter 50

"Good morning Leonardo, good morning Janice," Max Hastings said. "Once again I thank you for your more than generous contribution to the Fenton for President campaign. My God, five billion dollars? I've never heard of such a lavish political contribution. So, what brings you good folks here today?"

"Janice and I are volunteering to work full-time on Admiral Harry's campaign. As we know, Martin will soon begin spreading lies about the admiral. It's my goal to box that bastard into a corner with my research."

"God bless you two. With your money you can lead a life of leisure, but instead you volunteer to throw yourselves into the middle of a stormy sea of stress. From everything I've read about the subject, you've been Admiral Harry's biggest fan ever since you served with him in the Navy."

"You got that right, Max. I am the Admiral's biggest fan, along with Janice here."

"Keeping our country safe from that bastard Bartholomew Martin is something you're obviously committed to. Have you discovered anything new with your research?"

"Yes, Max, we have," Leonardo said. "We've discovered that Bartholomew Martin controls hundreds of dummy corporations, and through them, he's seeking control of the world's shipping industry. I've already told our government all about this. The result is gigantic amounts of cash flowing into Bartholomew's coffers, cash that will be used to spread lies and slander about Admiral Harry, not to mention Meg. I don't want to brag, Max, but Bartholomew has never seen the likes of Leonardo and Janice Murphy."

"But you and Janice are still on active duty in the Navy. With your okay I'll make some phone calls to get you relieved of your active duty status so you can work on the campaign. Admiral Harry will call the White House if necessary. President Blake listens to the admiral."

"Please make that happen as soon as possible, Max. Janice and I are anxious to get started on Admiral Harry's campaign. We're worried that the Bartholomew Martin smear announcements are about to begin. Our lives are committed to Admiral Harry as the next President of the United States. He'll be the best president our country has ever seen."

Chapter 51

I t looks like you've taken to tweeting, honey," Meg said.

"What? I haven't looked at Twitter in six months. It's a waste of time."

"I said it *looks like* you've taken to tweeting. Obviously, it's not you. Let me read a few tweets that apparently came from your Twitter account. Stand by."

- "Sex is better when done in groups."

- "When I think of all the women I've ever laid, I want to do it again."

- "I find 12-year-old girls to be the sexiest people on earth.

- "There's nothing like a good blow job to relieve stress."

- "I hate faggots."

The phone rang.

"It's Max," Meg said. "Max, I'm putting you on speaker. Harry is next to me."

"Obviously I'm calling about that tweet-storm last night. Have you read any of them?"

"Meg just read me a few of the missives. I'm almost speechless. I thought Twitter had taken all sorts of steps to prevent a person's account from being hacked. Looks like it didn't work. If you believe those tweets, Max, Harry the pervert has just weighed anchor."

"Harry, Meg, when I first read these tweets, I was furious. But a few of us have huddled this morning and we all came up with a different take on the matter. One thing we seldom see from Bartholomew Martin's people is stupidity, but that's exactly what we're seeing. If somebody hacked your account, they could certainly spread a lot of misinformation and lies. But when I read those tweets, I thought I was reading a parody, like a script from *Saturday Night Live*. Anybody who reads them would say to himself, 'You've got to be kidding.' I think the Martin people have overplayed their hand, something they seldom do. This could work in our favor and gain sympathy for our cause. Nobody, even somebody who doesn't like you, Harry, would ever believe those tweets came from you. In five minutes, I'm going to be on a call-in with *Good Morning America*. They want to talk to me about the tweets. I'm going to discuss the obvious—that your Twitter account has been hacked and the utter nonsense is just that, nonsense. Expect this story to dominate the news for the next couple of days. The positive side is that we'll get a gigantic amount of free publicity. The Bartholomew people blew this one."

Chapter 52

What idiot is responsible for those ridiculous tweets last night, James?"

Bartholomew Martin was at his Manhattan penthouse, meeting with his assistant, James Brent.

"Miles Conklin, Bartholomew, that new guy who works in our publicity department. We thought he was a talented copywriter, which he is, but those tweets are, as you say, ridiculous."

"We've been made to look like fools, James, the last thing we can afford. What have you done about the idiot?"

"Miles has been repurposed, Bartholomew."

"Repurposed? Speak English, James."

"He has been killed, Bartholomew."

"James, I don't want anything like this to happen again. I fully expect that our campaign will become the butt of late-night talk show comedy in the coming weeks. I hold you personally responsible for vetting the credentials of anyone on our staff."

"I'm sorry, Bartholomew, it won't happen again."

Chapter 53

Meg and I flew to Norfolk to tie up my affairs as Commanding Officer of Carrier Strike Group 14, as well as my job as Commander of United States Fleet Forces.

As we walked up the gangway to the quarterdeck of the *Ford*, I expected to hear 'United States Fleet Forces, arriving,' the traditional Navy way of announcing a senior officer's presence, along with his title. Instead, we heard, 'Future President of the United States, arriving.'

"That's outrageous," I said, turning to Meg. "This is a Navy ship, not a political installation."

"Hey, lighten up, honey. It's just another indication that people love and respect you."

We went to my office adjacent to the flag bridge where Admiral Bob Molloy, my replacement, waited for us, along with Admiral Peter Jones, Chief of Naval Operations.

"Good morning, gentlemen. I must say that I'm embarrassed by the way I was just announced."

"Well, it *was* against regulations, Harry, but don't sweat it," Admiral Jones said. "I know I speak for the vast majority of the people on this ship, certainly for Bob Molloy and myself, when I say that I hope those words are true—that you *are* the future

President of the United States. Harry, you've done one hell of a job with CSG-14 and U.S. Fleet Forces Command. I look forward to having a five-star admiral in the Oval Office. If it weren't against regs, I'd volunteer to serve on your campaign staff in a Navy Minute. You make us all proud, my friend."

"Thanks for your kind words, Peter, but I should point out that the lady next to me has had everything to do with this turn of events."

"Harry, I know you didn't come here for unsolicited advice, but I'd recommend that Meg would be an outstanding Secretary of Defense, or at least Secretary of the Navy."

"Hey, Admiral Peter, give me a break," Meg said, "this is all about Harry, not me."

We spent the next two hours giving Bob Molloy the rundown on CSG-14. Meg, my encyclopedia-brained chief of staff, provided most of the details of the operations of a carrier strike group. I always like to leave a command in good shape, and I think our briefing of Admiral Bob did just that.

After our meeting wrapped up, Meg and I took a flight from Norfolk to New York, where my campaign headquarters would be located in mid-town Manhattan.

"I think you're going to miss the Navy, Harry."

"You?"

"Yes, I think it's gotten into our blood. As one of the top dogs in the Navy, you sure left it in a hell of a lot better shape than when you started."

"You mean, 'when *we* started.' Remember, we're *America's Twofer.*"

"God, I love that phrase. But the strange thing is, I often think of us as one, not two."

"That's because we *are* one, baby. How about a kiss before we land?"

Chapter 54

Good afternoon, ladies and gentlemen, and welcome to the *Pete Peters Show*. I'm your host, Pete Peters. We have with us this afternoon, a woman, Gladys Porter, who has a shocking story to tell."

The Pete Peters Show is one of the most popular shows on daytime television, with consistently high ratings. The reason for the high ratings is easy to understand. The show caters to a basic instinct of a lot of viewers—voyeurism. We had been tipped by a friendly insider at CBS about the subject of the show.

Meg and I were peeled to the TV. I hated to watch this crap, but Max Hastings convinced us that we should take careful notes to pick out discrepancies in the person's account.

"Gladys, please tell us your story," Peters said. He almost had a look of glee on his face.

"I was sexually molested against my will at a house party in Pearl Harbor. I was a Navy Ensign at the time."

"And when did this occur, Gladys?"

"In July of 2013, Saturday, July 13th to be exact."

I looked at Meg.

"We were deployed in the Sea of Japan that entire summer,"

Meg yelled as she jotted a note.

"And who was the person who molested you?"

"Admiral Harry Fenton. He was a captain at the time."

"I cannot fucking believe this, Harry. You were a vice admiral in 2013. You'd think those idiots would have done some basic research before they made up their lies."

"I was with another woman. Captain Fenton invited us into a small lounge area off the main room. 'How about a threesome?' he said."

"Harry, you waskilly wabbit. I guess this ties in with your group sex tweet, honey," Meg said, laughing.

"Shush, hon. We need to take notes."

"And then what happened, Gladys?"

"The other woman walked out, and I wanted out of there too. I tried to open the door, but that's when he grabbed me by the breasts and flung me onto the couch."

"You always were a frisky hunk, baby."

"We need to pay attention, Meg."

"Did you resist?" Peters asked.

"Yes, but he was a very muscular powerful man."

"At least she got *that* right, honey."

"Do you recall where the party was, Gladys?"

"No, I had a bit to drink, and I don't remember where the house was. I think Fenton spiked my drink with something."

"Always the playful devil, hon," Meg said.

"Do you recall who the other woman was?"

"No. It's all a blur." She dabbed a tear from her eye and blew her nose.

"Thank you for coming forward with an emotionally difficult story, Gladys."

"How's that for hard-hitting journalism?" I said. "She didn't recall where the house was or who the other woman was, and the guy didn't even follow up with a single question."

"The purpose of this creep show, Harry, is to produce hard-ons, not hard-hitting news. I scratch this up as a win for our side."

Gladys Porter had just been disconnected from her microphone and was walking out of the studio.

"Good afternoon, Ms. Porter. My name is John Kendall, attorney for Admiral Harry Fenton. I'm hereby serving you with a summons and complaint for slander in the *Matter of Harry Fenton vs. Gladys Porter*. I recommend that you hand this document to your attorney as soon as possible. Failure to answer this complaint will result in a default judgment against you in the amount of one million dollars. Have a good day."

Chapter 55

Meg and I sat in Max Hastings's office at the Fenton Campaign Headquarters. John Kendall, my attorney, had just arrived.

"So, I guess you two watched our favorite TV show," John said. "I served her with a summons and complaint immediately after the show. Max, I suggest you issue an immediate press release about the fact that Harry has filed a lawsuit for slander. Harry, Meg, please fill me in on any observations you have, especially any discrepancies in the woman's statements."

"Well, first is this," Meg said. "When Harry allegedly raped this bitch in July of 2013, we were deployed in the Sea of Japan that entire summer. Also, she said Harry was a captain at the time. Not so, he was a vice admiral. Just check Navy records or do a Google search. Harry's in the newspapers a lot. Also, I notice that she didn't recall where it happened or who else was there, only that it happened on July 13, a date when Harry and I were overseas."

"This show was so ridiculous it's almost funny, but before we laugh, I need to warn you about a couple of things. First, Ms. Porter is an attractive woman,"

"I don't think she was attractive," Meg said.

"Shush, honey," I said, "let John continue."

"Of course, we're going to do a lot of research on this woman,"

"You mean this *bitch*,"

"Meg, stop."

"Something tells me she has professional acting experience in her background," John said, "because she seemed genuinely upset, or *acted* like she was genuinely upset. The factual discrepancies you pointed out are excellent, but remember, she kept saying that she couldn't recall the details. At trial, she might testify that she *thought* Harry was a captain at the time."

"John, she stated that she was a Navy ensign, a trained officer," I said. "She certainly would have known the difference between a captain's stripes and those of an admiral."

"True, and we're going to check to see if she actually *was* a Navy ensign," John said. "The fact that she seemed certain of the date is a big point for us, because the records will show that Admiral Harry was a couple of oceans away from the scene of the alleged deed. The only thing I caution you about is that she did appear to be a sympathetic witness. Remember the Judge Kavanagh confirmation hearings? His accuser came close to keeping him off the Supreme Court because she appeared to be sincere. But all told, I'd say we have an excellent case."

"So, one at bat and one base hit," Max said. "I like those stats."

Chapter 56

Three weeks went by. The statutory time for Gladys Porter to answer my complaint expired. John Kendall's research disclosed some interesting stuff. Records from the Bureau of Naval Personnel showed that a Gladys Porter was never in the Navy for one thing. John isn't even sure her name is Gladys Porter. A search of public records disclosed no such name. She had said that she never married, so it couldn't have been a question of a maiden versus a married name. He tried to get her address from CBS but they refused, so, he got a court order compelling disclosure. The CBS execs swore under oath that they didn't have her address.

John stopped by my office, where Meg and I were sipping coffee.

"So, we started out with a lawsuit, but now it's been transformed into a story, a very powerful story for the Fenton Campaign," John said. "I'd love to file a default judgment for a million, but, of course, I don't have an address where I could serve her. I'm going to draft a story that I think Max Hastings will love. Harry, it portrays you as the victim. You, a presidential candidate, were framed, or to be more accurate, somebody *attempted* to frame you. I think the news outlets will find this story fascinating. This dumb stunt will actually help our side, and I'm talking politics, not law. If the story had a title it may be something like: 'Hey, what are those bastards doing to good old Admiral Harry?' "

"John, do you expect to see any more fraudulent accusers on TV?" I said.

"Like a lot of people, Harry, myself included, I've tried to anticipate what Bartholomew Martin will do. This Gladys Porter fiasco gave him a black eye. So, to answer your question, no, not in the near term anyway. In the final weeks before the election, all bets are off."

"Expect to see legions of Boy and Girl Scouts coming forward claiming that you molested them," Max Hastings said.

"Naval warfare is a lot more civilized than this shit," Meg said as she threw a ball of paper into the wastepaper basket.

"I agree, hon. I'd like to order a rocket attack, but I'm sure John Kendall here would object."

"I might be persuaded to counsel exactly that, Harry."

Chapter 57

The Republican National Convention was a month away, and nobody has stepped forward to oppose me. It seemed that a lot of people were willing to hold my jacket for this fight.

Jack Riordan, Governor of Florida, had accepted my offer to join the ticket as my running mate. My "political handlers" were delighted that he accepted and so was I. Meg and I had dinner with Jack and his wife, Loretta. He not only has a great resume, he's a hell of a nice guy and Loretta is charming and well-spoken. I looked forward to working with him.

Max Hastings jolted me when he said that none other than Frank Bertone, head of the Democratic National Committee, is scheduled to speak. Max said they're toying with the idea that Bertone may actually give the nomination speech. I began to feel like hot shit, but then I reminded myself that a lot of my support is motivated by hatred of Bartholomew Martin.

The polling numbers uniformly showed me way ahead, by a 70 to 30-point margin. Although that's a comfortable lead, I had a hard time wrapping my head around the idea that 30 percent of eligible voters actually prefer a proven dictator to be their president. I miss the Navy. At least there I could lead people into not screwing themselves.

Max Hastings stopped by my office.

"Harry, you have what would normally be described as an insurmountable lead. But with Bartholomew Martin in the picture, the word 'normal' doesn't fit the equation. Admiral, you've been under attack before while you served our country. You were attacked with missiles, bombs, rockets, and torpedoes. But all that is nothing compared to the shit storm that will soon head your way."

"Thanks, Max, for the heads up. Yes, from everything I've heard about Martin, he will try to portray me as an evil child-molesting sexual monster, just like he tried with President Blake. Yes, it bothers me, and it sure as hell bothers Meg. But we knew what we were getting into, and we're ready for anything else that bastard comes up with. Having good people like you on my side will help me overcome this crap."

"And there's a lot of crap heading your way, Admiral Harry."

Chapter 58

Hello everyone, I'm Dana Perino, along with Greg Gutfeld, Jesse Watters, Juan Williams, and Jedediah Bila. It's five o'clock in New York City, and this is *The Five*. Election season is heating up, to say the least, and we've been following it closely. Although the Republican National Convention is a month away, it's no secret who the Republican nominee will be—the famous naval officer and war hero, Admiral Harry Fenton. With the general election just five months away, Admiral Fenton has a commanding lead in the polls, with 70 percent of eligible voters in his corner."

"Admiral Fenton is one great American, no doubt about it," Greg Gutfeld said, "but the reason he's so far ahead has as much to do with that evil bastard he's running against as it has to do with him."

"Hey, Greg, watch your mouth. We're on national TV," Perino said, chuckling at Gutfeld's earthy remark.

"Sorry, Dana, I meant to say that evil son of a bitch. What torques my brain is that Bartholomew Martin polls with 30 percent. Don't people realize what happened to our country a few short years ago, when we went from a democracy to a dictatorship overnight? Thank God the admiral is the likely nominee to oppose him, because Fenton is probably the best presidential candidate we've seen in a lifetime. The guy's a genuine war hero and a brilliant strategist."

"Yes, he's one heck of a guy," Jesse Watters said, "but I fear what he's going to be up against as we head toward the election. I can't believe the Martin people hacked into the admiral's Twitter account and put out a batch of insane tweets, expecting the American people to believe they came from Admiral Fenton. I mean come on, one tweet talked about how the admiral is supposedly fond of 12-year-old girls. And then that bimbo was on TV talking about a supposed affair with Fenton, not bothering to check out that the admiral was commanding a carrier strike group in the Sea of Japan when the incident supposedly happened in Hawaii."

"And she couldn't remember exactly where it happened or who was there," Jedediah Bila said. "And even though she was a naval officer at the time, she didn't realize that Fenton was an admiral, not a captain. You can't make this nonsense up, although she tried—or someone did."

"And she was served with a lawsuit immediately after the show," Dana Perino said, "which I thought was a brilliant move on the part of the Fenton people. The crazy thing is that Admiral Fenton's lawyer hasn't been able to find her. It looks like a totally fictitious story. Navy records show that nobody named Gladys Porter was ever in the Navy, and a public records search shows nobody by that name even exists."

"We're about to take a commercial break," Juan Williams said. "We have a super-special guest this evening, so make sure to stick around."

———◆———

"It gives me special pleasure to introduce our guest this evening, a truly great American, former Navy Commander Meghan Fenton, Admiral Fenton's wife."

"It's my pleasure, Dana," Meg said. "Admiral Harry and I watch *The Five* every night, either live or on DVR."

"Meg, you and the admiral are famous for your heroic actions in the Navy, but you're also well-known for your close marriage. President Blake refers to you as 'America's Twofer.' I've heard many times that you two constantly joke and banter with each other. I've also heard that you and the admiral communicate with one-word sentences, and sometimes just a glance."

"Yes, it's safe to say that Harry and I enjoy each other's company. And yes, we often communicate with a word or a glance. When I urged him to run for president, my message consisted of one-word followed by a question mark, 'Harry?' He knew exactly what I meant."

"Can you tell us about the decision to run for president?" Dana Perino said.

"Besides me, Harry had somebody else urging him to run—President Blake. I remember it like it was yesterday. The President said, 'Harry, there are two words that explain why you should run for president—Bartholomew Martin.' No way would my Harry risk another Martin presidency. That man is the most evil (she almost said scumbag) person on earth."

"Can you tell us a bit about what it's like to run a big political campaign," Jedediah Bila said. "President Blake once said that Admiral Fenton is the greatest fighting admiral in American history. I guess that prepared him—and you—for this political fight. It must be extremely stressful."

"Yes, it is stressful," Meg said, "but one thing makes it easier— the nature of our marriage. Harry once said that sometimes he and I disappear and become one person. Harry has a great way of saying sweet things."

"Commander Meg, thank you so much for joining us on our show," Perino said. "Although we're not supposed to be overtly political, I want to tell you that we're all cheering for you and Admiral Fenton."

"You got that right, Dana," Juan Williams said.

"So, set your DVRs ladies and gentlemen," Perino said, "and never miss an episode of *The Five.*"

Chapter 59

Meg and I were on our way to the Waldorf Astoria where I was scheduled to give a speech before the U.S. Chamber of Commerce.

"Hey, I thought you were great on *The Five*, honey. You could have your own TV show."

"Well, it *was* fun, but a bit embarrassing. My God, those people are crazy about you, Harry. I thought I was sitting in on a cheerleading practice."

"Max Hastings was happy as hell you were booked on that show. They have one of the best ratings on TV and millions of people saw you. Max is working on booking the both of us on friendly shows."

"Friendly shows? Is there any group in this country that isn't friendly to my Harry?"

"It's an interesting phenomenon, Meg. I'm sure there are a lot of people who don't want me in the White House, but nobody would go public in support of my opponent."

"The most evil scumbag on earth."

"Somehow I knew you'd say that."

We walked down a crowded hallway to the rear entrance to the ballroom where I'd give my speech. A lot of friendly well-wishers reached out to shake my hand. A few patted me on the back.

"I'll be happy when the convention is over next month, honey," Meg said. "Then you'll get a Secret Service detail. All these people get me nervous."

"Don't worry, hon. They all look friendly."

We were about to walk through a door when we heard a man scream "*GUN,*" followed by the sound of gunshots.

Instinctively I grabbed Meg and wrestled her to the floor, positioning my body on top of her. We heard five shots in rapid succession. I felt a searing pain in my right leg. I looked to my left and saw a man lying on the floor with a cop standing over him. Then I looked down at my leg and saw it was covered in blood.

"Everyone against the wall," another cop screamed. Obviously, they weren't sure there was only one shooter.

Two other cops and a guy with a stethoscope around his neck ran over to Meg and me.

"I've been hit, honey, but I don't think it's too bad."

Two guys with a stretcher came running to us. One of the EMTs wrapped a tourniquet around my bloody thigh. "It doesn't look too serious, Admiral, but let's get you to the hospital."

They carried me down the hall and outside to a waiting ambulance. I guess I won't be giving a speech tonight, I thought.

We were taken to NYU Medical Center, where they whisked me through the emergency wing to a private room. Two doctors walked quickly through the door. "I hate to say you were lucky to a man who's been shot, but you were definitely lucky, Admiral. It's just a graze wound. You probably won't even have a scar. We'd like to keep you here for a couple of hours for observation, sir. Mrs. Fenton can stay with you, of course."

Meg sat next to my bed. I could see tears running down her face.

"Hey, why so quiet, baby?"

"Harry, this is the second time I've seen you shot."

"Hey, it's not so bad. You heard the doctor. I probably won't even have a scar."

"Harry, that bastard wanted to fucking kill you. How can you be so calm?"

"I'm calm because it was me that got hit, not you."

The phone rang. Meg picked it up.

"He's right here, sir."

"It's President Blake."

"Harry, I'm about to do something that's unprecedented. Actually, I did it already. Although you're not yet an official candidate, I'm assigning a Secret Service detail to guard you. They should be there in a few minutes. I spoke to the doctor, and it seems like the news is good, as good as news can get when somebody's been shot. Get some rest, Harry. I'll talk to you later."

The phone rang again.

"Hi Meg, it's Leonardo. Please put the admiral on."

"Admiral, it was Bartholomew Martin's people who tried to kill you," Leonardo said. "I intercepted three phone calls and four text messages. I was about to call you when it happened.

It looks like he's not satisfied hacking Twitter accounts and hiring bimbos. Janice and I are at our house in Manhattan. We'd like to invite you and Meg to stay with us tonight. You'll have your own private suite and there's plenty of room for your Secret Service detail."

"How did you know I'm getting a Secret Service detail? I just found out myself."

"Max Hastings told me. He was notified by the White House. News travels fast about you, sir. Admiral, I hope you'll accept my invitation to stay here. As you know, Janice and I have had some security concerns over the years. We designed this place to be safe and defensible. It's safer than a hotel room—and a lot more luxurious."

"I accept your gracious invitation, Leonardo. You're a good friend. I'll have one of my Secret Service guys grab our bags from the Waldorf. What's your address?"

"I'll send a car to pick you up, sir. My house is on 66th and Fifth Avenue."

"Wow, 66th and Fifth. Pretty nice neighborhood. We'll see you shortly."

———◆———

My leg was wrapped in bandages. Meg, always the efficient chief of staff, went to a store to buy me a new pair of pants. When she got back to the room, I was walking as the doctor recommended. It hurt like a bitch, but I made a conscious effort not to limp. Stiff upper lip and all that.

So, I survived another assassination attempt. This shit is getting old.

Chapter 60

Leonardo's huge Bentley limousine brought Meg and me, along with our three Secret Service guys, to the Murphys' house. We stared at the beautiful building, a classic Upper East Side brownstone. My leg was feeling a little better, and I was able to avoid limping.

My God, what opulence, I thought. Leonardo, with his billions, likes to do things in style.

Meg looked at me.

"Secretary of the Treasury?"

"I agree. Think he'll accept?"

"He will if *you* ask him."

Janice greeted us at the door and led us into the den, which was more like a ballroom. Meg and I have a few bucks, owing to Meg's huge trust fund from her dad as well as our book royalties, but I wasn't accustomed to such lavishness as the Murphy's house. It obviously belonged to a couple of billionaires. A butler—yes, a butler—walked in to take our bags up to our suite. Meg walked over to look at a large mural on the wall of the den.

"Oh, dear Lord, this painting is beautiful," Meg said. "It's exquisite. You guys have great taste. Look, Harry, two beautiful mountains with a lake in the valley. It reminds me of a Hudson River School painting."

"Lee gave it to me for my birthday two years ago. He painted it himself after he took a few art classes."

He painted it himself? I walked over to the painting, being careful not to limp.

"Leonardo, you never cease to amaze me. I think this is the most beautiful painting I've ever seen. And you did it after a few art classes? And look here, Meg, that's Janice in the painting, walking toward us smiling."

We sat on a sumptuous leather couch. Janice brought me a cushion to put on the ottoman. "You should keep your leg raised, Admiral."

I lifted my leg (without wincing) and rested my foot on the cushion.

"Janice and I would like to bring you up to date on our Bartholomew research," Leonardo said. "I've already updated Max Hastings. As I told you on the phone before, sir, I've concluded that the man who shot you is one of Bartholomew's hired guns. Admiral, Bartholomew Martin wants to kill you. It's great that President Blake assigned you a Secret Service detail. One positive thing is that we're getting close to being able to spot his moves before he makes them. It surprises me that they're so clumsy. Those insane tweets, supposedly sent by you, became an overnight national joke. And that bimbo Gladys Porter doesn't even exist as far as the records show. No doubt about it, Bartholomew is a brilliant man, but I think he's surrounded by a bunch of idiotic yes-men. Nobody dares to oppose him, and the result is a lot of stupid actions."

"Leonardo," Meg said, "does your research indicate anything

that he may be up to as we get closer to the election?"

"Good question, Meg," I interrupted. "I met with Max Hastings recently and he predicts that we'll see Boy and Girl Scouts in brigade strength accusing me of molesting them. I think he was exaggerating, but what do you think, Leonardo?"

"As brilliant as he is, Bartholomew is accustomed to doing things his way and nobody else's. What's the old saying about power going to one's head? He tried to pull the same stuff with President Blake's campaign. Dozens of women accused him of molesting them, and the voters saw right through it. I predict that the next woman who takes to the air will become an overnight laughing stock. He does have the money to buy lies, but, being the megalomaniac that he is, he can't see how his actions can backfire on him. His arrogance will help to undo him. The press isn't fond of him, to say the least. Without any prompting from us, they'll call him on his crap."

"Meanwhile," Meg said, "we'll all be on bimbo alert."

Chapter 61

Meg and I were at the Fenton campaign headquarters about to meet with Max Hastings. Max ran, literally ran into the room, grabbed the TV remote and clicked it.

"I just got word about this from a friend at CBS. We're about to see another bimbo attack. I called your attorney and he's on his way there."

We looked at the TV as a commercial was ending.

"Welcome to the *Pete Peters Show,* ladies and gentlemen. I'm your host, Pete Peters. We have with us today a brave young woman who refuses to bow to power, and who has a shocking story to tell us. Nancy Berringer is a computer software engineer and lives here in Manhattan. Nancy, please tell us what happened to you."

"Oh shit, here we go again," Meg said.

"Three years ago, almost to the day, I was hired by the Navy to consult on a revision of one of their databases. I was assigned to the *USS Gerald R. Ford* as a base of operations. The man in charge of the carrier strike group, Admiral Harry Fenton, called me into his office next to the flag bridge. I didn't think anything about it, because I was often called by senior officers to update them on my progress. As soon as I walked in, Admiral

Fenton walked over and padlocked the door. He invited me into a bedroom adjacent to his office. He said he had a computer in there and wanted me to look at it. As I looked at the machine, he tore off my blouse and began to fondle my breasts. I was about to scream when he put his hand over my mouth, and said, 'If you ever want to see another Navy contract, I suggest you cooperate.' Then he pushed me onto the bed, pulled off my skirt and panties, and forcibly raped me."

"We need to take a quick break, folks. Stay tuned."

"Holy shit!" Meg said as she threw a bunch of papers into the air. "I cannot fucking believe this crap. Three years ago we weren't even in the Navy. Harry and I had retired, and we were running our Leyte Hall resort in Rhode Island at the time. Another lying bitch who didn't bother to get her facts straight."

"I just got a text from your lawyer, John Kendall, Harry. He's on his way now to serve her with papers."

"Welcome back folks. Ms. Berringer will continue her story. Nancy, was that the only time the admiral molested you?"

"No, he repeatedly raped me during the remaining month of my assignment. He kept threatening me with loss of Navy contracts unless I cooperated. I rely heavily on Navy contracts in my practice and was frightened that I'd lose my livelihood."

"Nancy, why did you wait three years to tell this story?"

"Well, as you know, Admiral Fenton is running for president. I couldn't live with myself unless I let the American people know just who that man is—a malicious rapist."

"Were there any witnesses to these events?"

"No, and I kept my mouth shut because I didn't want to lose my business. But now, I feel better that I got it into the open."

"Nancy, the women of America thank you for telling your troubling story. Sexual misconduct, especially by a superior who holds an economic advantage, is something that should never be tolerated."

"Stay tuned for our next segment, folks."

Max Hastings' assistant walked into the room. "It's *The New York Times* on line one for Admiral Harry."

"Go ahead, Harry. Tell the simple truth," Max said.

"Good afternoon, Admiral, Frank Blanchard for *The New York Times*. By any chance, sir, did you see the *Pete Peters Show* today."

"Yes, Frank, I was forewarned that a…"

"*Don't say bimbo,*" Max whispered loudly.

"…that a woman would be on the show accusing me of misconduct."

"Do you have any comment about what she said?"

"I certainly do. Not only was I not on the *Ford* at the time of this alleged incident, I wasn't even in the Navy. My wife and I had retired to run a resort that we bought in Rhode Island."

"Yes, Leyte Hall. Lovely place," Blanchard said. "My wife and I stayed there a couple of years ago. So, you say that you weren't even in the Navy at the time the incident supposedly happened?"

"That's correct, Frank. Don't take my word for it. You can check Navy records. Actually, you can search *The New York Times*, which ran a feature article in the magazine section about our running Leyte Hall. No, I was nowhere near the *Ford* at the time of this alleged incident. I have never seen Ms. Berringer in my life."

"Admiral, as a reporter, I shouldn't be saying this, but someone is out to get you, and I think we both know who it is. That last incident on the *Pete Peters Show* turned out to be a sham, and it seems that this is a fraud as well. Don't worry, sir, this story will never see the light of day, not in *The New York Times*, anyway. I never go with a story unless it's corroborated by at least two witnesses, and Ms. Berringer said that nobody knew about it. Besides that, you weren't even there. Now I'm going to say something else that I shouldn't. I look forward to voting for you. Good day, Admiral, and sorry for the bother."

I had put the phone on speaker, so everybody in the room heard it.

"Yesss," Max said as he jumped up and fist-pumped the air. Political pros, I've observed, are a lot like athletic coaches, always watching the score.

"I can't believe Bartholomew Martin can be such a clumsy asshole," Meg said. "That woman never checked her facts."

The phone rang

"It's your attorney, John Kendall."

"Hi, John, I'm here with Max and Meg. I'm putting you on speaker."

"Well, I nailed the bitch, I mean woman. She has three weeks to answer my quickly-drawn complaint. *The Matter of Harry Fenton vs. Nancy Berringer* is now a lawsuit for slander. Anything you can tell me, Harry?"

"Yes, sweet and simple. I was not on the *Ford*, nor even in the Navy at the time she alleges. Let's hope this one doesn't disappear like Gladys Porter. I can't believe Bartholomew

Martin would be so sloppy."

"Harry, I think it's just a case of hit and run. A lot of people who saw that show will not see the corrections and retractions, so they made their point. We'll talk soon. Hey, don't send out any tweets."

"On another subject," Meg said after John hung up, "how's your leg feeling, honey."

"Much better, just itchy from the healing."

"I'll have to give it a kiss."

"That would be nice."

"Would you two like me to leave the room," Max said, laughing.

"Get used to us, Max," Meg said. "We go on like this all the time."

"It's been a hell of a week," Max said. "First, Harry was almost assassinated, and now another bimbo eruption. I'm getting a few more gray hairs working with you two."

"I wonder what Bartholomew Martin is planning next," I said.

Chapter 62

The *Cape Fear* was a large Canadian bulk carrier. She was steaming to Canada with a cargo of iron ore from Latin America. Like most bulk carriers, she had a small crew of only 30 people. The captain, Loretta Paxton, was on her second cruise with *The Cape Fear*. Paxton, age 42, had served 15 years in the United States Navy before she was offered command of this ship at a salary far bigger than her pay as a Navy lieutenant commander.

"Good morning, Captain Loretta," said James Bigelow, her first officer. "Beautiful day I must say," as he handed her a cup of coffee.

"I'm feeling a bit more relaxed about the ship attacks, Jim, but just a bit."

"There hasn't been a report of an attack in over a month, Captain. Maybe whoever is running the show has decided it sank enough ships."

"Hey, what's that, Jim?"

She pointed toward the sky off the ship's starboard side.

"It looks light a flight of helicopter drones. I count 15 of them. What the hell are they doing out here on the ocean?"

The drones aimed straight for *The Cape Fear*. Paxton and

Bigelow were both surprised at how silent the aircraft were.

"Shit, they're aiming for us," Paxton said. "What the hell can they be up to?"

Five drones dropped bottles of nerve gas near the 12 men on deck. They succumbed instantly to the gas, each man falling to the deck, dead.

Ten drones then flew toward the air intake towers on the ship, firing bottles of nerve gas into the huge scoops.

Within 10 minutes, the entire crew was dead, including Captain Paxton and First Officer Bigelow, asphyxiated by the powerful nerve gas.

A helicopter landed on the forward deck. Its crew, the replacement team for *The Cape Fear*, went to their appointed stations. They threw the dead bodies overboard and changed course for the coast of Concordia. The latest addition to the Concordian merchant fleet would soon be at dock in its new homeport.

Chapter 63

ood evening everyone, I'm Brett Baier, and this is *Special Report*. Tonight's show is indeed special, because we have with us an honored guest, Admiral Harry Fenton, a man who's running for President of the United States and appears likely to capture the Republican nomination in a few weeks. I say it appears likely because he's running unopposed.

"I'm not exaggerating when I say that Admiral Fenton is an authentic American hero, one who President Blake refers to as the greatest fighting admiral in American history. He is the first five-star admiral since Chester Nimitz, the World War II naval leader. Admiral Fenton actually wears the pentagram-shaped admiral's bars that Nimitz wore. President Blake ordered the bars to be removed from the museum at the Smithsonian Institution and attached to Admiral Fenton's uniform. Like many people, President Blake is a big fan of Harry Fenton.

"Admiral Fenton went on to become the Chief of Naval Operations and then the Chairman of the Joint Chiefs of Staff. He headed up an operation to prevent the detonation of an EMP, an Electromagnetic Pulse, over the United States. Like most of his missions, that was successful. The story took a scary turn, however. At a cocktail party celebrating the defeat of the EMP conspiracy, a man drew a gun and fired at Admiral Fenton's head. Fenton's wife, Navy Commander Meghan Fenton, drew her service revolver and killed the man before he could fire another round. The low caliber bullet struck the forward part of Admiral Fenton's skull, causing no permanent damage.

"The Fentons have a reputation as being a close and loving couple. President Blake calls them 'America's Twofer.' But besides all that stuff, I can personally attest to another thing about Admiral Fenton. He's just a plain, simple, likable guy, the kind of person you want as a neighbor.

"So, tell us, Admiral Harry, what motivated you to throw your hat in the ring and run for President of the United States?"

"Two words, Brett—Bartholomew Martin. As we all remember too well, he was America's first dictator. He turned our democracy into a totalitarian state in a matter of months, and he wants to do it again. Few people lined up to run against him, probably because of the viciousness of his attacks on his opponent, as President Blake soon realized. My wife, Meg first sprang the idea on me, and that was followed by a personal appeal from President Blake himself. I've grown accustomed to battles, so I decided to give it a run. Already my Twitter account was hacked and a bunch of crazy tweets went out, supposedly from me. And to date, two women who I never met have accused me on daytime TV of sexually molesting them. Their stories were riddled with factual discrepancies and they have been totally discredited. My opponent, shall we say, does not fight by the Marquess of Queensbury Rules. It's going to be an interesting few months."

"And let's not forget, Admiral, that another assassination attempt was made on you recently at the Waldorf Astoria, just before you were due to give a speech. Fortunately, you received a minor graze wound to your leg. You are one tough guy, Harry Fenton."

"Maybe, but not bullet-proof."

"In an amazing bit of political history, I understand that you are going to be cross-endorsed by the Democratic Party."

"In a way it's not amazing, Brett. Nobody, Republican or Democrat, wants to see a repeat of the Martin dictatorship. The backing of the Democrats, which I deeply appreciate, will give me a big advantage in the election."

"Speaking of advantage, Admiral, the most recent polls show you with a commanding 75 percent of eligible voters backing you."

"Yes, Brett, that is a comfortable lead. But it has us all wondering what Bartholomew Martin will have up his sleeve next."

"Admiral, thank you so much for joining us this evening. As you know, ladies and gentlemen, this is a news show, not a program of opinion, but I think you can all guess who I'm voting for."

Chapter 64

Hi Meg, it's Leonardo. I need to see you and Admiral Harry right away. I'm at campaign headquarters."

"We're heading there now, Leonardo. We'll see you in a few minutes."

Leonardo was waiting for us in my office at headquarters. He didn't say anything but handed each of us a piece of paper.

"Read it," he said. "It's an email message I intercepted from Bartholomew Martin."

"James, this is unacceptable. I paid Smith a small fortune to get the job done, and what did he do? He missed. Fenton is still alive. I want a full report on how this simple matter went wrong.

"Bartholomew."

"This is the smoking gun we've been looking for," Meg yelled.

"Not quite," Leonardo said. "I showed it to my father at the FBI. He said that because I obtained it illegally, it can't be valid evidence, and besides that it's difficult to prove where it came from. But it does tell us what we've suspected, that Bartholomew Martin wants to kill you, Admiral. I'm happy to see that Secret Service guy posted outside your office. But if there's one thing we know about Martin, he's persistent. He won't stop."

"That son of a bitch has tried twice to take my Harry away from me," Meg said. "I'm not going to let that happen."

I've been worried about Meg lately. Unlike her usual effusive self, she's been quiet, almost sullen. She keeps saying, "That bastard wants you dead Harry. If I kill him it won't happen."

"Calm down, honey. Don't talk like that," I would say.

"Okay, I won't talk. I'll act."

"Meg, I want you to take a couple of days off and relax. Why not go out to your folks' house in East Hampton? A little ocean air will do you good."

"I don't need any fucking ocean air. I've got things to do."

This was definitely not my Meg.

Chapter 65

Wife of Presidential Contender Arrested for Attempted Murder

Michael Bogart for *The New York Times*

Meghan Fenton, the wife of presidential hopeful Harry Fenton, has been arrested and charged with an attempted murder of her husband's political opponent, former President Bartholomew Martin. The incident happened at the Martin campaign headquarters in Manhattan. The police report indicates that Mrs. Fenton drew a gun and fired it at Mr. Martin. He ducked behind his desk and the bullet missed. The arraignment is scheduled for today.

———◆———

"Attorney Robert Stone, you may approach the bench," Judge Shapiro said.

"Your honor, I respectfully move that this case be dismissed with prejudice. My client, Mrs. Meghan Fenton, a former Commander in the United States Navy, is licensed to carry a firearm and she does so at all times. Her testimony is that, while meeting in his office, she saw Mr. Martin suddenly open his desk drawer and reach inside. She had the reasonable belief that her life was in danger because he was going to pull a gun on her. Therefore, her action was clearly in self-defense.

The police report indicates that, indeed, there was a gun in Mr. Martin's desk."

Judge Miles Shapiro had been on the bench of the New York State Supreme Court for 20 years. He remembered the administration of Bartholomew Martin, a time when his job as a judge was essentially taken away from him. If he wanted to approve of a settlement in a civil case, he was required to submit a request to the Martin Administration, and the approval would take as long as six months. If he didn't submit the approval form, he would be charged with a felony. He remembered that his job became one of rubber-stamping Martin's executive orders and watching helplessly as democracy disappeared. Although he kept it to himself, he vehemently detested Bartholomew Martin with a festering hatred that never let up, and he feared what another Martin presidency could mean for the courts and the country.

"Counsellor, you have made strong and compelling argument that Mrs. Fenton's action was a matter of self-defense. I hereby grant your motion. Case dismissed. You are free to go, Mrs. Fenton. You may retrieve your weapon at the property clerk's office. I apologize for your inconvenience."

Stone couldn't believe his ears. Strong and compelling argument? he wondered. All the hell he did was repeat what his client said. Not only did he expect his motion to be denied; he expected to argue against a staggering bail amount. This Bartholomew Martin bastard sure doesn't have a lot of friends, he thought, the least of whom is Judge Shapiro. And the prosecutor said nothing. He just sat there with a smile on his face.

I was sitting in the back of the courtroom, along with Max Hastings and Leonardo Murphy. When I heard the judge dismiss the case, I felt like I'd pass out. Meg stood and was about to walk to the back of the courtroom. We hugged as if Meg had just landed safely on the flight deck of a carrier.

"Let's go back to our apartment and talk, honey."

Chapter 66

Meg and I sat in our dining room holding hands.

"Honey, why did you do this?"

"You heard the judge, Harry. I acted in self-defense."

"I'm your husband, not a judge. What were you doing there? How did you get in?"

"I wore a wig and made up a story that I was a newspaper reporter and I wanted to interview Martin. I figured I'd take the risk that they wouldn't inspect my briefcase. They didn't. Idiots."

"And I noticed you weren't carrying your Glock but a Colt 45—a hand-held cannon."

"My intention was to blow his fucking head off from the neck up."

"So, you went there to kill him?"

"I went there to talk to him, to reason with him. Yes, I also thought I might shoot him if he tried anything—or if the opportunity presented itself."

"My God, honey. You were lucky his security people didn't immediately shoot you."

"I studied a lot of the research that Leonardo did on the relationship between Bartholomew Martin and his employees. Most of his subordinates hate him. The only thing that secures their loyalty is money. After I fired the gun, two guys came running into the room and ordered me to drop it, which I did of course. I was amazed at how polite the men were. One of them even asked my permission to put me in handcuffs. I had the distinct impression that those guys were disappointed that I missed."

"Baby, you can't take the law into your own hands," I said.

"Hey, Harry, we're military people, we're warriors. And what do warriors do? They kill the enemy, that's what they do. That bastard is your enemy; he's my enemy; he's the country's enemy. I mean, shit, he's the enemy of humanity. Harry, you're not part of my life, you *are* my life. You and I have been through the hell of warfare, Harry, and I'll be goddamed if that scumbag takes your life away from you—and me. That bastard tried to kill you twice, and Leonardo thinks he's planning another attempt. No way in hell would I let that happen. But now I've managed to fuck up everything. Your campaign was going great, but what's going to happen to it now?"

"Something tells me this incident won't have a negative impact," I said. "Max whispered to me in the courtroom that the country will think of you as a hero who tried to slay the dragon. A lot of people hate Martin, as we saw this morning. I can't believe the judge dismissed the case without so much as a hearing. I almost expected him to say, 'next time shoot straight.' Remember what your lawyer told you?"

"Yes, whenever the subject comes up I should say, 'self-defense.' I'll do just that. But if that scumbag makes another move against you, there will be consequences."

"Hey, babe, let's put this behind us. We have a campaign to work on."

Chapter 67

Meg and I walked into the main room of the Fenton For President campaign headquarters. About 100 people were busy at their desks. As if someone blew a whistle, they all stood and gave Meg a standing ovation, accompanied by loud cheering. The ovation went on for five minutes.

Meg walked up to the microphone at the back of the room.

"It was self-defense, nothing more, nothing less," she said, following her attorney's advice. "That's all I have to say."

The crowd heard it, but they didn't buy it. Another five-minute standing ovation.

We walked into Max Hasting's office. Max was grinning ear to ear.

"As I predicted," Max said, "Meg's ill-advised action is getting us nothing but positive press."

"It wasn't ill-advised, Max," Meg said. "It was self-defense."

"Of course," Max said, giving Meg a wink. "Harry, I know you don't like Twitter, but get a load of just a few of the thousands of tweets since yesterday, and these are typical."

• "Meg Fenton, that brave woman, needs target practice."

• "I look forward to a First Lady with balls."

- "No greater love can a woman show her husband. Too bad she missed that bastard."

- "Meg Fenton, my hero."

- "Next time use a machine gun, Meg."

"You're not the only hero in this campaign, Harry," Max said. "Yes, I know it was self-defense, Meg. I'm a lawyer myself. But on a personal note, I'm in awe by the love you showed for your husband. But, hey, please don't do that again."

"If that scumbag makes one more attempt on Harry's life, I just may have to defend myself—again."

"Meg, please don't say things like that," Max said.

"Okay, I won't say it. But you can't tell me what I can think, Max."

"Tomorrow you're due to give a speech in Chicago, Harry. I suggest you two take the afternoon off and go back to your apartment and chill out a bit."

Chapter 68

Meg, Max Hastings, and I walked into the Palmer House Hilton on Monroe Street in Chicago. I was about to give a speech to the American Bar Association. The ABA is known for its liberal positions, and many of the leadership were wary of my conservative views. But one thing united them, their hatred of Bartholomew Martin, a man who once made a sham of the American legal system.

"Good afternoon, ladies and gentlemen. As you all know, I'm a sailor not a lawyer. But one thing we all agree on is that our great legal system can never again be trashed as my opponent did during that horrible time he occupied the Oval Office. None of us will ever forget the Bartholomew Martin administration. Every day we saw another of our precious rights eroded. A 'knock on the door' became a startling reality for millions of Americans. Instead of laws enacted by our elected representatives, we were treated to a daily flurry of 'executive orders,' orders that could not be undone because of his veto-proof majority in both houses of Congress.

"And he wants another term of office, another opportunity to turn this great nation into his private playground. President Blake has referred to me as a 'fighting Admiral,' and this is one fight that I won't duck. Our strength comes from our freedom, and it's my intention to see that freedom preserved and enhanced. God bless this great nation."

Wow, they gave me a standing ovation.

"Perfect, honey, just perfect," Meg said. Sometimes I think Meg would say that if I belched.

"Meg's right, Harry," Max said. "You hit just the right pitch, and you kept it brief as they had requested. Just two weeks to the convention, then it's on to the general. This morning's polls show you with a 75-point lead. Admiral Harry, I look forward to calling you Mr. President."

I wondered what Bartholomew Martin looked forward to calling me.

Chapter 69

Good afternoon, ladies and gentlemen, and welcome to the *Pete Peters Show.* I'm your host, Pete Peters. We have with us this afternoon a remarkable young lady who has a startling message to tell. Amy Watson is 13 years old and will tell us about an incident that happened to her when she was 10 and in the Girl Scouts. I must warn you, what you're about to hear is shocking. Amy, please tell us your story about an incident between you and a Navy admiral."

"Accuser number one from the Girl Scout Brigade," Max said as he threw a folder onto the table. We were all crowded around the TV in the main office.

"She's really cute, honey. You always did have excellent taste in little girls," Meg said.

"Shush, hon, we need to take notes."

Amy Watson appeared to be extremely nervous. She didn't speak when prompted but seemed to be gathering her thoughts.

"I have nothing to say."

"I'm sorry Amy, but could you tell us your story?" Peters said.

"There is no story. It never happened. It's a pack of lies. I never met Admiral Fenton. Some guy gave my parents $25,000 and handed them a printout of a story that I was supposed to memorize. It's all made up. I admire Admiral Fenton and his pretty wife. I wish I were old enough to vote because I'd definitely vote for him. I think he'll be a wonderful president."

"We're going to take a quick commercial break, folks," Peters said. "Please stick around for our next guest."

Pandemonium is too mild to describe the mood at Fenton Campaign Headquarters. Papers were flung everywhere, and a few people danced on desks. Max grabbed the microphone.

"I think we should invite young Amy Watson to give the keynote speech at the convention. That brave kid just showed the world what our opponent is up to. My God, $25,000 to memorize and spout a bunch of lies. I think the clumsiness and stupidity of the Martin people is starting to work in our favor."

———◆———

That night I was scheduled to appear on the *Tonight Show* with Jimmy Fallon. For his monologue he wore a Girl Scout uniform and began by saying, "I'm looking for a handsome admiral to play with." The audience went wild.

When Fallon interviewed me, he held back on the comedy. Although he was still wearing a Girl Scout uniform he opted instead for a straight-forward interview.

"You have served our country with honor and courage, Admiral Fenton. It must be a shock for you and your lovely wife to be the subjects of so many lies and slanders."

"It is a shock, Jimmy, but I think people are beginning to see through what's going on."

"I think you're right, Admiral. People are seeing these

accusations for what they are—lies. Thank you, sir, for appearing on my show, and best of luck with your campaign."

I couldn't believe it, he actually called me "sir." He didn't even crack one joke at my expense. I think I have another fan.

Meg, Leonardo, and Janice were waiting for me outside the studio after I was done taping the show.

"I think we may have seen the last of the TV slander attacks," Leonardo said. "As arrogant and thick-headed as he is, Bartholomew must realize that he's making a fool of himself. Jimmy Fallon in a Girl Scout uniform nailed it. The country is on your side, Admiral Harry."

Chapter 70

The Republican National Convention was held on the last four days of August at the Houston Astrodome. It was hot as hell, with the temperature in the high 90s for all four days. Because, as anticipated, I was the only candidate, I thought it was a waste of money to have a regular four-day convention. But, as Max reminded me, traditions have their own demands. One tradition is that "favorite sons" have their names placed in nomination and make speeches, even though I'm running unopposed. According to the same tradition they would all throw their support for me.

Bartholomew Martin hadn't been heard from in two weeks. It almost seemed like he had given up on the election. The polling numbers showed me in the lead by an unbelievable 90 percent.

I was scheduled to be nominated on the final night of the convention. As Max had hinted earlier, Frank Bertone, Chairman of the Democratic National Committee, would be the man to put my name in nomination.

Hiram Gibbons, Chairman of the Republican Party, introduced Frank Bertone. The crowd—the Republican crowd—cheered wildly for their favorite Democrat.

"Although our views may differ on certain matters," Bertone began, "one thing is certain. I am about to nominate a truly great American, a man who seeks to provide the great leadership he has shown during his years of courageous military service. Ladies and gentlemen, it is my privilege and honor to present to you, the future President of the United States, Admiral Harry Fenton."

As if on cue, the crowd freaked out. I could see why people go into politics. The feeling of having a large crowd cheering for you is a moving experience.

"*Fen-ton, Fen-ton, Fen-ton,*" the crowd screamed for five straight minutes.

An often-seen ritual at a nominating convention is for the presidential and vice-presidential candidates to walk around the platform, holding hands with their wives, waving to the cheering crowd. A cameraman gave us a thumbs-up, a prearranged signal that we should put on the classic pose of a political ticket. So, Meg and I and Jack and Loretta faced the camera with our locked-together hands in the air.

The shock wave from the explosion hurled the four of us backward off the platform onto a crowd of cheering people. Meg cracked her head against somebody's camera.

I looked toward the site of the explosion and saw a sickening vista of dead and mangled bodies. I glanced to my left and saw the crumpled body of Frank Bertone, the man who had just put my name into nomination minutes before. His dead eyes stared at the ceiling. Although I was temporarily deafened by the sound of the blast, I could hear hundreds of people screaming. I looked at Meg. She buried her face in the crook of my neck, sobbing hysterically. Max Hastings pawed his way through the crowd to us. Three of my Secret Service guys ran to our side. The fourth lay dead 10 feet from us. I'd been in more naval encounters than I can remember, and I know the sights and sounds of combat, but I'd never seen anything like the horror in front of me.

A large crew of first responders worked their way through the crowd, trying to save as many lives as they could. I noticed them slipping on the sea of blood and body parts that covered the floor. One guy slipped and landed face-first in a pool of blood.

The TV control booth, suspended from the ceiling, was a shattered hulk of broken glass and dangling wires. The booth was positioned above the site of the bomb. The body of a cameraman was slumped over the edge, blood dripping from his face to the floor below.

We thought it was over when we heard another gigantic explosion, this one at the back of the hall. I saw no fewer than five bodies hurled through the air. I admired the courage of the cops and Secret Service people as they ran to the various piles of bodies, trying to render assistance. I especially admired their courage because none of them knew if another bomb was about to detonate.

The fun, happy sounds of a political convention were replaced by the screams of the wounded and dying, and the sirens of emergency vehicles.

So, the race to the White House was on. I wondered if I'd live to see Election Day.

Chapter 71

B rett Baier for *Fox News* ladies and gentlemen. There is only one story tonight, a story of horror and tragedy. Last night at the Republican National Convention in Houston, two huge bombs were detonated in the middle of the convention floor. Experts say that the bombs were intended to inflict maximum damage, as the weapons were laced through with nails and ball bearings, a design intended to kill. And kill it did. The bomb exploded in the middle of a large cheering crowd. The latest death toll is 395, with 84 people in critical condition, and hundreds with injuries of all sorts.

"The explosion came two minutes after Admiral Harry Fenton was nominated to run for president. Admiral Fenton and his wife, Meg, were hurled from the stage by the blast wave, along with Vice Presidential candidate, Florida Governor Jack Riordan and his wife, Loretta. We're told that the Fentons and Riordans are okay with minor cuts and bruises. Speculation is rampant that the blast was intended to kill Admiral Fenton. If so, this would be the third assassination attempt on the admiral's life.

"Frank Bertone, the Chairman of the Democratic National Committee, had just put Admiral Fenton's name into nomination in a historic cross-endorsement. I'm sad to say that Mr. Bertone perished in the explosion.

"The general election is just a bit over two months away.

Admiral Fenton's opponent, former President Bartholomew Martin, hasn't been heard from in weeks. It's as if he's given up on his campaign. Here at *Fox*, we don't like to speculate without evidence, but I can report that the FBI has centered its investigation of the bombing on the Martin campaign.

"I've just received a report that the death toll has climbed by 17 to 412 dead.

"We will bring you updates as they occur. Stay tuned to *Fox News*."

Chapter 72

Meg and I were back at our apartment in New York. Our Secret Service detail of four men occupied the apartment next to ours. One of the men was new, replacing the poor guy who was killed in the explosion. Meg still wore a bandage on her forehead from slamming against a camera when we were blown off the platform. My left hand was bandaged from being cut by some flying debris.

"Honey," Meg said. "That bastard is out to kill you, and he just came close. He almost got me too. Is this worth it?"

"I hear you, babe, but think about what you're saying. Do you want me to cede the election to that psychopath?"

The phone rang.

"It's Leonardo, honey. He sounds happy about something. I'm putting you on speaker, Leonardo."

"Admiral," Leonardo said, "I'll get right to the point and work backwards. Bartholomew Martin is in jail. He's been hit with 412 counts of first-degree murder and a few thousand counts of attempted murder. The judge refused to set bail at his arraignment this afternoon."

"Oh my God," we both screamed. Meg, head bandage or not, stood up and did a cartwheel. "When did this happen, Leonardo?"

"As you know, sir, I've been working my algorithm to death. I found incontrovertible evidence that not only the Martin people, but Martin himself, planned that bombing. I took it to my dad and the FBI hit the panic button. The last time I gave them evidence my father said it couldn't be used in a criminal case because I had obtained it illegally. But this time I gave them a ton of evidence, a lot of which was right there on the Internet. Dad and the other FBI honchos decided to cast doubt to the wind. He doesn't think any judge in the country would disallow that evidence. And it *was* presented, this afternoon at Martin's arraignment. Martin's people tried to keep it from the press, but they couldn't keep it from me. Did I mention that the judge refused to set bail? Martin, with his billions, could cover any amount he set. Admiral Harry, soon I'll be calling you Mr. President. I better get off the phone. I know Max Hastings will be calling you. I hope I've made your day with this good news, Meg."

"Meg's busy doing cartwheels around the living room, Leonardo. Yes, it's safe to say that you've made our day, my friend."

"As Leonardo predicted, it's Max on the phone, honey. I'll put him on speaker." She was out of breath from her cartwheels. She didn't even break anything. Well, except for that table lamp.

Meg kept walking around the room slapping her thighs, tears running down her face as she said over and over, "*Yes, yes, yes.*"

"President Fenton, Max Hastings here."

"Hey, let's not get ahead of ourselves, Max, the name's still Harry, although with the great news from Leonardo it looks like my chances are pretty good."

"Yes, Admiral Harry, I agree that your chances are *pretty good*," he said with a laugh, "even though the Democrats just announced they're withdrawing their cross-endorsement of you."

"Why the hell would they do that?" Meg yelled.

"Don't fret Meg," Max said. "I fully expected that. As we know, the only reason they cross-endorsed Harry was because of Bartholomew Martin. With Martin out of the picture, they had no reason to throw their support to Harry. But I wouldn't sweat it. They haven't named a candidate yet, and they haven't done any fund raising. And they sure as hell don't have Leonardo Murphy money. God knows what their campaign platform would be. The election is in two months, not enough time for them to mount a credible race. It's against my political instincts to say this, but you're in, Harry."

After we got off the phone with Max, Meg sat on my lap and put her arms around me.

"Honey, I don't know about you," Meg said, "but I feel like I've just gotten my life back, not to mention yours. That evil scumbag is where he belongs—behind bars. I think we should start brainstorming your cabinet and other appointments— because you, baby, are the next President of the United States."

"I think you'll be my first appointment. Admiral Jones had an excellent idea. How would you like to be Secretary of Defense?"

"Well, it would freak my mother out, honey, but I have a better idea. I think you should keep me on as your chief of staff."

"My God, I was hoping you'd say that, Meg. In my wildest imagination I can't think of a better chief of staff than you.

Hey, it's one of the most important jobs in Washington."

"Speaking of your wild imagination, why don't we go to bed and, you know, *carry on?*"

"Only the best chief of staff in the world would come up with such a great idea."

Chapter 73

Election day is next week. The Democrats nominated Jerry Malone, Governor of Louisiana, to run against me. He's a nice guy, but he waged a campaign best described as unfocused. My polling numbers are still solid. I dropped from 90 percent to 85 percent, when a few anti-Bartholomew Martin people decided to switch because Bartholomew was out of the picture. But 85 percent is still what Max Hastings calls an insurmountable lead.

Max, Hiram Gibbons, Meg, and I sat in my office at the Fenton for President campaign headquarters. We were going over cabinet picks and other appointments.

"I think your idea of Leonardo Murphy for Secretary of the Treasury is brilliant, Harry."

"Meg and I thought of it at the same time" I said.

"That doesn't surprise me," Gibbons said, laughing. "America's Twofer. You'll be a wonderful First Lady, Meg."

"Meg will also be my Chief of Staff. I can't imagine one better than her."

"Wouldn't that put a strain on your marriage?" Max said.

"Nothing puts a strain on our marriage, Max. Nothing," Meg said. "Remember, we went through the Battle of Leyte

Gulf together."

"Bill Carlini has announced he's resigning as Director of the CIA," I said. "I think Buster would be an excellent replacement."

All three loudly agreed.

"Max, I think you'd make an excellent Attorney General," I said. "The Justice Department can use your wisdom."

Max sat there, slack jawed.

"I won't let you down, Admiral Harry."

"Hiram, how would you like to be Secretary of the Interior?" I said. "I recall that you grew up on a farm and I've heard you speak with authority about environmental matters."

"You flatter me, Admiral. I gratefully accept."

"I think we've got a head of steam going," I said. "Please give me your lists of other recommendations. Better yet, give them to Chief of Staff Meg here."

Chapter 74

Election day was finally upon us. Rather than mail in absentee ballots, we thought it would be appropriate for us to vote in Norfolk, still our legal residence. It was Meg's idea, of course. We took an early morning flight, along with our Secret Service detail, and voted at the Naval Station Norfolk headquarters. The poll watchers had a hard time convincing people not to cheer for me in the voting room. Meg and I were in our element—a Navy installation. We boarded the plane for our trip back to New York.

"Damn, it's 1100," Meg said. "Ten hours till the polls close in the East. I don't know why I feel agita, but I do."

"That's because my pretty chief of staff always sweats the details."

———◆———

At exactly 2100 (9 p.m. Eastern time), all the major networks, including the big cable networks, *Fox* and *CNN*, called the election for me. Governor Jerry Malone, my opponent, phoned and graciously congratulated me.

Max, Meg, Hiram Gibbons, and I sat in Gibbons' office at campaign headquarters.

"Harry, if these numbers hold true," Max said, "we'll be

seeing the biggest presidential landslide in our lifetime. Job well done, Mr. President."

My cell phone rang.

"Let me get it, honey," Meg said. "You need to get used to other people answering your calls."

"Fenton for President Headquarters, may I help you," Meg said.

Her face turned white, white as snow. She held the phone against her chest, looking at me wide-eyed.

"It's Bartholomew Martin, that slimy fuck," she said.

"How the hell did he get hold of a phone in jail?" I said, reaching for the cell phone.

"Money talks," Max said. "It talks loudly and in many dialects."

"Harry Fenton here," I said. "Something tells me you're not calling to congratulate me."

"No, I'm not calling to congratulate you. I'm calling to warn you. As I have told many people in the past, don't make the mistake of thinking that you have defeated Bartholomew Martin. I shall never be defeated."

"Well, you're in jail, facing 412 counts of first-degree murder as well as thousands of counts of attempted murder, you tyrannical piece of shit. That sounds like defeat to me."

"Good night, Admiral Fenton. Until the next time."

"His name is *President* Fenton, asshole!" Meg screamed. But he had already hung up.

"I spoke to Jake Arnold at the White House earlier," Max said. "They're painfully aware that Martin has the money to bribe his way out of prison. No way will President Blake allow that to happen. On orders right from the Oval Office, the security detail guarding Martin's cell has been tripled, and is under the direct supervision of the Justice Department. Also, they're going to be rotated regularly and randomly to ensure that Martin's lackeys don't get the opportunity to pay somebody to look the other way. Also, I spoke to the Attorney General. He's ordered that the prosecution be in a Texas court because the scene of the crime was in Texas. As we know, Texas has the death penalty. So, although I thought I'd never say this, I believe Bartholomew Martin's power is gone and his days are numbered. Mr. President, I just heard him say to you, 'until the next time.' For once I'm confident there will be no next time. He's fucking toast."

"He's facing 412 counts of first-degree murder," Meg said. "I wonder if they can execute the bastard 412 times. I wish they'd prosecute the son of a bitch in Oklahoma, the only state that allows execution by firing squad." Meg said. "I'd be happy to volunteer."

"Hey, pretty First Lady, make nice," I said. "This horror is finally behind us. We have much better things to think about than Bartholomew Martin."

Chapter 75

January 20 is a crazy day to hold an event in the Northeast, especially one that takes place mainly outside. I recalled that President William Henry Harrison died of pneumonia just 31 days after he contracted it at his inauguration in 1841, and back then Inauguration Day was on March 4, a chilly day with temperature in the 40s. But old traditions die hard, and Inauguration Day is January 20 ever since 1937. What's wrong with late November a few weeks after the election? I thought. The temperature was 20 degrees Fahrenheit with a stiff wind on the day of my inauguration.

Chief Justice John Roberts and I stood there freezing our asses off as he prepared to administer the oath of office for President of the United States. Meg, who thought of everything as usual, bought me a pair of light-weight long johns to wear under my suit. But I was still cold. I shouldn't complain because Meg wore a dress and an overcoat according to protocol, not a pantsuit.

Precisely at noon, Justice Roberts held out the Bible and asked me to raise my right hand.

I do solemnly swear that I will faithfully execute the office of President of the United States, and will to the best of my ability, preserve, protect and defend the Constitution of the United States. So, help me God.

I'm pretty good at keeping my emotions under control, a

talent I picked up in many a sea battle, but I found that saying those words was one of the more moving experiences of my life. I've had some big assignments in my career, but now it's my job to *preserve, protect, and defend the Constitution of the United States.* Wow. Thank God Meg is my Chief of Staff.

Time for my inauguration speech. My first major task was to keep my teeth from chattering. As I walked up to the microphone, the crowd applauded loudly and long. I think they were trying to keep their hands warm.

I began with the traditional thanking of the dignitaries.

"I thank Vice-President Jack Riordan, Chief Justice John Roberts, etc., etc., etc..."

I then inserted something that wasn't in my written speech, but something I felt I had to say.

"I first want to thank the most important person in my life, the First Lady of the United States and my Chief of Staff, my wonderful wife, Meg Fenton."

Meg was shocked. She had gone over the speech with me countless times, and she wasn't expecting what I said. After I thanked her, I looked into her eyes. She blew me a kiss, then mouthed the words, "carry on."

"In recent years, our nation has gone through some of its most trying times, times that tested our resolve, times that made us fearful, times that made us doubt we would overcome the forces against us. Those times are over. As religious leaders always tell us, there *is* such a thing as evil in the world, evil that seeks control through power, evil that has no respect for basic human rights. The epitome of that evil is now in prison, facing 412 counts of first-degree murder and thousands of counts of attempted murder. You know who I mean."

As we wrote the speech, Meg and I agonized over my mentioning Bartholomew Martin, and we decided that I would do it without naming him. I even discussed it with the Attorney General. No way did I want my words to be used as a defense by that monster, claiming that I prejudiced any potential jurors against him. But the AG assured me that the evidence against Martin was so strong and widely publicized, nothing I said would make a difference. I felt that I had to mention him, at least by description, the 800-pound gorilla who almost destroyed our country, the man Meg was accused of trying to murder, although I definitely wouldn't bring *that* up.

"Often, in a speech such as the one I'm giving, we hear a warning that there are treacherous times ahead. I won't say that. I thank God on bended knee that I am fortunate enough to have as a wife, a woman who gives new meaning to the phrase positive thinking." This wasn't in the speech either, but I didn't care. I wanted the world to know how much Meg means to me—and to the country.

"Meg's positive attitude has rubbed off on me over the years, and I intend for it to continue, and I encourage you all to think like Meg. We're blessed to live in a wonderful country, the cradle of liberty, the font of hopefulness. We saw our precious freedoms eroded a few year ago, but that has now passed. It's my intention as your president, not only to defend our liberties, but to expand them."

The crowd went nuts when I said that last sentence, as Meg and I expected when we wrote the speech.

"Just as my great predecessor, President Matt Blake, I intend to keep restoring our wonderful freedom that was seriously attacked a few short years ago."

I still had about three pages to go, but I could see that people were freezing, and I didn't want them to catch pneumonia, as poor President Harrison did. So, I decided to wrap it up.

"God bless you, my fellow Americans, and God bless America."

———◆———

Meg and I climbed into the presidential limousine, affectionately known as *"The Beast,"* a huge Cadillac SUV that has enough armor in it to take on a tank. We were happy that the driver was thoughtful enough to warm it up before we got in.

In an amazingly choreographed move, the Blakes' belongings were moved out of the White House just before ours were moved in. As career Navy people, Meg and I never acquired much "stuff," so our move-in went a lot quicker than the Blakes' move-out.

Jake Arnold, our friend and former White House Chief of Staff, took it upon himself to show us everything we needed to know about living in the White House. It wasn't so friendly when Matt Blake moved in after Bartholomew Martin.

Beginning at 7 p.m., Meg and I would begin making the traditional rounds of Inaugural Balls. We had four to attend. It's a good thing we keep in good physical shape, because this day was exhausting. It was a day of nonstop walking, waving, handshaking, and smiling.

When we returned to our new home at 11 p.m., we both showered. Meg walked up to me, wrapped her arms around my neck and said. "Wow, I can't wait to *carry on* in the White House."

That said, we both fell fast asleep as soon as we hit the bed.

The next morning, I would discover that I had nothing to feel relaxed about.

Chapter 76

Early the next morning after we had a quiet breakfast to ourselves, Meg and I sat in the Oval Office going over her plans. I guess I shouldn't have been surprised, Meg being Meg, but she had my entire day lined up for me.

"When did you find the time to do all this?" I said. "We didn't have a moment to breathe yesterday."

"You know me, Mr. President, I love to multitask."

"Mr. What?"

"Sorry, I meant baby."

"Much better."

"Aren't you going to tell me to carry on?"

"Later, sexy lady, we have work to do."

"Mr. President, it's Treasury Secretary Murphy for you on line one, sir," my assistant, Nancy Cochrane said. "I tried to find out what he wanted, but all he said is that's it's urgent."

"Hi, Leonardo, always good to hear from you, my friend. I'm here with Meg and I'll put you on speaker. What's up?"

"This has nothing to do with the Treasury Department, sir. Have you ever heard the name Antonio Martin?"

Meg and I looked at each other with an expression that said, "Who's he?"

"Martin? Any relation to my favorite jailbird?"

"It's his son, sir. Bartholomew Martin has kept this a closely guarded secret for years."

"So, tell us about this guy, Leonardo."

"To get right to the point, sir, Antonio Martin, age 42, intends to pick up where his father left off. In the overnight hours, three ships were attacked with nerve gas, killing their entire crews. All three were taken to Concordia."

Nancy Cochrane knocked and walked in.

"This message was just emailed to you, sir. I thought you'd want to see it right away."

Meg had counseled Nancy never to be hesitant about interrupting me with something she thought was important. Meg told her it would be an executive decision on Nancy's part, and her decision would never be questioned.

"Hold on, Leonardo, I just got an important message. I'll read it aloud."

Meg stood over my shoulder.

"Dear President Fenton:

"My father warned you, and now I shall warn you. Do not think that you can defeat the Martins. Others have tried over the years, to their peril. Our plans may have been delayed, but not thwarted. Last night, my forces acquired three more ships, ships that will carry the flag of Concordia. Once again, the oceans of the world will become a sea of fear.

Yours in victory,

Antonio Martin"

PART TWO

Chapter 77

On a warm June day, First Lady Meg Fenton walked with her three Secret Service agents toward the new Labor Department Building. She had an appointment to meet with the new Labor Secretary, and she insisted that it be at the Labor Department rather than the White House, so she could check the place out. As they approached the entrance, they heard a loud bang coming from the road in front of the building. Instinctively they all turned around, the agents drawing their guns. They saw an old model car drive slowly by when they heard another bang, accompanied by a puff of smoke from the car's tailpipe. Just a backfire, they were relieved to see. In the process of spinning around, Meg tripped backwards through an opening in a hedge but managed to keep from falling. Her foot struck a grate in the ground that was obscured by shrubbery. She felt the ground rumble under her feet. The daylight turned dark. In two minutes, the rumbling stopped, and the daylight returned.

Shit, she thought, I stepped on a goddam wormhole. She looked to her right and the new Labor Department building wasn't there, replaced instead by a row of one-story office buildings. She looked toward the street and thought she was in Havana. All the cars were models from the 1950's or early 60's. "Hank," she yelled to the lead agent, although she couldn't see him. He didn't respond. Obviously, she had travelled through time alone.

Meg had been through this experience enough times that she knew exactly what to do. To get back to where you came from, just recross the wormhole. She looked to her left and saw the storm grate about four feet away. Wow, she thought, I did some serious stumbling. She laughed. Meg had long ago convinced herself that she should treat her problem with clumsiness by seeing the humor in it. She was about to approach the wormhole grate when she was gripped by the normal reaction of any time traveler—she simply *had* to find out what year she was in before attempting to return to the present. She looked around, not recognizing the scene at all. Then she noticed a coffee shop across the street. She walked through the front door, grabbing a newspaper from the rack at the entrance. She sat down at a small table and ordered coffee. Then she looked at the date on the newspaper. June 9, 1961.

Thank God I hit the ATM before going to the Labor Department, Meg thought. I don't think my credit card would do much good because it has an expiration date of 2025. She paid for the coffee in cash—10 cents. Her first inclination was to call her husband, the President. Wait a minute, she thought, I don't think there are any cell towers in 1961. As she sipped her coffee, she heard President Kennedy giving an address on the radio. The café had no TV. Her intellectual curiosity on full alert, Meg toyed with the idea of walking around the city to see what life was like in 1961, a time long before she was born. But then her diligent Chief-of-Staff brain kicked in. This is bullshit, she thought. I've got to recross that wormhole *now*.

———◆———

I had been calling Meg on her cell phone for the last half hour, but not one call went through. That's weird, I thought. Meg is fanatical about keeping her cell phone charged and ready to receive calls at all times.

"Mr. President, Agent Jackson is here to see you, sir," my assistant, Nancy Cochrane said. "He says it's important."

Tom Jackson is the agent in charge of the White House Secret Service detail. What could he want? I wondered. The only time I ever see him is for regularly scheduled meetings.

"Mr. President, I'll get right to the point, sir. The Secret Service detail guarding the First Lady has lost contact with her. They last saw her in front of the Labor Department building where she was going for a meeting. They've cordoned off the area with crime scene tape."

"How the hell could they lose contact with her?" I said, feeling both pissed off and scared. "What's so complicated about Secret Service agents watching the person they're supposed to protect?"

"I'm sorry, sir, but I don't have an explanation at this point. I just dispatched 12 additional agents to report to the scene."

"I want to go there now, Tom."

"Sir, I'm not sure that would be advisable."

"Tom, I don't give a flying fuck what you think is advisable. Take me there *now.*" I realized I was being nasty, but I didn't care. My Meg is missing, and these bozos are in charge of protecting her.

"Nancy," I said to my assistant, "contact CIA Director Buster and tell him to meet me at the Labor Department building— immediately."

I knew I was stomping on agent Jackson's turf, but I didn't care. I have more faith in Buster than most people in government, and if Jackson feels slighted by having the CIA on his territory, tough shit. They shouldn't have lost Meg in the first place.

Chapter 78

I was taken in a Secret Service vehicle to the site where Meg disappeared. I didn't want to use *The Beast*, my presidential limo, because I didn't want to call undue attention to the operation. I just wanted to find Meg. Buster, not to my surprise, was already there. He had noticed a storm grate on the ground and told the agents to rope it off.

"Good morning, Mr. President," Buster said. "Something tells me that we're both thinking the same thing."

"A wormhole?" I said.

"Yes, sir. Watch this."

He tossed a stick at the storm grate. The stick disappeared.

"Sir, Meg is on the other side of that thing. I'm sure of it."

The Secret Service people didn't seem to know what to make of our conversation. Although all agents are briefed on the phenomenon of time travel, to the uninitiated it's still like science fiction.

I had a decision to make, as usual. Should I send someone through the wormhole to try and find Meg, or should we wait a while to see if she makes it on her own? Meg knows the drill with wormholes. To get back to the present, all you need to do is cross back over the wormhole. As Buster and I continued our conversation about five feet from the storm grate, we saw movement out of the corner of our eyes. Suddenly, there was Meg, *my* Meg. She walked up to me with a wide smile on her face. We wrapped our arms around each other and hugged, ignoring the crowd that surrounded us.

"What happened?" I said. Stupid question, maybe, but maybe not. I wanted to know what happened.

"Long story, honey. I bring you greetings from 1961, the year on the other side of that wormhole."

"Madam First Lady," Tom Jackson said. "The Secret Service owes you an apology."

"Don't be silly, Tom," Meg said. "It wasn't your guys' fault. It was a freak accident."

Meg then told us about the backfiring car, and how everyone instinctively looked that way. Hell, when they heard what may have been a gunshot, the agents' job *was* to look that way. They only did what they were supposed to do.

Meg is like that. She would never let other people think they were wrong when they weren't.

Then she described how she stumbled backwards and hit the wormhole. Although I was so inclined, I didn't even make a crack about her clumsiness.

Phil Blancato, Secretary of Labor, walked up to us.

"I'm sorry I was late for our meeting, Phil," Meg said.

"Not at all, Madam First Lady. It's only been a few minutes. Under the circumstances, I guess you'll want to reschedule our meeting."

"Yes, Phil, definitely. I've got some catching up to do with this guy," she said, putting a hand on my shoulder. "I'll have my assistant call and set up another meeting."

"Miss me?" she asked as she stroked my face.

"Miss you? Are you kidding? I felt like I was hit by a comet. It's great to have you back, honey. Come on, let's go to the White House."

Chapter 79

Meg and I lead interesting lives, no other way to put it, unless you substitute the word bizarre for interesting.

We had just finished breakfast and sat in the Oval Office to review my day's plans.

"I'm still trying to get over my upset when you did your little time travel journey yesterday. You must have been frantic, honey."

"No, I wasn't frantic at all, for one reason. You were on the case. When Harry Fenton is in charge, stuff happens."

"Well, nice of you to say that, hon, but I really didn't do anything."

"Didn't do anything? You immediately assembled the entire Secret Service, got hold of Buster, and came to save me. Turns out, I found my way back myself. But I wasn't worried. *You* were in charge."

Sometimes I think Meg flatters me too much.

"And that's why I'm not worried about our country despite all the crazy shit that's going on. The best President our country ever had will handle it."

"Speaking of crazy shit, hon, I assume you read the CIA briefing memo this morning."

"Yes, I did," Meg said. "Antonio Martin, that insane bastard, is busy rolling up the world's shipping industry as his private yacht club. I think he's every bit as evil as his father Bartholomew, maybe even worse."

I'll never forget the first time I heard of Antonio Martin. On my first day in office five months ago I received an email from him, letting me know that he had no intention of abandoning his father's plan to destroy the world's shipping industry. The message ended with the chilling words, "Once again, the oceans of the world will become a sea of fear."

"Admiral Mike Hamlin, Director of Office of Naval Intelligence, will be here in two hours to meet with you, honey."

"You mean meet with *us,* Meg. Sometimes I get the feeling that I can get a lot more done by just meeting with you alone. You have an amazing talent for cutting through bullshit."

"Thanks for the compliment, baby, but Admiral Hamlin is important. ONI is a key to helping us stop that goddam Concordian yacht club."

"Concordian yacht club? I love the way you put it, Meg."

"Because that's exactly how Antonio Martin views the world's shipping industry, as his own private club. Harry, that bastard is our enemy. Just last week, Concordia attacked and stole three more ships. The tactic they've been using recently is to attack with poison gas, the tactic that Leonardo told us all about. They've discovered, or created, a new type of nerve gas that dissipates quickly after killing its targets. That enables a boarding party to take over the ship after its crew has been killed. Three more ships for Antonio's fleet. You know I hate to put more pressure on you, hon, more than you're already under, but you're going to need to take some drastic steps with that prick."

Chapter 80

Treasury Secretary Murphy is here for his appointment, Mr. President. I'm sending him in, sir."

As Meg often reminds me, Leonardo is my biggest fan and he readily accepted the job of Treasury Secretary when I offered it to him.

"Good morning, Mr. President, good morning, Madam First Lady."

"Hey, Leonardo, the name's Meg. You should call this guy Mr. President, of course, but I'm still Meg. Good to see you as always."

"Leonardo," I said, "in your short time as Secretary of the Treasury, you're doing a great job as we expected of you. Meg told me all about how you reorganized the committees and appointed new chairmen. But I know you realize that the Treasury Department isn't what I wanted to see you about. Concordia, in a word, is the subject of this meeting. Antonio Martin is proving to be as big a threat as his late old man, Bartholomew. Meg, as usual, put it perfectly. Antonio Martin wants the world's shipping industry as his private yacht club, and he'll let nothing get in his way. In the past week he's attacked and stolen three more ships. I know your duties at Treasury have you busy, but with your brain you can keep a dozen or more balls in the air at any time. Leonardo, I want you to keep me up to date on what that bastard is up to."

"I've already been working on just that, Mr. President. I've taken that Bartholomew tracking algorithm that I wrote and have been tweaking it into an Antonio tracker. My objective is that we'll know what he's doing before he does it. Between him and his late father, they've destroyed the cruise line industry, but that isn't the end of the story."

"What *is* the end of the story, Leonardo?" I said.

"Well, sir, it's not the end, but the continuation. Every week we see an increase in advertising for cruise vacations. Concordia has burglarized the cruise line industry and has changed the appearance of the ships to look different from before they were hijacked. Bookings are building slowly because a lot of people are still fearful, remembering when Concordia attacked cruise ships with abandon. But they *are* increasing, and as no new attack reports on cruise ships hit the newspapers, the numbers will only go up. I've told you that Concordia keeps these maneuvers covered by layers of legal complexity. There are no fewer than 15 dummy corporations that own the vessels of Antonio's fleet, ships that were simply stolen from their former owners. And now that the cruise ship industry is in new hands, Antonio has set his sights on the rest of the rest of the world's shipping, just as his father intended to do."

"Do you think he has any political plans in the United States, Leonardo?" Meg said.

"All I can do is observe his actions and look for patterns. But I don't doubt for a moment that he has his sights on high office, meaning your seat in the Oval Office, sir. A trait that he inherited from his father, besides greed, is the lust for power. He certainly has power in Concordia, but my guess is that his sights are higher. Our Navy is going to be quite busy with Antonio

Martin. They've been careful to avoid direct confrontations with any of our ships, especially those in a carrier strike group like you commanded, sir. But their naval fleet is growing rapidly, as much as its commercial ships. I expect to see Concordia seeking confrontations, rather than avoiding them."

"Harry, Admiral Hamlin will be here in a half hour," Meg said.

"Leonardo, you're going to be the busiest Treasury Secretary in history."

Chapter 81

Milton, have you prepared the report I asked of you?"
Antonio Martin said to Milton Drake, his assistant.

"Yes, sir, I have."

"Sir? Milton, how many times do I need to tell you that my name is Antonio, not sir, or any other name you choose for me."

"Yes, Antonio."

One of the many traits Antonio Martin inherited from his father was a strict code of communication. He insisted that all his subordinates be called by their first names, and never nicknames. James was James, never Jim. Milton was Milton, never Milt. And Antonio was Antonio, not sir or Mr. Martin. He also insisted that his subordinates never use adjectives or adverbs when making a report. He wanted to be free to put his own highlights on subjects, better to enable him to do the analyzing, not some eager-to-please subordinate.

"As you are aware, Antonio, the White House is now occupied by a man with vast experience in naval warfare. Expect that experience to be used against us. I expect us to see confrontations from the American Navy on a regular basis. President Fenton wants to stop us, Antonio, and his actions in the past lead me to believe that nothing will turn his eyes from that task."

"On the subject of naval matters, Milton, tell me about our latest preparations with our navy."

"Antonio, in the past month we have acquired three frigates from the Chinese navy, four destroyers from the Russians, and most important of all, our first aircraft carrier, which we also obtained from China."

"If I understand you, Milton, soon we will be able to fulfill my objective of confronting the American Navy directly."

"Yes, Antonio, I see that day coming. No less than four months from now."

Milton Drake felt sick to his stomach. He was paid a huge salary by Antonio Martin, over a half million dollars a year, far more than he could earn at any other position. But a nagging feeling in the pit of his stomach kept screaming that maybe he was on the wrong side. An American by birth, Milton never lost his affection for his old country. And nothing prevented his growing revulsion for his keeper and benefactor, Antonio Martin.

Chapter 82

"Mr. President, Admiral Hamlin is here for his meeting with you, sir," my assistant said.

"Good afternoon, Mr. President, Madam First Lady."

"Just before the election a few short months ago, Mike, we thought we had rid ourselves of that evil bastard Bartholomew Martin," I said. "By the time I took office the son of a bitch was safely in jail awaiting execution—or as it turned out, assassination. We may be rid of him, but we soon discovered that we had somebody just as bad, maybe worse. I'm talking, of course, about his son, Antonio Martin."

"I think he *is* worse, honey, I mean Mr. President," Meg said. "From our daily intelligence briefings, it almost seems that he *wants* his name in front of you."

"Meg's right, Mike, he is worse than his father, although I have a hard time even saying that. Bartholomew Martin was the cruelest bastard in history, and it's amazing that somebody else is competing for that honor. Mike, I need to work with the facts in front of me. To change the conversation a bit, your aide told Meg that you had something urgent to tell me. Enough with the suspense, what is it?"

"I'm about to tell you something that we've been keeping

super top secret. Of course, nothing is secret from you, sir; I just wanted to deliver the news personally. Here it is. No fewer than 50 F/A 18 Hornets have been stolen."

"Stolen?" both Meg and I yelled.

"Mike, how the hell do you steal a fighter jet, not to mention 50 of them?" I said.

"Bribery is the answer, sir, we believe. The ONI began an immediate update on the service records of the last known pilot on each of the planes. The planes have, in a word, been hijacked."

"When did these thefts occur?"

"Just last week, sir. All of the planes were taken over a three-day period."

"Last week?" Meg said with considerable volume in her voice. "Why wasn't President Fenton or me as his Chief of Staff notified immediately?"

"We wanted to sort it all out and present you with as full a report as we could assemble, rather than feed it to you piecemeal."

I looked at Meg. Those beautiful blue eyes can register many emotions, including anger and rage, which is what she showed.

"I'm surprised the CIA didn't tell us about this in any of our morning briefings in the past few days," Meg said.

"The CIA doesn't know about it, sir. I wanted to tell you myself," Hamlin said.

"You've got to be fucking kidding me!" Meg shouted.

I was furious, so angry that I felt like punching the guy. I stood and walked across the room, if only to let off a little steam and get control over my anger. I walked back to my desk and sat, taking a deep breath as I did.

"Of course, we don't have conclusive evidence," I said, "but I think it's obvious we're looking at Concordia. As you know, the CIA has found out that Concordia acquired its first aircraft carrier about a month ago from China. What can you tell us about the carrier, Admiral?" Although I usually address subordinates by their first name, I was too pissed with this guy to be informal.

"Not a lot as of now, Mr. President. ONI is working on it."

"Working on it?" I said.

"Shit!" Meg yelled as she slammed her hand on the table.

"Let me get this straight, Admiral. A month ago, we find out that Concordia acquired an aircraft carrier. Then last week we had 50 carrier-based fighter jets stolen from under us. And you tell me that ONI is 'working on it?' The shit I'm hearing from you this afternoon sounds a hell of a lot like dereliction of duty. Consider yourself warned, my friend. Any more of your secretive bullshit and you'll be facing involuntary retirement— or worse. The 'I' in ONI stands for *Intelligence*, of which I haven't seen any evidence in this conversation. I mean, holy shit, Admiral, Concordia acquired an aircraft carrier a month ago and ONI is 'working on it?' Completely unsatisfactory. This meeting's over. I want you to report to my Chief of Staff here as to what steps you've taken to correct these errors, and your report better be thorough."

After Hamlin left, Meg walked behind me and put her arms around my shoulders.

"Hey, baby, calm down. Your face is beet red."

"You look a bit pissed off yourself."

"Yes, I am pissed off. I mean what the hell does Hamlin think the United States Navy is, a private club? And the Office of Naval *Intelligence* doesn't know diddly squat about the Concordian aircraft carrier. You know who we need to see?"

"I agree, Meg. Call him."

"Nancy, please get the CIA Director on the phone," Meg said.

—◆—

"CIA Director Atkins is here, Mr. President."

"Good afternoon Mr. President, Meg. You wanted to see me, sir?"

"I'll let Meg explain, Buster. I'm too pissed off to talk straight."

"I've known you for a long time, sir," Buster said, "and I must say I've never seen you look so angry."

"Buster," Meg said, getting right to the point, "are you aware that 50 F/A 18 fighter jets have been stolen?"

As a seasoned spy, Buster is an expert at putting on a poker face, to keep his feelings hidden from the person he was talking to. But he didn't even try for the poker face when Meg told him about the missing planes. His jaw literally dropped, and he just sat there, mouth agape. Meg then told him about our entire conversation with Admiral Hamlin.

"Mr. President, I've never heard of such a breach in national security. Days have gone by, valuable days when we could have been chasing leads and simply trying to locate the planes."

"Tell me what you know about the Concordian aircraft carrier, Buster," I said.

"That project is in the hands of ONI. I didn't object, because they do have a lot of naval and shipping expertise. I have asked for a report, as little as a week ago, but I still haven't received anything."

"That's because they have nothing to give you, Buster," Meg said loudly as she threw a pen to the table. "Since we heard about that carrier, ONI hasn't done jack shit."

"And they've managed to keep the CIA in the dark too. Today is Admiral Hamlin's today last day on the job," I said. "I told him I was giving him a warning, but now I realize it's time to let the idiot go."

"Let me take care of firing him, honey, you've got a lot to do."

When Meg gets angry about something, she likes to take personal action.

"So, we find ourselves in an interesting position," I said. "Fifty of the most sophisticated fighter planes in the world get stolen, like a cat burglary, and Concordia has the ship from which to launch them. All of a sudden, the balance of power in the world has taken a new direction. Buster, do you have anybody to recommend to me to replace the lackadaisical Admiral Hamlin?"

"Yes, sir. Tim Clayborn, Deputy Director. He's a hard charger and smart as hell. I've tried to convince him on a few occasions to come over to the CIA. I'm going to call him to my office this afternoon to see what he can tell me about this jet-stealing fuck up. I hope he can pull himself away."

"Don't worry, Buster. In less than five minutes he will be the new Director of ONI. I'm sure he can give himself permission to take the time to meet with you."

Chapter 83

Tim, it's Buster. I guess I should begin by saying congratulations, Mr. Director."

"Thanks Buster. I just got off the phone with the President. I hope I don't sound like an egotistical asshole when I say that I think President Fenton has made a wise choice."

"It *is* a wise choice, Tim. You were my recommendation."

"The President told me that, Buster. Thank you, my friend. I know you want to see me. I'll be at the CIA in a half hour."

"The Director of ONI is here to see you Bust...I mean Mr. Director."

"Tim, good to see you. I'm delighted that we have you as director of one of our more important intelligence agencies. You're a guy who doesn't walk around with his head up his ass like your predecessor. The main thing I want to talk to you about, on direct orders from the White House, is that cluster fuck last week where we lost 50 of our best fighter jets. Why all the secrecy? Why wasn't I told? Why wasn't the White House told?"

"Buster, I came damn close to resigning over that fiasco. I almost called you, but I thought it would have been a breach of trust with my then boss. He assured me that he was in touch with the White House, and that's the only reason I backed off.

But we now know that was a lie. I don't want to be overly critical of my predecessor, but the guy had a penchant for tidiness. He wanted every i dotted and t crossed before he would go to you or the White House."

"And the result was a fucking breach of national security," Buster said. "I mean, shit, we lost valuable days when we could have been tracking the planes down—or their pilots. And what about the carrier that Concordia has acquired? I left it in the hands of ONI, only to find that nothing has been done in over a month."

"Yes, Buster, it was in the hands of our Bureau of Shipping Data. My first official act when I return to ONI will be to fire the head of that bureau. Good God, our sworn enemy acquires an aircraft carrier, and the Bureau of Shipping operatives treated it like a minor item on their to-do list. And what about the goddam pilots? We should have had a detailed dossier on every one of them within an hour, but it still isn't complete."

"Don't worry about the records on the pilots, Tim. The CIA already put together the info as soon as we got the names, which was this afternoon. Unlike ONI, the CIA works fast. All the pilots are men and they're all unmarried, which leads us to believe they were targeted because they didn't have typical family obligations. We have no idea yet how much they were bribed, but with Antonio Martin money in play, we're sure it was a lot. The worst part is we don't know where the planes are, thanks to the tidiness of ONI. Tim, you've got a lot of ass kicking to do when you get back to your shop. But I digress. Tell me what you know, if anything, about the aircraft carrier."

"Well we do have some basic research, but nothing that you can't find on Wikipedia. It's the third carrier that China launched. They don't classify their carriers like we do in the States with names like *Nimitz* or *Ford* class, but with numerical designations. So, the carrier in question is a Type 001A. We don't know its name, but I'm sure Concordia will come up with something if it hasn't already. She's just over a thousand feet long with a beam of 246 feet. She's more than capable of carrying and launching F/A 18 Hornets. With skilled pilots at the controls, she can pose a major threat."

"As far as pilots, Tim, my prediction is that all of them will be assassinated after they've trained their replacements. Like his father before him, Antonio Martin doesn't trust anybody. I'm going to be working closely with the White House on this matter. When it comes to operations involving naval warfare, we have the world's expert in the Oval Office, none other than former five-star Admiral Harry Fenton. His wife and Chief of Staff, Meg, a former Navy Commander, also knows everything there is to know about naval matters. I want you to get to know First Lady Meg, Tim. She's bright as hell and is great to work with."

Chapter 84

Good evening, ladies and gentlemen, and welcome to *The Story with Martha McCallum.* I have a report that I find touching. President Harry Fenton has ordered his five-star admiral's bars to be returned to the Smithsonian Institution where they'll be placed next to a photograph and biography of the person who originally wore them, Admiral Chester Nimitz. President Fenton was the first five-star admiral since Nimitz, and President Blake, Fenton's predecessor, ordered them to be placed on Admiral Fenton's uniform when he promoted him. I contacted the White House for a comment, and, to my shock, the President himself spoke to me. "These bars belong to the American people, Martha. I was only privileged to wear them," he said. Then I contacted the director of the Smithsonian Institution. He told me that the bars will be in a glass case between the photo and biography of Admiral Nimitz and a photo of President Fenton in his admiral's uniform, along with his bio. As we've learned recently, we have a classy guy in the Oval Office."

———◆———

"Honey, I think that was so sweet that you returned your admiral's bars to the Smithsonian Institution," Meg said. "And you didn't even ask me about it."

"I didn't want you to try to talk me out of it. I meant what

I said that I consider them to be the property of the American people."

"I wouldn't have tried to talk you out of it, honey. I agree with Martha McCallum. We have a classy guy in the Oval Office. And that gorgeous photo of my handsome hubby in his dress uniform will be right next to Nimitz."

"I wish you could be in the photo with me."

"So, anything new from Buster, Harry?"

"Yeah, he met with Tim Clayborn, the new Director of ONI, a half hour after I appointed him. Wow, did we ever need a new director at that agency. Buster filled me in on just how off-the-job Clayborn's predecessor was. It seems he liked to keep things secret, not only from the White House, but also from the CIA. Apparently he was obsessed with tidiness and wanted to present all his findings to me as a whole, rather than in pieces."

"I enjoyed firing that asshole, Harry. So where are we now?"

"We're in trouble, that's where we are. The little bit ONI learned about the Concordian carrier is that it's big and is capable of launching F/A 18s. And we don't know where the planes are, thanks to the foot dragging by ONI. Like it or not, it looks like you and I will be talking a lot about naval warfare."

"Between you and me, hon, I think we know a hell of a lot more about naval warfare and strategy than the rest of the admirals in the Navy combined. Hey, honey, to change the subject, tomorrow you and I are scheduled to discuss more of your appointments."

Chapter 85

Meg had her list of appointments I needed to make along with a photo and biography of each person. Meg loves to do things right.

My mind sometimes goes in a direction all its own, whether I steer it that way or not. I guess most people are that way, but that morning I could think of only one subject—Meg, my wife. When I gave my inaugural address, I think a lot of people wondered why I went on and on about not only Meg, but about my relationship with her. Most of those remarks were off-script, and I think Meg was surprised because she helped me write every word of the speech. But I felt I just had to let the American people know how much she means to me as well as the country. But to be honest, most of those words were addressed directly to Meg.

"You look pensive this morning, Harry. Care to share your thoughts with me?"

"Yeah, I'd love to share my thoughts with you. Do you realize we've been married 10 years and we're hardly ever away from each other except when one of us goes to the bathroom."

Meg laughed. "You have such a romantic way of saying things, baby."

"I'm serious, hon. For 10 years we've been husband and

wife, commander and aide, and we're still together in the same way. When you're away from me, and forget my dumb bathroom crack, I feel a strange emptiness, sort of like I'm missing something. I mean, hell, if we were a 'normal' couple after 10 years of nonstop contact, we'd be getting on each other's nerves, bickering constantly, and complaining to each other about habits that annoy us."

"Okay," Meg said. "Why don't we try some bickering and see if we've been missing anything? Let's say something critical of each other. You go first."

"Sometimes you forget to say, 'God bless you' when I sneeze. Your turn."

"You sneeze too much. How am I doing?"

"Well if this is bickering, it's sort of fun," I said. "But seriously, it seems to me that our relationship is sort of strange after all these years."

"It's not strange, honey, it's beautiful," Meg said. "We should just thank God that we have a marriage this close. I love you more than life, honey. I love you more and more each day. I love you more now than I did when I woke up this morning."

We wrapped our arms around each other, something we never tire of.

"Wow, it feels like you're coming to attention, Admiral. Hey we have work to do. Let's make an appointment to 'carry on' later."

"I always obey my Chief of Staff. We've got a date. Okay, honey, time to go to work. As soon as you take your hand out of my lap, we'll go through the list in the order we discussed."

"Chairman of the Council of Economic Advisors."

"Your dad, Boyd Johnson, of course, one of the most brilliant businessmen our country has ever seen."

"Didn't you say you thought about my mom for something?"

"Yes, Secretary of Education. Hey, we named a sailboat after her, so why not a cabinet position? I think she'll do a great job."

"Oh my God," Meg said, "I can hear her screaming now."

"National Science Foundation?"

"Roger Cramer, and his wife Janey as Deputy Director."

"Perfect call, honey."

"National Endowment for the Arts?"

"Leonardo Murphy's wife, Janice. I think she'll be perfect for the job. She's smart, organized, and has an encyclopedic knowledge of American arts and culture."

"I agree, honey, Janice is perfect. And she's one of your biggest fans."

"Mr. President," my assistant Nancy interrupted. "CIA Director Buster is on line one, sir. He says it's urgent."

"What's up, Buster?"

"Sir, the USS *Abraham Lincoln* has been attacked by five F/A 18s. It hasn't hit the press yet. I just heard about it."

"Damage?"

"Extensive, sir. They hit the bridge with rockets and bombed the flight deck, causing extensive damage. She can't launch aircraft, which was the apparent goal of the attack. The *Lincoln* shot down three of the planes and two escaped."

"Do we know where they came from, Buster, was it a carrier?"

"We don't know yet, sir. The *Lincoln* was steaming about 300 miles from Concordia, well within range of land-based Hornets. Radar had just picked them up when the attack began."

"Contact me immediately with any updates, Buster. We'll talk later."

"I cannot believe this, Harry, a direct attack on one of our carriers," Meg said. "This is just what Leonardo predicted. Any thoughts you want to share with me, honey?"

"Yes, I suddenly realize that I don't have a choice."

I stared at Meg and she stared back. We were having one of our wordless conversations.

"You're declaring war on Concordia, aren't you?"

"Yes, a formal declaration of war. Put your negotiating hat on, hon. We need to start rounding up votes in the Senate. I'm going to destroy that country."

Chapter 86

Meg works fast, amazingly fast. She began calling senators first thing this morning. At noon she walked into the Oval Office, tripping over the door sill as she did.

"Let's have a nice quiet lunch, honey. We need to celebrate."

"Celebrate what?"

"We need to celebrate 75 votes in the Senate, much more than you need to ratify a declaration of war. It's time to stomp that little shit into the ground."

"Call the Senate Majority Leader, hon, and tell him I need an emergency meeting this afternoon at three. On second thought, call the Speaker of the House too. I want this to be a joint meeting of both houses of Congress, even though only the Senate will vote for ratification."

———◆———

"Ladies and gentlemen, it is my honor to introduce The President of the United States."

A small band from the Congressional Orchestra played *Hail to the Chief.* Neat tune, but I prefer *Anchors Aweigh.*

Standing ovation. Wow, a lot of these people are as pissed

off as I am. Just like his father before him, Antonio Martin has no talent for winning the minds and hearts of people.

"Mr. Senate Majority Leader, Mister Speaker, my fellow Americans. We all know why we're here this afternoon. Our nation is under attack by a small band of savages from a tiny country, a country that means us nothing but harm. You've all heard of the unprovoked attack on the USS *Abraham Lincoln* yesterday by five of the jets that were stolen from us recently. For a short while last year, we thought our problems with Concordia were over when Bartholomew Martin was imprisoned and assassinated in his cell. But we now find that his son, Antonio Martin, is just as evil as his late father, perhaps even more so. In a matter of months, Concordia destroyed the world's cruise ship industry, and has now set its sights on the rest of the shipping business. My Chief of Staff and First Lady, Meg, says that she sees Antonio Martin's actions as trying to turn the world's shipping into his private yacht club, and I think that's an accurate way of looking at this problem. On my first day in the Oval Office I received a message from Antonio Martin, basically threatening what we saw happen to the *Lincoln*. This stops now.

"I hereby declare war on Concordia, and I respectfully request that the Senate ratify my decision."

Another standing ovation, this one going on for 10 minutes. I'd like to believe that all my speeches will end up this way, but of course that won't happen.

Chapter 87

Meg and I were having a quiet breakfast by ourselves in my private dining room. Although meals are a good time for meeting with a variety of people, Meg and I agree that breakfast is our time, our quiet time.

"Hey, you look kind of tired this morning," I said.

"After our carrying on last night, yes, I admit that I'm a bit worn out."

"We just need to do it more often," I said.

"Roger that, baby. Hey for the Leader of the Free World, you're pretty frisky, I must say."

"Around you, it's difficult not to feel frisky. Hey, we've got a lot to do. You can start by not rubbing my thigh under the table."

"Whoops, sorry. Later."

"I'm concerned, Meg, that now that we're involved in a naval war, I'm going to forget myself and put my nose where it doesn't belong. I need you to keep reminding me that I'm the Commander in Chief, not a seagoing admiral. Your thoughts?"

"You're right on target, honey. I don't think it would be appropriate for you to meet with the fleet commanders alone. You should include the Secretary of Defense and the Secretary of the Navy. Hell, you know more about naval tactics and strategy than any of them, but it's important to communicate cooperation and not just give orders."

Meg contacted all the eight admirals in charge of the carrier strike groups in the Caribbean and Atlantic, as well as the head of the US Fleet Forces Command, my former job. She also called the Secretaries of the Navy and Defense. Meg tells me that calling a meeting from her office as Chief of Staff to the President is a snap. She never needs to utter the words, "if that works for you." When the word comes from the Oval Office, it better fucking work for you.

Chapter 88

I assumed that our meeting with the Defense and Navy Secretaries as well as the Navy brass would be held in the Roosevelt Room, a conference room in the West Wing. But Meg, as usual, had a better idea. Because a lot of these people had never been to the White House before on official business, Meg thought it would add some drama to the event if it were held in the Oval Office. Her idea was to communicate urgency. So, the plan was for me to give an opening speech in the Oval Office, and then move to the Roosevelt room and its conference table, more conducive to note taking and reading through materials. She announced that plan at the start of the meeting, then introduced me.

"Yesterday, as you all know, I declared war on the nation of Concordia, and my action was overwhelmingly ratified by the Senate. This will be a Navy war, gentlemen, something I'm quite familiar with."

Meg loudly cleared her throat when I said the word "gentlemen." One of the admirals, the Commanding Officer of Carrier Strike Group 12, was Admiral Ashley Patterson, very much a woman. I was doubly embarrassed because Ashley and her husband Jack are good friends of ours. When we were both stationed at Norfolk, we would often have dinner together. Ashley made headlines a few years ago when she was a captain and commanding officer the *USS California*. She became famous, as did the entire crew, when the ship hit a wormhole in the ocean and time traveled from 2013 to the Civil War. The incident became known as *The Gray Ship*, because that's what the southerners called the *California*. Ashley and Jack wrote a book about the incident and introduced the world to the phenomenon of time travel. Just like I shortened World War II at Leyte Gulf, Ashley shortened the Civil War. Ashley Patterson is good people, one of the best admirals in the Navy, if not *the* best. Now I need to remind myself not to call her a gentleman.

"I'm terribly sorry, Admiral Patterson, for including you in my address to 'gentlemen.'"

"That's perfectly okay, Mr. President. I'm used to being thought of as one of the guys." Among her other qualities, Ashley Patterson has a good sense of humor.

I continued. "The events of the past few weeks convinced me that I had to take the step of a formal declaration of war. Fifty of our sophisticated F/A 18s were hijacked right from under our noses. The crew of the *USS Abraham Lincoln* got a bitter taste of that action when she was attacked by five of the Hornets. We also know that Concordia has acquired its first aircraft carrier, obtained from China. The CIA advises me that the ship is now named the *Concordian Advance*. I am also told that the ship is capable of launching F/A 18s. As your Commander in Chief, it is not my objective to micromanage naval tactics and strategies even though I've had a lot of experience in that area. No, you fine people will lead our war against Concordia. This will not be an easy fight, as our friends on the *Abraham Lincoln* learned. But it is a fight that we will win. Before we adjourn the meeting to the Roosevelt Room, are there any questions?"

My old friend Mike Jamison, Secretary of Defense, stood. Mike is a tall black guy at 6'5," well known for the force of his personality and his powerful speaking voice.

"Mr. President, I don't have a question, but I would like to make a comment. Your predecessor, President Blake, referred to you as the greatest fighting admiral in American history. I just want to say that it's an honor to serve under you. I know I speak for everyone in this room when I say, we won't let you down, sir."

Standing ovation with whoops and cheers. Wow, great way to start a meeting. I wondered if Meg orchestrated Mike Jamison's dramatic comment.

Chapter 89

Meg and I were having our usual breakfast in my private dining room.

"I think yesterday's meeting was terrific, Harry. Wow, Mike Jamison sure teed up the ball for you."

"Did you put him up to that?"

"Who me?" she said, smiling.

"Yes, I think the meeting went well, except that I forget Ashley Patterson was a woman, as pretty as she is. Thank you for your thoughtful throat clearing, hon. There was a lot of detail in the meeting, which I like. The plans are in place and everybody is ready. Those officers are good to go, but we know one thing. No meeting ever won a war. Now the shooting starts as we enter the fog of war. What is it that the German General von Moltke said? 'No battle plan survives contact with the enemy.' We're in for some scary times, Meg."

"I'm not scared, baby. With my Harry running the show, this shit will be over in no time."

"I hope you're right, hon."

Chapter 90

The *USS Nimitz* (CVN 68) is a supercarrier, the first of the *Nimitz* Class carriers, launched in 1975. She and the other *Nimitz* class carriers will be gradually replaced by the newer *Ford* class ships. She steamed off the coast of Honduras in the Caribbean Sea. The *Nimitz* is the Flagship of Admiral Ashley Patterson, Commanding Officer of Carrier Strike Group 12. The CO of the ship is Captain Mike Johnston.

"Captain, we have a flight of possibly six enemy aircraft flying five miles off our port beam," the officer of the deck said to Johnston.

"Air ops, bridge, launch six Hornets and prepare to interdict bogies off our port beam," Johnston said to the commander of Air Operations.

Admiral Patterson walked onto the bridge.

"Attention on deck," the OOD yelled.

"As you were," Admiral Patterson said. "What have we got, Mike?"

"Six bogies incoming fast."

Within two minutes all six of the Hornets launched off the flight deck. The pilots locked onto the incoming planes with radar and commenced firing missiles. All six of the incoming jets were destroyed. None of the enemy missiles found its target. The Hornets returned to the *Nimitz.*

"What do you think, Admiral?" Captain Johnston said to Patterson.

"I think this is good news, Mike. Those enemy pilots couldn't have been more inexperienced. They didn't even fall into attack formation. Whoever trained those guys set them off on their own too soon. Tell our pilots to join me in Ready Room Three so I can debrief them and prepare my summary. I'm under orders to report any enemy contact directly to the White House."

"I bet Harry Fenton wishes he could be out here with us," Johnston said.

"Our country is lucky to have that man just where he is—in the Oval Office," Admiral Patterson said.

Chapter 91

The *Sea Devil* was a large Canadian freighter, laden with containers of pallets of various goods from small cars to racks of lumber. Her American captain, Roger Sloan, stood on the bridge, his binoculars trained on a patch of sky about a half mile off the ship's starboard side.

"They appear to be drones, Captain," First Officer Philip Magnussen said.

"But they're not headed our way, Sloan said. "They appear to be circling as if they're looking for something. Alert the *Nimitz*, Philip."

Ever since the declaration of war on Concordia, standard procedure for all commercial vessels was to stay aware of any nearby American warship, and to contact the ship in the event of any threatening action from a Concordian vessel.

"Foxtrot Bravo, Foxtrot Bravo," Magnussen yelled into the radio, using the code sign for the *Nimitz*.

"This is Foxtrot Bravo, read you loud and clear," the officer of the deck on the *Nimitz* said.

Captain Sloan grabbed the radio from Magnussen. "We see a large flight of drones, about 15, a half mile from our position."

"I'm sending a flight of F/A 18s now," said Captain Mike

Johnston, CO of the *Nimitz*. "They will be overhead in 10 minutes. We have your coordinates."

The flight of four F/A 18s approached the *Sea Devil*, and the flight commander, Lieutenant Bryce Alexander, spotted the drones. The rules of engagement, ever since the declaration of war, were simple: Attack and destroy any enemy ship or aircraft. They would attack with Hellfire missiles and cannon fire.

"Engage, engage, engage," Alexander shouted into his radio.

In less than three minutes the entire flight of drones crashed burning into the sea.

The latest contact with the enemy was a success. But nobody had reported any sightings of the *Concordian Advance*, the newly acquired aircraft carrier.

Chapter 92

Mr. President, the CIA Director is here for his appointment, sir."

"Good morning, Mr. President, Good morning, Meg," Buster said. "I guess we have good news to discuss, based on the latest intelligence."

"I take it you're referring to the flying skills of the Concordian F/A 18 pilots, Buster," Meg said.

"Yes, that's exactly what I'm talking about. Our spies on the ground tell us that all the Hornet pilots speak native Spanish, so it appears the American officers who hijacked the planes are out of the picture."

"Do we know what happened to them?" I asked.

"Although we don't have conclusive evidence, sir, our moles believe they've all been assassinated."

"Typical of Antonio Martin," I said. "Act impetuously and worry about the consequences later."

"Yes, and it's also typically stupid. As an F/A 18 pilot myself," Meg said, "I can tell you it's one monster of an airplane, but it's also complicated. They should have at least kept on the hijackers as regular trainers and consultants, pretending to pay them millions of dollars. We've shot down eight of the planes so far, leaving 42 owned by Concordia. But the way I look at it is this: with an untrained pilot at the controls, an F/A 18 is about as dangerous as a Piper Cub. Having said that, Concordia's ability to launch Hornets off an aircraft carrier can still mean big problems—assuming, of course, the pilots learn how to fly them."

"And we haven't gotten any word about the location of the *Concordian Advance*," I said. "I can't believe that our satellites haven't spotted her by now."

"We think that the ship isn't located in Concordia, Mr. President," Buster said. "We believe she's tied up in port somewhere, covered by camouflage. They don't want to take any chances losing their prized possession."

"I want to get this show over with," I said. "My latest briefings from the fleet tell me that we sank three frigates and four destroyers in the past week. Good news, but not good enough. I want to put that bastard into a corner with the only way out being surrender."

"You mean the Fenton Doctrine, honey, I mean Mr. President."

"Yes, exactly, the Fenton Doctrine. Remove the enemy's options."

"Just like you did at Leyte Gulf?" Buster said.

"Why not?

"That asshole should know better than to mess around with my Harry," Meg said. I'm glad Buster's a good friend. He's grown accustomed to Meg's constant flattery of me.

Chapter 93

Antonio Martin met with his aide, Milton Drake, at his inherited mansion in La Punta, Concordia.

"Milton, it appears that the valuable acquisition of those fighter planes is not proving as positive as I expected."

"The problem, Antonio, is that the pilots received insufficient training. The American pilots who hijacked the planes have been executed, as you know. That means that whatever training our pilots received will be the last. They do have basic knowledge of the aircraft, but the flight controls are quite complicated."

"If I wanted excuses, Milton, I would have asked for them. In the two engagements between our planes and the Americans, the enemy came out on top. We were moderately successful with our attack on the *USS Abraham Lincoln* because we had the advantage of surprise. But since the declaration of war, we can expect no surprise opportunities. Milton, I order you to begin a regime of constant training flights with our Hornets. The pilots' lack of knowledge will be filled in by constant training— and I mean constant."

"It will be done, Antonio."

"And what can you tell me about our prized possession, the aircraft carrier *Concordian Advance*."

"She is at a pier in Madagascar off South Africa. We have her covered with camouflage, so she can't be spotted by satellite. Of course, until our Hornet pilots reach a minimum degree of proficiency, the carrier will not do us much good."

"That puts emphasis on our accelerated pilot training, Milton. It must happen, and it must happen fast. I expect another full report in two days. That is all."

Chapter 94

War or no war, Meg and I felt that we needed a break from the nonstop stress. We went to Camp David, the official retreat for the President of the United States. But we wouldn't be away from command and control because the camp can be turned into a White-House-in-the-woods on a moment's notice. Camp David was built during the Franklin Roosevelt Administration and was completed in 1938. The camp got its name from President Eisenhower, who coined it after his father and grandson, both of whom were named David. I always thought the place made a hell of a lot of sense. Rather than launch a huge and complex security operation to schlep the First Family to a vacation spot, the idea is for the for the President and First Lady to get there quickly in a 62-mile helicopter ride to Thurmont, Maryland. It's in the hills of Catoctin Mountain Park. The official name of the place is the catchy title, Naval Support Facility Thurmont. It really is a military installation under the jurisdiction of the Navy, with heavy security already solidly in place. The staff is mainly Navy and Marine Corps personnel, making Meg and me feel right at home.

The late August weather was beautiful. Although it can sometimes be sultry and humid at that time of year, there was a gentle dry breeze that carried with it a hint of the coming autumn.

Meg and I decided to take advantage of the great weather and went for a long hike. As is normal at Camp David, our security detail didn't need to right be on top of us because the camp was armed to the teeth with security. Our two Secret Service guys walked about 30 feet behind us. We decided to head off the main path and take a side trail into the woods. Meg, my beautiful, elegant, clumsy-as-an-ox wife, tripped over a tree root, spun around and landed on her butt. She then slid down a steep hill. I ran behind her, and owing to the steepness of the hill, fell on my ass as well and slipped down after her. When we met at the bottom of the hill, we both cracked up laughing. Meg, an accomplished athlete, believe it or not, always comes out of one of her falls unscathed.

"Hey, we better hurry," I said. "We don't want you to be late for your ballet lesson."

"Stop picking on me, wiseass," she said, laughing.

"Mr. President, Mr. President," we could hear my Secret Service guys yelling. Suddenly their voices stopped. We felt a trembling under our feet, when suddenly it was pitch dark. After a couple of minutes, the trembling stopped, and the daylight returned.

"Holy shit," Meg said, "here we go again."

"Hey, let's go back across the spot. Obviously, it was a friggin wormhole," I said.

"But Harry, don't you want to see where we are in time?"

Meg was right. Ask any time travelers and they will tell you that you absolutely *must* find out where you landed. It seems to be part of the weird program of time travel.

"Obviously you're right, hon. Let's carefully memorize the

spot so we can cross it after we figure out where we are."

We both looked carefully at the location that contained the wormhole, orienting ourselves with the trees and surrounding shrubs, but stupidly failing to mark the spot with sticks.

"I notice the Secret Service guys are no longer calling us," Meg said.

"That's because they're not here, wherever the hell here is. I can see the golf course through the trees. Let's go and see if we can find anybody."

We came upon a guy about to tee off from the 18th green. We walked slowly so as not to mess up his swing.

Then we froze. Standing in front of us with his golf club raised, was Dwight David Eisenhower, 34th President of the United States.

"Hey, who goes there?" a guy with a pistol on his hip said. He didn't even take his gun out of the holster. Security, I noticed, wasn't as tight as in our day. If somebody stumbled across the President of the United States on a golf course in the present, he would have been tackled to the ground and handcuffed. But wait a minute, I thought—*I'm* the President of the United States. Well, we're obviously on the other side of the wormhole.

The guy with the gun walked over to us, still not removing his weapon from the holster.

"I assume you folks are guests here at Camp David, but I don't recognize you. We're shown photos of any people on the guest list, and I don't recall seeing you."

Eisenhower walked over to us.

"Let's go back to the house, Jack," he said to his Secret

Service man. "It's too damn hot out here. I'll finish this game tomorrow."

He was right, we both noticed. The weather was hot and sticky, nothing like the beautiful day we set out on a short while ago.

Eisenhower walked up to me.

"You look awfully familiar," he said. "I think I've seen your photo somewhere. What's your name?"

"Fenton, sir, Harry Fenton." I left out the 'President' part. "This is my wife, Meg."

"Fenton, Fenton," he kept repeating. "Oh my God, you're Admiral Harry Fenton, the hero of Leyte Gulf. You're that amazing time traveler who helped us end World War II."

"That's my guy, Mr. President," Meg said, grinning ear to ear.

"Yes, sir, I am that Fenton, and Meg here was my chief of staff at Leyte Gulf."

"Please join me for lunch, my friends. We have a lot to talk about."

Although Meg and I were itching to find the wormhole and return home, we couldn't resist the opportunity of having lunch with the 34th President of the United States. Have I mentioned that time travel is weird?

We were led by Hank Morton, Eisenhower's chief of staff. We walked into the President's private dining room, the same one that I use to this day (Use? Used? Will use?). I saw a newspaper on a table. The date was August 19, 1956.

"I wish First Lady Mamie could be here, but she's off visiting our son John and his wife. So, what brings you folks here?"

I decided it was time to stop playing around with the facts, and just lay them on the table for Eisenhower and let him sort it out.

"We come here quite often, sir," I said.

I glanced at Meg with a look that said, tell our story.

"Mr. President," Meg said, "Harry is—or was—or will be— the 48th President of the United States. We come to you from the year 2025. Yes, sir we have time traveled, 69 years into the past to be exact."

"Hank, get me that scrapbook of the Pacific war in World War II, the one with the photos," Eisenhower said to his chief of staff.

Morton returned with the large scrapbook in two minutes. Eisenhower flipped through the book until he came upon the photo he was looking for. It was from *Life Magazine* and the photo quality was still excellent even after many years. I remembered seeing the picture he pointed to. There I was, standing next to Meg, along with Admirals Halsey and Nimitz, shortly after the Battle of Leyte Gulf.

Eisenhower kept looking at the photo, then at us. Hank Morton did the same. Eisenhower had the reputation of being a calm, unflappable man, not easily overcome by emotion. But he looked like someone had just dropped a cat down his drawers.

"Admiral Fenton, Mr. President, hell I don't know what to call you."

"Harry will do just fine, sir."

"Harry, I'm not one who's easy to startle, but I am amazed at what I'm seeing. My friend, you made my job easier on D-Day because we had plenty of reinforcements from the Pacific after you thrashed the Japanese at Leyte Gulf. That was, let me see, 81 years ago from your time. You are one great American, my friend, and so is your charming wife. And here you are visiting us in 1956. How did you folks get here, if I may ask?"

Meg and I then explained the wormhole. Eisenhower wasn't totally unfamiliar with the concept of time travel, mainly because of the story about Meg and me at Leyte Gulf. That said, as a non-time-traveler, he had a hard time believing his ears—and eyes.

"If I may add, sir, Meg and I love this place. Like many a First Couple, we think of it as our second home. I don't need to tell you about stress of office, Mr. President. Camp David, which you graciously named after your father and grandson, is the perfect stress reliever. We planned to go back to the White House after five reasonably carefree days. I don't know if I mentioned, sir, but we're at war, a formally declared war against a rogue nation that is bent on destroying the world's shipping industry and converting it to its own."

"Well, Harry, I believe the United States has the perfect guy sitting (or should I say will sit?) in the Oval Office. Please pardon me, but this time travel stuff has me confused."

"Don't feel bad, sir, it confuses people who experienced the phenomenon as well."

Hank Morton sat there, speechless.

"So, tell me, Harry, and by the way, please call me Ike, how do you plan to return to where you came from? It sounds like you're badly needed in 2025, although I can't believe I just said that."

Meg and I then explained the fine art of reverse wormholing.

"So far, as we've learned, Ike, an immutable characteristic of a wormhole is that the way to go back is to recross the spot where you came in."

"Harry, I'd love to accompany you on your journey, but because your target date is 69 years into the future, I'd be long dead by the time we got there."

"Mr. President, Ike, because you're my Commander in Chief here in 1956, I'm in no position to tell you what you can and can't do, but let me just say this: One of the many unexplainable things about time travel, it that you carry your own age with you, as if it's your own private universe. If you wish to join us, you won't be any older than you are now when we get to our destination. Another strange part of the phenomenon is that only a short time will have passed where we came from."

"Mr. President, I'm concerned, sir," Hank Morton said.

"Don't worry, Hank. You can come too," Eisenhower said. "Would you give up the opportunity of a lifetime to see the future?"

After we finished lunch, we hopped onto a couple of golf carts, which I had read came to be widely-used beginning in the early 1950s.

We drove to the edge of the golf course where we knew the wormhole was located. Then we discovered we had a problem. As a lifelong sailor, I always knew my position. But suddenly I realized that I always knew my position because it came from lines on a chart or a digital readout based on an electronic, celestial, or satellite fix. Meg and I stared at the woods, not remembering where the wormhole was located, wishing we had poked a couple of sticks in the ground to mark the spot.

We thought we knew the location, but the view from the angle where we stood didn't look familiar at all. Time to start hunting, I thought.

"This may sound crazy, Ike, but I want you both to carefully observe Meg and me as we walk around the woods. You will see one or both of us literally disappear. Follow us exactly where that happened. You will notice a rumbling and the daylight will turn dark. After two minutes the daylight will return, and you will join us in 2025.

Meg disappeared. I followed her precisely and crossed the same spot. When we got to the other side after the daylight returned, we immediately turned around to look for Eisenhower and Morton. Eisenhower appeared, laughing out loud, flashing that world-famous smile of his. Morton then showed up, bent over and barfed, a common reaction for a first-time time traveler.

"My God," Ike said, "the weather's beautiful, nothing like the hot sticky day we just left."

"Time travel, Ike, occasionally has some pleasant side benefits."

"Mr. President," we heard one of our Secret Service guys shout, "oh my God, sir, we lost track of you two minutes ago. Are you okay?"

"Two minutes?" Ike said, laughing. "By my watch it's been seven hours."

"We're fine, Pete. We slipped down that hill and hit a wormhole." All Secret Service agents had been drilled on everything there is to know about wormholes. Agent Pete looked surprised, but not shocked. I told him to place golf hole flags all around the wormhole location, so our guests would have an easy time of returning.

"And who may I ask are these folks?" Pete said. "My God, sir, you are a dead ringer for Dwight Eisenhower."

"Pete, Mike," I said. "It's my pleasure to introduce you to the 34th President of the United States, Dwight David Eisenhower. And this is Hank Morton, his Chief of Staff."

They both adopted the typical slack jawed, wide-eyed pose of a non-time traveler.

Pete arranged for a golf cart to retrieve us rather than trek back up that hill. I didn't want Meg falling again. It was still early in the day, and we had just eaten lunch (in 1956) so Meg and I figured it would be fun to take Ike and Hank for a tour of the updated Camp David. I drove, and Meg insisted that Eisenhower sit next to me.

"What surprises me," Ike said, "is that the place hasn't changed much architecturally, except for a bunch of new buildings."

"Yes, sir, most of the new buildings were added during the Nixon Administration from 1969 to 1974," Meg said. "Nixon loved the place."

"Dick Nixon, Richard Nixon?" Ike said.

"Yes, sir," Meg said. "He was president from 1969 to 1974."

"Dick Nixon, that son of a gun, my vice president. Looks like he had his dream fulfilled."

"Well, his dream had some problems, sir," Meg said. But she didn't want to go into the Watergate story and interrupt our pleasant tour.

As it was getting close to 5:30, we went to the main lodge where we'd have supper.

About 15 employees were on duty at the main lodge when we entered. I could see that they were doing a slow-burn freak-out when they looked at Eisenhower. A few of them were too young to remember him, except for photos they'd seen. I decided to make their day and ordered my aide to call everyone into the main dining room.

"Folks, it appears that the First Lady and I have once again time traveled. You've heard many of our stories. Well, we have another one. It's my honor to introduce the 34th President of the United States, Dwight David Eisenhower."

As the vulgar old saying goes, they didn't know whether to shit or go blind. Meg broke the awkward silence by standing and applauding. They all joined in. Ike stood and thanked them. "My curiosity got the best of me," Ike said, "so I decided to join President Fenton and the First Lady on a brief adventure. I bring you folks greetings from the year 1956."

As we sat down in the dining room, Meg and I figured we'd entertain our honored guests by bringing them up to date on the years from 1956 to 2025.

We told them about photocopy machines, which didn't hit the market until 1959, modern rocketry, missile guidance, the personal computer, the Internet, email, Facebook, Twitter, Google, smart phones, iPads, IPods, and space travel.

To wrap a little history around the technology, we then discussed the Kennedy assassination, Ed Sullivan, the Beatles, the Rolling Stones, the moon landing, Vietnam, the Gulf War, 9/11, Iraq and Afghanistan, and the election of Barack Obama as the first black President of the United States. Just to bring him completely up to date, I told him all about our troubles with Concordia.

"Harry, it sounds like our country has a full plate of problems, more so than in 1956," Eisenhower said. "Let me ask you a blunt question my time-traveling friend. If you were me would you do anything differently?"

"Well, Ike," I said, "This doesn't really have anything to do with you but with your successors, mainly John F. Kennedy, Lyndon Johnson, and Richard Nixon. I would do whatever it takes to warn them to stay the hell out of Southeast Asia, specifically Vietnam. In the 1960s, that country was involved in a civil war, with the communists on one side and the nationalists on the other. Kennedy started to put our foot into Vietnam's door, and Lyndon Johnson jumped in with two feet in 1964 after an event known as the Tonkin Gulf Incident, an encounter between an American destroyer, the *USS Maddox*, and three North Vietnamese torpedo boats. In an exchange of gunfire, the *Maddox* received one bullet hole—that's right, a *bullet hole*. There were no American casualties. Reports soon surfaced that there was a Second Tonkin Gulf Incident, but those reports were later discovered to be false. To this day many historians believe the incident or incidents were a pretext for America's involvement in the Vietnam War. All this happened before I was born, but the effects of that war still reverberate in the country."

"It turned out to be a big mistake, Mr. President," Meg said.

"Meg, please call me Ike."

"It won't work, sir. I've always seen you as a larger-than-life part of our history. How about if I call you General?"

Ike laughed. "Whatever works for you, Meg."

"A few years into that war, General," Meg said, "it gradually started to dawn on America that we picked the wrong fight. It was a Vietnamese civil war, not a global war of free enterprise against communism. Although it was before my time, I've read extensively about the conflict. Our country found itself in a horrible time of riots and protests. Over 59,000 Americans were killed in the war. General, I completely agree with Harry. You should do whatever you can to prevent the Vietnam War."

"But let me ask the two of you," Ike said. "if I were somehow able to prevent the war, wouldn't that be changing history? And if I changed history, what would be the outcome?"

Meg looked at me, indicating that I should answer.

"Keep going, honey," I said. "Nobody can explain a complicated set of facts better than you."

"General," Meg said, "on the subject of changing history, let's get back to what we discussed before about the Battle of Leyte Gulf. That's how you learned about Harry and me and our weird time travel to World War II. The alternate history of that war, before Harry's actions at Leyte Gulf, included some things that will shock you. President Truman ordered the dropping of two atomic bombs on Hiroshima and Nagasaki, Japan, killing hundreds of thousands of men, women, and children. Also, in that alternate history, World War II raged on for another year. Because of what my husband did at Leyte Gulf, we avoided the horrible final battles of the Pacific war. There never was a Battle of Luzon, Manila, Iwo Jima, or Okinawa, battles that you never heard of because you experienced a different time. Yes, Harry changed history by convincing Japan that it was futile to continue the war. I think he changed history for the better, and saved a few hundred thousand lives in the process. Harry's predecessor, President Matt Blake, called Harry the greatest fighting admiral in American history. After what I just said, I think you'll agree."

"Ike, I hope Meg and I have convinced you that you shouldn't hesitate to change history if you can."

"You have convinced me," Ike said. "Hank," He said to his Chief of Staff, "I want you to prepare a timeline of actions I need to take, beginning with a conversation with that young Senator from Massachusetts as soon as he's elected president. Maybe I can also convince him to avoid Dallas on November 22, 1963, the day you folks told me he will be assassinated. If that doesn't work, I want to meet with Lyndon Johnson. The Tonkin Gulf Incident, from what you tell me, occurred in 1964, after Kennedy was assassinated. I want to convince Johnson that the Tonkin Gulf Incident was bullshit, and he shouldn't get our country into a hopeless war on false pretenses."

Meg and I were surprised when Ike used the word "bullshit." He was known for keeping his language cussword-free. I think we got his attention.

"Harry, Meg, you two are the most amazing people I've ever met, and two of the greatest Americans. I will do everything in my power to keep our country out of that Vietnam War. But now you have another war on your hands with that crazy Concordia nation you told me about. Our country is lucky to have America's greatest fighting admiral in the Oval Office. Well, Hank and I better get going—back to 1956. I can't believe I just said that. This time travel business will take some getting used to."

Our Secret Service detail accompanied us to the patch of woods near the golf course, where the wormhole was well-marked with golf flags. Ike, ignoring his usual persona as a man from the 1950s, gave both Meg and me bear hugs. We watched as our new friends disappeared into time.

Chapter 95

Antonio Martin and his assistant, Milton Drake, stood on the viewing platform overlooking one of Concordia's military air bases. They were discussing Drake's report on pilot readiness.

"Give me your report, Milton, and please no exaggerations. Tell me about your latest findings of our pilots' readiness to fly the F/A 18s. Tell me everything that we know to date."

"Well, Antonio, in the past three weeks we've lost no fewer than 10 of our jets, and I'm not counting the three that were shot down by the Americans. As of now, we have gone from fifty jets to 37. As we discussed before, it seems that our pilots have received insufficient training on the Hornet aircraft."

"Who ordered the deaths of the American pilots who stole the planes for us?"

"You did, sir, I mean Antonio."

"Why did no one object to their executions, Milton?"

Drake just swallowed hard. Like his father before him, Antonio Martin would never put up with being second-guessed by a subordinate. Nevertheless, if a subordinate didn't have an answer for why a problem occurred, he wanted to know why.

"I did recommend, Antonio, that we may have been

premature in assassinating the American pilots."

"I do not recall hearing any such recommendation, Milton."

"Yes, sir, I mean Antonio."

Antonio, like his father before him, was skilled in passing off his mistakes onto others.

"These men aren't stupid, Milton. Why are they having such a hard time learning to fly those planes.?"

"A major problem, Antonio, is that all of the instrumentation and instructions on the planes are in English. None of our pilots speak or read a word of English."

"Who picked these pilots, Milton?"

"I gave you a list of 100 pilots, and you selected every one of the pilots who fly, or try to fly, the F/A 18s, Antonio."

Antonio said nothing. He adjusted his binoculars to watch an F/A 18 as it taxied to its launch position. Hector Ruiz, the pilot of the plane that was about to take off, raced his jet down the runway. As the plane became airborne, he hit a switch that he seemed to recall controlled the afterburner to give the plane an extra boost to gain altitude. The switch he hit, however, was the release button for an external fuel tank. The tank, which was filled to the top with jet fuel, separated from the plane and hurtled toward three other aircraft that were taxiing. The ensuing explosion destroyed all three aircraft. The Concordian Hornet fleet was down to 34 planes.

Antonio looked at Drake and shook his head, simply saying, "This is unacceptable, Milton."

All employees of the government of Concordia were highly paid, a policy that Antonio Martin's father had instituted years before. Their high incomes guaranteed strict conformity, but it was unable to control what went on in the employees' minds. If there was a phrase that all subordinates thought of when contemplating Antonio, it was "blind arrogance combined with vicious cruelty." But no one would ever dream of letting Antonio hear that, nor would they even discuss it among themselves. Milton Drake quietly despised Antonio Martin.

Chapter 96

Marjorie Drake

My name is Marjorie Drake and I'm married to Milton Drake, the assistant to Antonio Martin. I call him Milt, which is frowned upon by Antonio, who hates nicknames. Milt and I are both 29 years old and have no children. I'm tall, at 5'11" with long brunette hair and blue eyes. And I'm a fanatic about staying in shape with a practice of constant exercise. Whenever I'm in the presence of Antonio Martin, he never takes his eyes off me, that repugnant bastard. He doesn't even do it coyly. He just stares at my body, obviously fantasizing. I fantasize about throwing acid in his leering face.

I'm a mid-level minister at the Concordia Department of State. Like most citizens of Concordia who have anything to do with the government, I detest Antonio Martin. With growing sadness, I watch my husband, an intelligent, self-assured man, reduced to a stuttering cypher by Antonio's demeaning treatment of him. If a person treated a dog the way Antonio treated Milt, he would be guilty of cruelty to animals. I never know when Milt will come home at night because his time is dictated by Antonio's whims. As if to pour salt on a wound, Antonio never allows Milt to call me with his cell phone to say he'd be late. I've tried many times since Antonio took power to convince Milt to resign, but he wouldn't hear of it. He's paid a half a million dollars a year, far more than he could earn anywhere else. Also, Milt fears for his life if he ever resigned. Antonio, he was sure, would see such an action as disloyalty. In Concordia, disloyalty results in death.

I'm American by birth, like many of the citizens of Concordia. Both English and Spanish are the official languages of the country, although Spanish is more widely spoken. Despite the strange circumstances of my new "allegiance," I still love the country where I was born, a wonderful democracy, not a fucking dictatorship. Milt was born in America as well.

I keep my thoughts to myself, as do most citizens of Concordia. When the United States declared war on Concordia, I was both fearful and hopeful. I fear the military might of my old country, but I'm hopeful that America will defeat Antonio and replace him and his henchmen with a new government, maybe even a democratic one.

I'm a distant cousin of First Lady Meg Fenton and, except for our hair color, we bear a striking resemblance to each other. Although we haven't seen each other in years, we occasionally corresponded by email, but not since Concordia was formed. Meg Fenton, I'm sure, has no idea of my connection to Concordia.

I walked into the living room, my mind racing. My thoughts were soon replaced by a single idea. I will defeat Concordia myself, and I have the means to do it. In a week I'm scheduled to travel to the United Nations, under cover of diplomatic immunity, along with four others from the Concordian State Department. Once we get to New York, I know what I have to do. Some people think I'm stubborn. Well, maybe, but sometimes stubbornness can be useful. This is one of those times. But there was one consideration that can interfere with my plan—Milt. I love him as much as I hate Antonio. We've been married only five years, and our relationship is one of closeness and affection. I can't simply abandon him. Getting Milt to quit his job is impossible. He's probably right that Antonio would interpret that as an act of disloyalty and kill him. Maybe he could somehow go into hiding for a time. Milt was once an infantry officer in the American Army and knows a bit about stealth. Will he go along with my plan? He really has no choice. If I don't return, Antonio will be likely to have Milt killed anyway. I sat on the edge of the couch, my hands pressed between my knees to stop them from shaking. What if Milt was found by Antonio's loyal robots?

A sometime novelist, I'm pretty skilled at blanking my mind and letting ideas show up rather than forcing them. I sat with my eyes closed, letting my mind come up with its own plans. Suddenly I stood and clapped my hands, something I often do when a sticky plot-point in one of my books just became unraveled. I've got a new plan. I won't stay behind in New York, but I'll return to Concordia with my colleagues from the State Department. All I need to do is make contact with the one person in Washington know I can trust—my cousin, Meg Fenton.

Chapter 97

Meg and I returned to the White House after our pleasant but short five-day vacation at Camp David, a vacation that included a brief trip to 1956. Time travel is weird, no other way to put it. I was still reeling from our meeting with Ike Eisenhower. Now it's back to the war with Concordia. CIA Director Buster was scheduled to meet in a half-hour with Meg and me to brief us on the latest developments. I got to the Oval Office first.

Meg walked into the office, tripping only slightly over the door sill.

"Come over here, honey. Sit on my lap."

She sat and wrapped her arms around my neck.

"I just wanted to give you an update on my feelings."

"I thought that's what our meeting with Buster is about," she said.

"I mean my feelings about you. So, here's the update. I love you. Gimme a kiss."

We sat there making out like a couple of teenagers. I figured that was a great way to preface what was likely to be a stressful meeting.

"CIA Director Atkins is here for his meeting, Mr. President."

Meg wiped the lipstick off my face.

We wanted to find out what was going on, but we couldn't resist telling Buster all about our time travel and our meeting with Ike Eisenhower. I began by handing him a photo of Ike, Meg, and me.

"Dear Lord," he said laughing. "Dwight Eisenhower? Mr. President, you and Meg have a way of making wormholes fun,"

"So, tell us the latest about our little enemy, Buster," I said.

"Let me get rid of the bad news first," Buster said. "We still have no idea where their carrier is located, even though we have a lot of operatives on the ground. The location of the *Concordian Advance* is a closely guarded secret. Now for what may be some good news. As our ace fighter pilot Meg here told us, the F/A 18 is a complicated aircraft. Our spooks on the ground tell us that none of the Concordian pilots speak or read a word of English— not one."

"Oh my God," Meg said. "All of the instructions and instrumentation are in English. That makes it a lot more complicated than I originally thought."

"And they're losing planes fast. In exchanges, we've shot down three, but they lost 10 before then on their own. My people tell me that Antonio has hit the panic button, realizing that he blew it by killing the American pilots who stole the jets. He's ordered constant and lengthy flight training sessions. Last week they lost seven on one day, bringing their total number of Hornets from 50 down to 30. One guy, thinking he was hitting the afterburner switch, lobbed an external fuel tank on top of three parked Hornets, destroying them. If we want to save money, Mr. President, we can just cool our heels and let the Concordian pilots themselves destroy the rest of their F/A 18 fleet."

"I can't get over how much Antonio is like his father, the late scumbag Bartholomew Martin," Meg said. "He's bright, but incredibly thick-headed, just like his old man. I mean, holy shit, he steals 50 of the most sophisticated planes in the world, and then kills the pilots who could teach his people to fly them. I wonder if he wants to run against you for president, honey. Wouldn't *that* be fun?"

"I don't want to make the mistake of underestimating this guy," I said. "Between him and his father, they destroyed the cruise ship industry. Naval Operations tells me that we sank 10 more Concordian warships just last week. I want that count to go up, and I said that to CNO Admiral Jones. Of course, we're still after the big prize, the *Concordian Advance.*"

"If those bozos keep crashing Hornets," Buster said, "pretty soon there will be nothing to launch off the carrier."

"Well, we have a lot to do," I said. "Good to see you as always, Buster. Keep up the good work."

Chapter 98

Admiral Ashley Patterson is the commanding officer of Carrier Strike Group 12, homebased in Norfolk Virginia. The *USS Nimitz* (CVN 68) was her flagship. The other ships in the group were *USS Antietam* (CG-54), a cruiser; USS *Bainbridge* (DDG-96), a destroyer; and *USS Carney* (DDG-64), a destroyer.

Ashley, a young beautiful African American woman, is on a lot of short lists to become Chief of Naval Operations. Her husband, Navy Reserve Lieutenant Commander Jack Thurber, a famous, wealthy author and journalist, was with her on the flag bridge. Ashley had long ago convinced the Bureau of Naval Personal that the *good of the service* was best served by her having Jack at her side. Besides his technical and tactical assistance, Ashley counts on Jack to help relieve the stress of command at sea.

Ashley was no stranger to naval warfare, and neither was Jack.

"Admiral Patterson, pick up please." It was Captain Mike Johnston, commanding officer of the *Nimitz.*

"What have we got, Mike?" Ashley said.

"Radar reports four ships cruising five miles off our port beam. I launched a couple of drones to check it out. One of the ships is a frigate and the other three are destroyers. We know they're definitely Concordian from the insignia on their decks. Awaiting orders, Admiral."

"Mike, our rules of engagement are to engage, and I intend to do exactly that. Launch a dozen Hornets and order the pilots to fire on the ships. Also, send our destroyers toward the flotilla. I want some of the bigger Harpoons from a surface ship."

The 12 F/A 18 Hornets dived at the Concordian flotilla, unleashing a barrage of Hellfire missiles as well as Harpoon missiles. Although not as heavy and powerful as the surface-launched Harpoons, they are still deadly.

The Hornets concentrated their fire on the large frigate. After three minutes of constant explosions, the ship began to list heavily to port.

"How's it going, Mike?" Ashley asked Captain Thompson. "Better yet, I'm coming to the bridge to watch the video feed from the drones."

"Attention on deck," the OOD yelled.

"As you were," Ashley said.

"As you can see, Admiral, our day is almost done. We sank two ships so far and the other two are about to go under. We lost one Hornet, but the pilot managed to safely eject. I just sent a launch to pick him up."

"I'm going to my office to prepare my report," Ashley said. "I'm under orders to report any enemy contact directly to the White House."

"I guess President Fenton can't get over his admiral's instincts," Thompson said.

"Yeah, but he's cool about it" Ashley said. "He may second-guess us on the line of fire, but he keeps it to himself."

Ashley and Jack walked into her office. Jack had already prepared a draft of her report.

"Admiral Patterson, the White House is on line one for you," her assistant said.

"Admiral Patterson speaking."

"Hi Ashley, Meg Fenton here. We've already heard about your successful engagement this afternoon. Congratulations. Harry, I mean the President, would like to see you and Jack at the White House. He already notified Naval Operations so as not to knock any noses out of joint. Harry thinks the world of you, and so do I. We'd like an in-person report from two people who were there. How about tomorrow morning at nine?"

"Washington is within range of the COD. We'll be there at nine, madam First Lady."

"Hey, Ashley, the name's Meg."

Chapter 99

Meg keeps reminding me that I'm the Commander in Chief, no longer a seagoing admiral, and that I shouldn't micromanage our naval war. That said, I wanted to huddle with Ashley Patterson, the Navy's best admiral in my opinion. She just had an encounter with Concordia and I wanted to hear about it from the source. Also, I had a surprise for Ashley.

"Admiral Patterson and Lt. Commander Thurber are here for their appointment, Mr. President," my assistant, Nancy said.

Ashley Patterson and Jack Thurber are two of my favorite people. They have a close, loving relationship and are totally dedicated to getting the job done. Jack is Ashley's chief of staff. He has a brilliant mind, a photographic memory, and an easy-going command style. They remind me of Meg and me, except with reversed genders.

"Good morning, Mr. President, Meg," Ashley said.

"Ashley, Jack, we wanted to meet with you two personally to discuss a few things," I said, "not the least of which is your recent clash with Concordian forces. As Meg keeps reminding me, it's not my job to micromanage our naval affairs, but I want to hear about the encounter from two of my favorite officers."

"Our battle with the Concordian navy was short, violent,

and encouraging, Mr. President," Ashley said.

"Encouraging?" I said.

"Yes, sir, encouraging. Simply put, the Concordian pilots don't know how to fly F/A 18s. My pilots tell me that fighting the Concordian jets is like shooting stuffed rabbits in an amusement park."

"Your thoughts, Jack?" I said.

"I agree with Ashley, sir," Jack Thurber said. "I interviewed each of our pilots and wrote a 25-page report which I have right here for you."

"Meg, as an F/A 18 pilot yourself," Ashley said, "I think you'll agree that those pilots had very poor training, and certainly not enough."

"I completely agree, Ashley," Meg said. "Our intelligence reports indicate that none of the Concordian pilots speak or read a word of English, and all of the switches and instructions on the Hornet are in English, of course."

"Ashley, knowing what you know, what would you recommend?" I said.

"Well, sir, making recommendations to you is above my pay grade."

"Don't be so sure about that," I said. "Go ahead and make a recommendation."

"I recommend extreme aggressiveness, sir," Ashley said, "just like we've seen from America's greatest fighting admiral in the past. That, of course, would be you Mr. President. I recommend that we launch constant and relentless attacks on every Concordian ship and air strip. I don't want to give them a chance to take a breath."

"That's exactly what I expected to hear from Ashley Patterson. Oh, about your pay grade, I'm appointing you a four-star admiral and putting you in charge of US Fleet Forces Command. I will recommend to the Secretary of the Navy and the CNO that you also retain command of Carrier Strike Group 12. I once handled both jobs, and I know you can, especially with Jack as your chief of staff. All of the eight strike groups will be under your command. Also, Meg checked with the Bureau Naval Personnel and found that Jack has the required time in grade. Therefore, and yes, I've cleared this through the Navy, I'm promoting Jack to the rank of full commander. Your brilliant husband and chief of staff will more than help you get the job done."

"Mr. President, you honor me," Ashley said. "I think you've known me long enough to know that when I say I won't disappoint you, I mean it. And thank you for promoting my handsome chief of staff too."

"Well, this is great," I said. "We have the Navy's best admiral in a position where she can make a big difference. Are we missing anything?"

"Intelligence," Meg said. "The Concordians may be dipshits when it comes to training pilots, but they're really good at hiding things. I think Ashley's idea about extreme aggressiveness is excellent. Problem is, how do you shoot at a target if you don't know where the target is. Honey, I mean Mr. President, we need better intelligence."

Chapter 100

M eg, a Marjorie Drake is on line one for you. She says she's your cousin, and that her call is urgent," her assistant said.

"Hi Margie. As the old saying goes, long time no see. My assistant said you have an urgent message for me."

"Meg, I'm embarrassed as hell because we've been out of touch for so long, and here I am calling you out of the blue. Please let me start by congratulating you and your wonderful husband on being America's First Family."

"Thanks, Margie. So I can put this in perspective, could you tell me what you've been up to in the past few years?"

"I'll get right to the point, Meg and work backwards. I live in Concordia. I'm a minister with the Concordian State Department. My husband is the personal assistant to Antonio Martin."

Meg stiffened when she heard that. *My cousin is an official with the government of my enemy—and her husband is the personal assistant to that scumbag Antonio?*

"I believe that provides me with enough background for the time being, Margie. I'll be asking you for a lot more detail shortly. Could you please explain to me what the urgency's about?"

"Is this phone secure, Meg?"

"Of course, it's secure. You're talking to the White House."

"The urgency I want to talk to you about concerns the war between Concordia and the United States."

"What about the war?"

"I believe I have a way that the United States can win the war—quickly."

Chapter 101

Marjorie Drake

My three colleagues and I from the Concordian State Department took a cab from Kennedy Airport to the Beekman Tower Hotel, a short walk to the United Nations Building where we will hold our meetings. I had told cousin Meg that I didn't want to talk on the phone, and asked if we could meet at my hotel room in New York. Fortunately, Meg was scheduled to give a speech at the United Nations during the time I would be there. Even if she wasn't so scheduled, I'm sure she'd fly to New York to meet me to talk about the amazing revelation I had given her.

I told my colleagues that I wanted my own room because I'm a restless sleeper and didn't want to keep them awake. The real reason I wanted a private room was to meet with Meg Fenton, the most important meeting of my life.

My phone rang. It was Meg, telling me she'd be right up. Meg wore a wig and thick rimmed glasses, trying to conceal her identity. Her three Secret Service agents accompanied her.

"Do they need to be here?" I asked, referring to the Secret Service people.

"Margie, dogs have fleas; I have Secret Service agents."

We exchanged a brief hug, brief, I'm sure, because I figured

Meg didn't know what make of me—an official of her country's enemy and the wife of the dictator's assistant. Meg took off her wig and gave her blond hair a shake. Then she removed her thick glasses.

"My God, cousin, you're more beautiful in person than on TV," I said.

"Thanks, Margie, you look pretty good yourself—for a woman who lives in a brutal totalitarian dictatorship. Hey, I'd love to chit-chat, but I need to know what you meant about the United States defeating Concordia—quickly, I believe you said."

We walked into a second bedroom of the suite, the Secret Service agents occupying the adjacent room. A woman Secret Service agent gave me a required pat-down, apologizing as she did.

"I'll get right to the point, Meg. The first thing you need to know is my deep hatred of that tyrannical piece of trash, Antonio Martin. I'm not a violent person, but if the opportunity presented itself, I'd be happy to kill him myself."

"I had similar warm feelings toward Antonio's father, Bartholomew Martin," Meg said. "I even tried it once, but that's a long story. Thank goodness he was assassinated in prison, so we no longer worry about him. But we do need to worry about Antonio."

"I'm not the only one who hates Antonio, Meg. My husband, Milton Drake, is Antonio's key aide and confidant as I told you on the phone. He detests him as well. Milt—oh, in Concordia I'm not allowed to call him Milt, only Milton—is a wonderful man, but Antonio treats him like a rabid dog. Antonio pays Milt a ridiculously high amount of money. That's the way it is in that lovely country. Antonio secures loyalty with money."

"Margie, not to be a pain in the ass, but what is the big secret you have for me?"

I handed her a flash drive.

"What's this?" Meg said.

"It's the key to a fast American victory in the war."

"You have my undivided attention Margie. Go ahead."

"On that drive are maps, charts, detailed statistics, and data. Let me tell you about the most important items on the drive. One map shows four military airfields all within ten miles of the capital city of Delfuegas. It also shows the hangars where the stolen fighter jets are housed. The second part of the drive contains the piers where all of Concordia's navy ships are located, along with their exact coordinates, not only in Concordia but in other countries as well. And finally, and I'm sure your husband will love this, is the exact location of a pier in Madagascar off the coast of South Africa. The ship tied up to that pier is none other than the *Concordian Advance*, the country's new aircraft carrier. Milt tells me everything, a fact that would get him killed if Antonio found out about it."

Meg's mind was racing. Can this be true? If not, why would Margie be doing this? Could it be a trap? If so, what could be Margie's motivation? Then, she had a simple thought, the thought of a fighter pilot. All it will take are a few air strikes to see if she's telling the truth.

"Margie, I know you told me before about your hatred of Antonio Martin, but could you please explain why you're doing this?"

"Meg, when a person's country has war declared on it, the normal response is fear, maybe anger, especially if the country declaring war is a superpower like the United States. But those weren't the emotions in Concordia after you husband declared war. Yes, there's fear, but the overwhelming emotion in Concordia is just like mine—happiness and hopefulness. The people of Concordia want to see that bastard gone, and a declaration of war by the United States makes it possible. Even Antonio's loyal lackeys will be happy for a change."

"I've got to get to the White House immediately. I'm thinking that we should get you and your husband into the Witness Protection Program, Margie. You need to be safe from Antonio."

"The problem will be getting us out of the country, Meg. I'm scheduled to return to Concordia tomorrow. If I don't show up, Milt is toast."

"We'll think of something. You're a courageous woman, Margie. I have one overriding piece of advice for you."

"What's that?"

"Keep your mouth shut."

Chapter 102

M eg's back from New York, Mr. President. She's on her way in."

"Wow, Secret Agent lady. I couldn't get two words out of you on your cell phone."

"That's because I want to blow your wonderful mind in person, Harry."

She held out the flash drive that Margie Drake had given her.

"What's this?" I said.

"The end of Concordia as we know it."

"I think Buster should be here," we both said simultaneously.

"The CIA Director is here, Mr. President."

Meg, Buster, and I walked into an alcove off the Oval Office, where there was a computer with a large monitor.

"Meg, honey, tell Buster what you told me. Buster, sit down so you don't fall over."

Meg told the whole story, beginning with her relationship

with her cousin Marjorie Drake. As she spoke, we looked at some of the maps from the flash drive.

"How well do you know this Marjorie Drake lady, Meg?"

"I know what you're thinking Buster, and for once I'm ahead of you. I kept wondering if this was some sort of a trap. I've known Margie for years, but we've never been what you would call close. But then I realized she had no reason to lie. Also, to test this out all we need do is launch a few air strikes at the targets on the flash drive. According to Margie, she wants to see Antonio out on his ass, and so do a lot of people in Concordia. Harry, Buster, this war can be over soon."

"This is about to turn into my favorite kind of war," I said—"a *short* one."

Chapter 103

U nconditional surrender is a pleasant way to start your day—certainly if you're on the winning side.

Meg and I agreed that we needed some R&R at Camp David after a few harrowing weeks of war. Well, it was mainly harrowing for Concordia. Armed with Margie Drake's targeting information, Admiral Ashley Patterson turned loose her eight carrier strike groups and hammered the living shit out of the Concordian navy, not to mention her aircraft. We destroyed 90 percent of Concordia's navy, and almost all her aircraft, certainly all the stolen F/A 18s. Ashley is without doubt the finest admiral in the United States Navy.

Undoing Concordia's stealing of commercial ships, including all cruise ships, was a complex and confusing matter. The legal complications, shrouded in secrecy, were astounding. Antonio and his father had set up dozens of dummy corporations to keep Concordia's shipping operations secret. So naturally I assigned the project to my genius Secretary of the Treasury, Leonardo Murphy, my brain on loan. If anybody can sort that shit out, it's Leonardo.

Maybe I have a nasty streak, but I couldn't resist ordering Ashley Patterson to personally deliver the unconditional surrender document to Antonio Martin. I knew what it would do to that bastard's mind—to be defeated by and surrender to—a woman.

Antonio Martin, I'm happy to say, is now in Federal Prison at Guantanamo, facing murder charges and war crimes. Attorney General Max Hastings showed me the indictments against him. The document was four inches thick. I was surprised that I had no opposition to locking him up at Gitmo. I got the impression that the world's leaders were just happy to be rid of the bastard.

Because it was an unconditional surrender, there were no surrender negotiations. Therefore, the United States government was free to try as best we could to introduce a new form of government to that little shit of a nation. The Senate leadership left it up to me. I appointed Margie Drake as the interim president of Concordia. Elections are scheduled a year from now. I asked Max Hastings, who was my campaign manager and is now Attorney General, to coach Meg's cousin on how to win an election in a democracy, and maybe help her find a campaign manager. Margie Drake is one hell of a woman, and nothing would make me happier to see her as the duly elected president of Concordia. If she doesn't get elected, I'll be happy to offer her a high position in the American government. She never did give up her American citizenship, nor did her husband, facts that were unknown to Antonio Martin. Margie's husband, Milton, or Milt as Margie calls him, has been sworn in as a CIA agent, and he'll be located in Concordia. He knows a lot of secrets, secrets that I want in our possession. Buster personally swore him in.

I had changed my mind about destroying the aircraft carrier, *Concordian Advance*. Although my heart wanted to sink her, I decided that we should take possession the ship so our Navy could learn the secrets of China's carrier-building skills. Spoils of war and all that. Instead of bombing the ship, we attacked with three companies of Navy SEALs. The battle was over in less than 30 minutes and we suffered no casualties.

———◆———

Meg and I were sitting on the terrace of our living quarters at Camp David. It was mid-September, and a warm breeze wafted over us.

"You did it again, honey," Meg said. "You took away the enemy's options. You shoved the Fenton Doctrine right up Antonio Martin's ass."

"Hey, baby you were right with me every step of the way. And that flash drive from your cousin made all the difference."

"Well, Harry, we would have won anyway, but that targeting data shortened the war. The war lasted three weeks, but once we got that information from Margie it was done in three days."

"You have a wonderful cousin, Meg."

"I love that you appointed her interim president of Concordia. I think she'll do a great job of bringing that country into the modern world."

"I agree. Margie is one hell of a woman. Your family has powerful genes."

Meg stood, walked around the table and sat next to me, putting her arm around my waist.

"Hey, Harry, to change the subject, I have a question, an important one. When was the last time we made love?"

"My God let me think. I really can't remember," I said.

"It was over three weeks ago, Harry, but it seems like an eternity. Since the war started it's been non-stop stress. Our intimacy consisted of a kiss in the morning and one at night. Honey, we need to get back to being ourselves, just us. That's the way it is with you and me, or it was that way until the friggin war started. But now the war's over. I want you in my arms and me in yours. I won't even use our cute little code phrase, 'carry on.' No war, no crisis, no bullshit. Hey, baby, let's go inside, go to bed, and just be who we are—Harry and Meg."

CHARACTERS *A SEA OF FEAR*

Arnold, Jake – Chief of Staff to President Blake

Berringer, Nancy - Accuser

Blake, Dee – First Lady of the United States

Blake, Matt – President of the United States

Blitzer, Wolf – Anchorman, *CNN*

Boland, Philip – Governor of Maine

Brunilla, Luis - Concordian official

Bruno, Orlando – President of Concordia

Buster – CIA Agent aka Charles Atkins

Clancy, Tim – Resort manager

Cramer, Janey – Professor, Roger's wife

Cramer, Roger – Professor, Janey's husband

Dormand, Michael – CO of the *USS Gerald R. Ford*

Drake, Marjorie – Concordian official and wife of Milton Drake

Drake, Milton – Assistant to Antonio Martin

Eisenhower, Dwight – 34th President of the United States

Fenton, Harry – Admiral, United States Navy, Meg's husband

Fenton, Meg – Commander, United States Navy, Harry's wife

Fleming, Otis – Secretary of the Treasury

Gibbons, Hiram – Chairman of the National Republican Committee

Hamlin, Mike – Admiral. Director of the Office of Naval Intelligence

Hastings, Max – Political consultant

Hoffman, Franz – Captain, *Splendor of the Seas*

Jamison, Michael – Secretary of Defense

Kendall, John – Attorney for Harry Fenton

Lansbury, Walter – First Officer, *Splendor of the Seas.*

Lopez, Hector – Concordia vice president

Martin, Antonio – Bartholomew's son

Martin, Bartholomew – Tyrant

McCallum, Martha – TV show host

Murphy, Janice – Leonardo Murphy's wife

Murphy, Leonardo – Genius – Secretary of the Treasury

Patterson, Ashley – Admiral, United States Navy

Peters, Pete – Talk show host

Peterson, Michael – CEO of the Darnell Corporation

Porter, Gladys - Accuser

Portillo, Juan – CIA spy

Riordan, Jack – Governor of Florida

Rove, Carl – Political consultant

Sanchez, Eduardo – CIA Agent

Smith, Shepard – Anchorman, *Fox News*

Thurber, Jack – Commander, Admiral Patterson's husband

Watson, Amy – Girl Scout

THE BOOKS OF RUSS MORAN

All books are available on Amazon.com, and also as ebooks on The Kindle or a Kindle app on your smartphone or iPad.

The Gray Ship – **Book One** of *The Time Magnet Series*
http://amzn.to/16GPumH

"This provocative, intensely powerful novel is a must-read for sci-fi fans and Civil War aficionados, though mainstream fiction readers will find it heart-rending and inspiring as well. A rare read that's not only wildly entertaining, but also profoundly moving." — Kirkus Reviews

The Thanksgiving Gang – **Book Two** of *The Time Magnet Series*
http://amzn.to/1NzBs7N

"I had never read a book before written in an efficient, minimalistic prose. Instead of writing what most readers want to read, he gives voice to life-like characters, with their flaws and prejudices. They are not infallible superheroes. It's always nice to find a new voice in fiction and to enjoy creativity at its best." — C. Ludewig. "Breakneck pacing and virtually nonstop action" – Kirkus Reviews

A Time of Fear – **Book Three** of *The Time Magnet Series*
http://amzn.to/1zdjaG9

"His story is fascinating, and adds even more depth to this already cavernously deep novel. Amazingly unique, chilling and well written, Moran weaves a future that is both desperate and hopeful. Blending modern fears with science fiction results in a tale that will keep you reading long into the night." Five stars!" —Heather

The Skies of Time – **Book Four of** *The Time Magnet Series*
http://amzn.to/1CCC3jg

In *The Skies of Time*, you will recognize the two main characters, Ashley Patterson, now an admiral, and her husband, Jack Thurber. They met and fell in love in *The Gray Ship*, and now they're in for the adventure of their lives in *The Skies of Time*. Ashley and Jack have been such prominent characters in all four books of The Time Magnet Series that I feel like they're old friends. You will also recognize some of the other characters. But if I told you who they are, it would ruin the fun.

"I'm big fan of this series and this one may be the best. I hope there is another book to this series since it keeps getting better. There are a few questions I have about certain events that makes the next one even more suspenseful. These are great books to binge read one after the other." — Time Travel Fan

The Shadows of Terror – Book One of the *Patterns Series*
http://amzn.to/1IDQzJS

A novel that explodes off the front page of your newspaper.

Terrorism has a new face, a face that's obscured in the shadows. The radical forces of destruction have learned to make themselves invisible to the West, and preventing a terrorist attack has become almost impossible.

A new war has begun, World War III.

Rick Bellamy, an FBI agent who specializes in counterterrorism, is engaged in his own war, a war with no end.

Bellamy's wife, Ellen, a prominent architect, discovers that she's in the middle of the greatest terror plot to date.

To defeat the enemy, Bellamy first has to uncover the clues, to shine a light on the shadows. He has to find patterns – before it's too late.

"Move over James Patterson and Mary Higgins Clark. There's a new guy in town. Russ Moran's new book – *The Shadows of Terror*." — Frank O.

The Scent of Revenge - **Book Two in the** *Patterns Series.*
http://amzn.to/1UvDRmw

The world is at war with the forces of terror. FBI Agent Rick Bellamy and his wife, Ellen, find themselves in the middle of a sinister terrorist plot.

Someone is attacking young prominent women, inflicting a horrible disease.

Nobody knows its origin, nobody knows how to stop it, nobody knows how to cure it.

Rick Bellamy and a team of scientists want to go on the offense. But how?

Will the lives of the women be changed forever? When will the attacks stop?

"Heart pounding, can't put down thriller that will force you to look at terrorism in different light. Life in America will never be the same." —Cold Coffee Cafe

Sideswiped - Book One in the Matt Blake series of legal thrillers. http://amzn.to/1MkxX35

Trial lawyer Matt Blake took on a perfect case.

It involved a sideswipe collision in which his client's husband, an investigative reporter, was killed. The evidence of negligence was overwhelming. Eyewitnesses testified that defendant was talking on his cell phone when he hit the other car.

But was it negligence? Was it an accident?

Or was it murder?

Matt uncovers evidence that the act may have been intentional. Somebody wanted the man silenced. Somebody wanted the man dead.

Somebody had a lot to hide.

The signs started to point to the highest levels of government.

An open-and-shut personal injury case suddenly became a vast conspiracy of terror.

"This book hooks you in from the first line. *Sideswiped* draws you into the world of Matt Blake and you become emotionally attached to him and his journey. The story itself is so well-written and moves quickly there is never a dull moment." — Sarah Elle

"Moran demonstrates the depth of his writing talent by developing a new genre with *Sideswiped*, a legal thriller. Branching out from his previous novels dealing with time travel, Moran goes in a whole new direction with Book One in the Matt Blake series. He creates a wild but totally believable story of modern day intrigue and suspense. Moran also deftly weaves into this book some of my favorite characters from his prior novels. I am looking forward to starting Book #2 - *The Reformers* — Frank from Lynbrook on August 16, 2016

The Reformers - Book Two of the Matt Blake series of legal thrillers, is the sequel to *Sideswiped*.
http://amzn.to/2m8uMdu

The forces of radical Islam are on the run.

Their leadership has been decimated, their ranks thinned, their power disappearing by the week.

Their recruiting efforts have been cut off, the radical websites shut down, and the attraction of jihad is losing its appeal among the young.

With targeted assassinations, military strikes, as well as the loss of oil fields and gold mines, radical Islam is fast losing power.

But who is responsible?

It isn't the United States Government. It's a new force the world has never seen before.

Lawyer Matt Blake and his wife Diana find themselves in the middle of the most gigantic plot the world has ever seen, a conspiracy that's only begun to grow.

"I've been a fan of the author, Russell Moran, since reading *Sideswiped* a few months ago, so I admittedly went into this book with quite high expectations. That being said, I had no idea that "*The Reformers*" was going to play out in the way that it does and I can see myself giving this book a re-read in the future. In fact, I am even more impressed by the storyline of this read than the last and it has left me excited to see more." Lucidity.

The Keepers of Time – Book Five of the Time Magnet Series
http://amzn.to/2wjVSTt

Admiral Ashley Patterson and her husband Jack have done it again. They've traveled through time, 200 years into the future—aboard a nuclear aircraft carrier, Ashley's flagship.

They discover a new world, a strange new world—a post-nuclear war world—one that is both a beacon of hope, and a cry of despair.

They meet a group of people who call themselves *The Keepers of Time,* an organization dedicated to preserving history and culture amid the horrors of a dystopian future.

The world around them has harkened back to a primitive and savage past, one that includes human sacrifice.

Ashley knows they must have to get back to the present to warn the government of the unspeakable horrors that await.

But finding the way back to the present is their greatest challenge, an almost insurmountable one.

"A wild time travel yarn that starts fast and doesn't slow down until the end."

A Reunion in Time
http://amzn.to/2tneIsg

What if a 37-year-old adult travels back 20 years in time and finds himself in high school, followed by his 36-year-old wife? They're now teenagers, 17 and 16.

Adults in teenage bodies, they struggle to convince the people from their past that they are real, not apparitions. With the benefit of hindsight, they know the history of the past 20 years, and it isn't pretty.

Rick and Ellen are married, and now have to adjust to married life as teenagers in 2001. Rick is a senior FBI official and Ellen is a famous architect.

But everybody sees them as kids. Nobody believes that they're married, and nobody believes their stories—until Rick and Ellen predict 9/11.

How do they find their way back to the year they came from? How do they warn the authorities of the cataclysm that will occur in the future? The answer is to find the time portal—the wormhole—that brought them to 2001. But the site has changed. It's no longer the place where they crossed the wormhole. Will they live out the balance of their lives beginning as teenagers? "We've all wish we could go back to earlier times with the mind we have now. This Russell Moran book takes you there and it is a fun creative romp well worth reading. *A Reunion in Time* is highly recommend!" Kindle Customer.

The President is Missing – Book Three of the Matt Blake series. http://amzn.to/2t9v7wu

While he was addressing the nation from a submerged nuclear submarine, President Blake's message is suddenly cut off. Anyone listening heard an explosion. The explosion was followed by floating debris five minutes later.

First Lady Dee Blake has doubts, which she shares with naval high command and the new president. She thinks the explosion and the debris were a ruse to make people think the sub was destroyed, and her husband with it.

Could the sub have been hijacked and the president kidnapped?

But who would commit such an act? What is its purpose?

Was it Russia, China, Iran, or a shadowy group of freelance terrorists?

The new president appoints Dee as his Chief of Staff, with explicit instructions to find the missing submarine—and President Matt Blake.

Her life, and the life of the nation, suddenly take a horrifying turn.

Robot Depot
http://amzn.to/2zXW7C2

Mike Bateman is a visionary businessman, the creator and CEO of the fabulously successful chain of stores, Robot Depot, a company dedicated to selling robots and Artificial Intelligence machines for a variety of uses.

The company is a darling of Wall Street and is the most

popular destination for consumers and businesses looking for labor saving devices.

But the company caught the eye of ISIS, the terrorist Islamic State. They discover a great way to deliver bombs – using the products of Robot Depot to kill people.

Robot Depot changed from being a popular company to an object of fear because of the tampered products it sells. The terrorists use the company for "terror spectaculars," including the destruction of a skyscraper, a drone attack on Yankee Stadium, and the bombing of a children's sailing regatta.

Mike Bateman and the FBI are in a race to stop his products from becoming weapons, a race to stop the wanton killings. His wife and partner, Jenny, discovers the true meaning of terror one horrible summer day.

A Climate of Doubt
https://amzn.to/2OSwcHR

A book that looks at the horrors of climate change, and how it became a weapon of terrorism, was published in May of 2018. It's Book Four of the Matt Blake Series. Matt and Dee Blake take on their biggest challenge to date, along with our old friends, Rick and Ellen Bellamy.

The Maltese Incident – A Story of Time Travel (Book One of the Harry and Meg Series), the prequel to *The Violent Sea*.

The story of a cruise ship, captained by Harry Fenton, that travels 100 million years to the past. Published in June 2018. https://amzn.to/2RclZCT

***The Violent Sea – A Story of Time Travel Book Two of the Harry and Meg Series*, the sequel to** *The Maltese Incident.*

Instantly you find yourself with Admiral Harry Fenton, 76 years in the past, just before the Battle of Midway. When he returns to the present, Lieutenant Meg is waiting for him.

———◆———

ABOUT THE AUTHOR

In addition to the 15 novels discussed above, I also published five nonfiction books: *Justice in America: How it Works—How it Fails; The APT Principle: The Business Plan That You Carry in Your Head; Boating Basics: The Boattalk Book of Boating Tips; If You're Injured: A Consumer Guide to Personal Injury Law; How to Create More Time.* My latest nonfiction book is *The Novel - A Writer's Guide - Discover the Joy of Writing Fiction,* published in November 2018.

I'm a lawyer and a veteran of the United States Navy. I live on Long Island, New York, with my wife and editor, Lynda.

A Personal Request

I hope you enjoyed reading *A Sea of Fear* as much as I enjoyed writing it. Please consider leaving a brief review on amazon. com.